"You know what separates the strong from the weak?" she says.

I wait for her answer to this question, but she shakes me.

"Do you?" she says.

Nervously, I shake my head.

"The strong can eat bitterness, stomach the suffering," Mom says. "But even the strong will grow weak and sick and die. I know you think I will live forever. That's how I felt before Popo died. But now I see the truth, that life is fragile, short, and brutal.

"We must help each other to survive. You must get into Berkeley and get straight As. That way, you can get into medical school and become a doctor. You will make lots of money and buy us a nice house so I can quit my job and tell your father's family to go to hell. With your medical skills, you can even cure the illness I have now. You can only accomplish this if you are focused. No distractions. No sports or other after-school activities. No socializing or running around with boys."

As she talks, she squeezes harder, her nails digging deeper into my skin. "This is our pact," Mom says. "You understand?"

I nod.

"Answer me!"

"Yes," I say, my voice barely a squeak.

Bitter Melon

CARA CHOW

EGMONT
USA
NEW YORK

EGMONT

We bring stories to life

First published by Egmont USA, 2011
This paperback edition published by Egmont USA, 2012
443 Park Avenue South, Suite 806
New York, NY 10016

1 3 5 7 9 8 6 4 2

www.egmontusa.com

THE LIBRARY OF CONGRESS HAS CATALOGED THE HARDCOVER EDITION AS FOLLOWS:
Chow, Cara
Bitter melon / Cara Chow.
p. cm.
Summary: With the encouragement of one of her teachers, a Chinese American
high school senior asserts herself against her demanding, old-school mother and
carves out an identity for herself in late 1980s San Francisco.
ISBN 978-1-60684-126-6 (hardcover) — ISBN 978-1-60684-198-3 (eBook)
[1. Mothers and daughters—Fiction. 2. Self-actualization (Psychology)—Fiction.
3. Child abuse—Fiction. 4. High schools—Fiction. 5. Schools—Fiction.
6. Chinese Americans—Fiction. 7. San Francisco (Calif.)—History—
20th century—Fiction.]
I. Title.
PZ7.C44639Bi 2011
[Fic]—dc22
2010036630

Paperback ISBN 978-1-60684-412-0

Printed in the United States of America

Bitter Melon

Prologue

"Fei Ting, you are my reason for living," Mom says to me. "You give me a purpose for my suffering."

Fei Ting is my Chinese name. *"Fei"* and *"ting"* mean "fly" and "stop" respectively. So to me, my name sounds like it means to stop flying, though I know that is not what Mom meant when she named me. When my mother took me to get naturalized, she was trying to come up with an American name that sounded like my Chinese name, hence Frances. I looked up the name Frances in a baby name book recently and found that in Latin, it means "free." So my American name seems to mean the opposite of my Chinese name.

Mom and I are in the living room of our small one-bedroom apartment. Mom is lying on our dilapidated dark green couch. She is short and slightly plump and looks as if she is wearing two small life preservers around her waist. Her hair, which is cut into a bob, is thin at the top of her head and white at the roots. Though I would never admit this to her, I am afraid of looking like her when I get older. Like her, I am thick waisted, with a long torso and short legs. Mom is very proud that I inherited her ears. However, she is less happy with my nose, which is too flat; my cheeks, which are too big; and my eyelids, which lack creases.

All these characteristics, she says, I inherited from my father.

Mom's bouts of stomach pain have become worse since my grandmother died two months ago from stomach cancer. I am kneeling beside my mother on the cold, hard linoleum floor, massaging her abdomen in little circles, pushing up the gas from her stomach as she periodically lets out little belches. Her belches sound like Chinese syllables or exclamations, *"Gnuh, gnuh,"* gagging sounds that make me want to throw up. But I keep rubbing, even though my fingers and wrists are tired. When her stomach goes into spasms, it fills with air, forming a big balloon in her middle. It hurts her so badly that she has to curl forward like a shrimp when she stands or walks. The only relief for her is to lie down on her back and have me push the air out.

I've been doing this for the last hour. My knees hurt from kneeling, and my back aches. I can't stand this any longer, but I'm afraid to ask for a break.

Mom lets out her final belch. *"Gwai nui,"* she says. That means "good girl," or "obedient girl." That also means that she's feeling better, and I can stop. "Because you were good, Mommy feels better." She is more relaxed and half smiling. On the outside, I ignore her praise. Yet a hidden part of me smiles.

Once Mom's bloating subsides, we wait at the bus stop on Balboa and 32nd, which is located in the Richmond District of San Francisco, just north of Golden Gate Park, facing the ocean. This is the foggiest part of the city. Tomorrow is the first day of school. Because of Popo's death, Mom did not have the energy to buy school supplies. That's why we have to go today. Just the thought of school creates a heavy stone in my chest that weighs down my whole body. It is hard to endure boring classes and to come home to a long night of tedious studying just to prepare for more tests I will have to ace.

The icy wind whips us left and right as we wait in the fog, barely sheltered by the bus stop structure, which has once again been shattered by vandals.

"My seams are coming apart." That's Mom's way of saying that she's exhausted and in pain. "My stomach hurts and my knees and back hurt. The cold only makes the pain worse."

Finally, the bus arrives. Silently, we board the bus and head to Walgreens.

⚭꙰꙰⚭

At Walgreens on Clement Street, Mom chooses my school supplies. She picks Bic ballpoint pens, even though I would prefer the Pilot rolling balls. She chooses the generic notebooks, though I secretly covet the ones with pictures of flowers or puppies. The ugly stuff is cheap. That's why she gets it. It seems unfair that other kids get the fun school supplies. I still think in this selfish way, even after getting a senior sweater.

Afterwards, I walk towards the 38 Geary bus stop to go home. But Mom has other plans.

"Let's take the Clement bus to the bank," she says.

"I thought we went to the bank yesterday."

"We did."

"Why are we going again?"

"I want you to see something."

What does she want me to see? And why can't she tell me what it is? I am itching with curiosity. But I know better than to ask her.

The Clement Street bank is a bright red fake-brick building. The builders did not go out of their way to make the brick facade look real. It isn't brick red but an orangey Chinese red. The glue holding the "bricks" together is too straight and too white. It reminds me of dentures. Despite the tacky look, this bank seems to have good business. The customers like that all the tellers are Chinese and that the building is a good luck color.

After waiting for twenty minutes, we finally get to the head of the line and go to Minnie's window. Minnie is Mom's favorite teller. As her name suggests, Minnie is very petite, about five feet two and probably a size two. Her hair is cut in a stylish bob that is shorter in the back and longer in the front. Her bright red dress suit contrasts with her quiet voice and demure manner.

"See?" Mom says to me. "Minnie is a student, yet she is working to help her family. You should be like her."

I blush with embarrassment. She says this every time she sees Minnie. The last time she said this, I offered to get a job, but Mom replied that work would distract from my studies.

Minnie smiles shyly. "Good morning, Ching Tai Tai," she says in perfect Cantonese.

"Listen to how beautiful her Cantonese sounds," Mom says to me. "Not like you with your *gwai lo* accent." "*Gwai*" means "ghost" or "devil," but she is referring to my American accent.

"You're too generous," Minnie says. "My Cantonese isn't really that good." Actually, that's not true. Her Cantonese is great. It's her English that has a slight accent, only Mom can't hear it.

"And see how modest she is too," Mom adds.

Mom then tells Minnie that she wants to see her safe-deposit box. I didn't even know she had one. I'm not even sure what that is. Minnie escorts us into the vault.

The air-conditioning is blowing against the back of my neck, making the hairs stand on end. The fluorescent lighting makes Mom's pale skin look gray, as if she were dead. The walls of the vault are lined with little gray metal rectangles arranged in perfect rows and columns. They look like wall-to-wall library card catalog boxes. Each rectangle has two keyholes. Mom points to one, and Minnie sticks her key into one of the keyholes. Mom pulls a key out of her purse and inserts it in the other keyhole. Then she pulls it out and removes the lid, revealing a long box filled with shiny orange, red, pink, and turquoise silk pouches, the kind made for storing Chinese jewelry. They shimmer and glow under the lights.

We're supposed to be poor. Why do we have all this jewelry?

Mom picks up the pink pouch, unsnaps the flap, and unzips

the zipper. She pulls out a gold bracelet. I can tell that it's twenty-four karats, because of its garish yellow. It's just a few inches long. The only hint that it's a bracelet is the S clasp. But I can't imagine anyone's wrist being small enough for it.

Mom's eyes are glowing. "Do you remember this?" she says.

Quickly, I nod. I don't want to upset her by letting on that I don't remember.

Then Mom picks up the orange pouch. She opens it and pulls out a tiny green jade O. It looks just like a normal bracelet, except it is about an inch and a half in diameter, again too small for any normal wrist.

Mom holds up my wrist next to the jade O. "Look how much you've grown," she says. Only then do I realize that this is baby jewelry, my baby jewelry.

"I want you to see this, to remember your origin," she says. "Your Yeh Yeh, he refused to have a red egg party for you because you were a girl." "Yeh Yeh" falls from her lips like bitter poison. My paternal grandfather is a relative on my mother's blacklist, along with my father. "He looked down on us because of my family situation," Mom says. "But still, I made sure that everyone knew that you were important. Everywhere you went, you wore the gold bracelet on one wrist and the jade on the other. Both hands full of riches. No hand left naked, empty, grasping. Unfortunately, your skin was too delicate for gold. So every day I switched your gold and jade bracelets, before a rash had a chance to develop."

Then Mom pulls out another silk pouch, which reveals

another jade bracelet, only this one is large enough to fit a five-year-old. Jade comes in different colors, but I usually see it in jewelry stores in shades of marbled green, white, and purple. The most expensive color is green, the greener the better. They say that if you're healthy, the longer you wear it, the greener it gets. This bracelet is a brilliant green, the greenest shade I've ever seen, with some streaks of white.

This one I remember. I wore that one when I was six. Because I wore my Mickey Mouse watch on my left wrist, Mom put the bracelet on my right wrist, so it wouldn't scratch the watch. But I was right-handed. It pressed mercilessly against my wrist as I wrote or drew. When I brushed my arm against any surface— a desk, a dining table, or a monkey bar—it inevitably struck the surface, making a hard knocking sound. When Mom was nearby, I always got hit. "How many times do I have to tell you to be careful?" she screamed. "This is valuable. If you break it, I'll make you eat it."

Soon I was afraid to write, draw, or play, fearful that I would break it and have to swallow the jagged pieces. When my first-grade teacher said, "What a beautiful bracelet!" I was sure she agreed with Mom that I was careless and disobedient to threaten such a treasure. I was afraid she would tell on me every time I knocked it against my desk. I began writing with my left hand to avoid trouble. When Mom caught me using my left hand, however, she hit me again. She watched me carefully from that day on, making sure that I did things only with my right hand. I had a difficult time that year, unable to reach for things with my left hand yet unable to make noise with my right.

This sudden flood of memories makes my ears burn, as if Mom were still pinching and twisting them as she did years ago.

"You wore this until you were seven," Mom continues. "I knew I had to remove it before you got too big, but it looked so pretty on you that I delayed taking it off. Then, one day, it was too late."

We were in the kitchen. She held my arm down on the cutting board. The other hand held a hammer hovering just a foot over my wrist. The hammer was shaking. I was so scared that I forgot to cry. At the last moment, she put the hammer away and dragged me to the bathroom.

"I got your hand and wrist all soapy, and then, finally, I was able to slide it off!"

That was when I remembered to cry. I screamed in agony as she made several attempts to force it over my hand. It must've taken a half hour. Afterwards, I couldn't move my throbbing hand for several minutes. I thought she had broken every bone in it.

"Thank goodness!" Mom says. "At least we didn't have to break the bracelet!"

Mom then opens more pouches, revealing saltwater and freshwater pearl necklaces, more twenty-four-karat gold necklaces and bracelets, gold and jade pendants, and two giant gold bangles with the double happiness character and the dragon and phoenix, the symbols of marriage. The yellowness of the gold brands itself onto my eyeballs. They are so yellow that they look fake, like the gold paint that lines many a Chinese banquet hall.

"I think you are old enough to see this now," Mom says. "I know when you look at me, you see this haggard woman who wears outdated fashions."

I bow my head in shame. I cannot face her, afraid she will see confirmation of her statement in my eyes.

"But that is not who I was supposed to be," Mom says. "And that's not who you are supposed to be either. If your Gong Gong hadn't abandoned us, we would be wealthy." Gong Gong is my mother's father. He left my mother's family for another woman. "If your rich father hadn't abandoned us, we would be even wealthier," she adds.

Suddenly, we are no longer paupers subsisting in a dingy apartment. We are royalty, exiled from our homeland, waiting to reclaim our birthright.

"I deserve better because I work hard and I am good," Mom says. "You deserve better because you are my daughter. I hate God for abandoning us, for letting life be so unfair. They all make me sick, sick!"

Mom's eyes are bulging. She flares her teeth as she says *"beng, beng,"* the word for *sick*. She looks like a wolf defending against attack or pouncing on her prey. Yet underneath her wolf exterior, I see her shrimplike spine curled up on the sofa, her stomach a balloon filled with air, ready to burst. I see all the bad people in our family making her sick, the injustice eating away at the lining of her stomach so that no drug can cure her.

"God won't help us, so we must help ourselves," my mother says. "Together we can change our lives. That's why I work all the overtime. Overtime is one hundred fifty percent pay. Also, I have to show those devil managers that I can work harder than everyone else. That's why every time there's a merger, others get laid off but never me. Because I am the best! I know my health would be better if I worked less, but it's worth the sacrifice so that you can get the best education.

"But you have to sacrifice too. You have to work harder. This is your most important year. You must improve your grades. You only got an A-minus in chemistry and math. This year, you have a chance to redeem yourself in physics and calculus. You must ace those classes and pass the AP physics and calculus exams with at least a four. You must improve your SAT and get at least twelve hundred."

I took my SAT last year and got 1050. When Mom found out that Theresa Fong got 1350, she flipped and is now on a mission to make me keep up with her.

Mom continues, "Ms. Costello said that because of aff— affirmation—"

"Affirmative action," I say.

"—affirmation action, it's much harder for Chinese to get into Berkeley these days. Competition is tough. Even one A-minus can cost you when hundreds of other Chinese students can get perfect As."

I tried telling her that so she wouldn't be too hard on me if I didn't get into UC Berkeley, but she never believed me until she spoke with Ms. Costello, my academic counselor. But instead of being easier on me, she's even harder on me now than before, expecting me to jump over the ever-rising bar. Every Chinese family thinks that Berkeley is the only good college besides Harvard, Stanford, and Yale.

"I've been doing a lot of thinking since Popo died," Mom says. "Your second uncle, the one who took care of Popo, had planned to be a doctor. I paid for his schooling. But he ended up becoming a businessman. He said that he liked business better than medicine. Perhaps, had he stuck with medicine, he would have seen the early signs of her illness and provided her with better care. Maybe Popo would still be alive today." Mom stares past me as she contemplates this possibility. Her eyes grow dark, then light again as she refocuses on me.

Mom suddenly grabs hold of my arms, as if drowning and holding on to me for life. "You know what separates the strong from the weak?" she says.

I wait for her answer to this question, but she shakes me.

"Do you?" she says.

Nervously, I shake my head.

"The strong can eat bitterness, stomach the suffering," Mom says. "But even the strong will grow weak and sick and die. I know you think I will live forever. That's how I felt before Popo died. But now I see the truth, that life is fragile, short, and brutal.

"We must help each other to survive. You must get into

Berkeley and get straight As. That way, you can get into medical school and become a doctor. You will make lots of money and buy us a nice house so I can quit my job and tell your father's family to go to hell. With your medical skills, you can even cure the illness I have now. You can only accomplish this if you are focused. No distractions. No sports or other after-school activities. No socializing or running around with boys."

As she talks, she squeezes harder, her nails digging deeper into my skin. "This is our pact," Mom says. "You understand?"

I nod.

"Answer me!"

"Yes," I say, my voice barely a squeak.

"Yes who?"

"Yes, Mommy."

Finally, she lets go of me. She leaves four white ovals on each arm where her fingertips were. Gradually, they fade, leaving behind four crescent indentations from her fingernails.

"No one can love you like your mother," Mom says. "Just remember that." Then she holds one of the boxes to my face. "I know you won't fail me. And when I die, all this will be yours!"

The sparkle of the jewels, like the sound of Mom's voice, is dizzying. I look around at all the safe-deposit boxes lining the walls like the ash containers in Chinese cemeteries. What treasures from the past lie hidden in all those little boxes? What hopes and dreams for the future?

As we exit the bank, I open the door for Mom. The harsh wind makes it heavy, almost impossible to open. The wind cuts right through my jacket and turns my cheeks and fingertips to ice. Silver rays of light peek out from behind the clouds as the sun melts the thick layer of white-gray overcast that blankets the city most days of the year. When the East Bay finally cools down, leaving a little summer for us, it will be late September or October. We'll have our long-awaited Indian summer, a week of azure blue sky and golden sunshine, temperatures in the eighties or above. But we'll be back in school by then, buried under books and deadlines, no time to see the blueness of the sky or feel the warm rays bake our cold skin. And by the time school is over and we run out to the beach in shorts, we'll be met with the bitter fog, a big white dragon pulled in from the ocean by the ninety-degree heat of the inland cities of Oakland, Concord, and Walnut Creek.

"Could you spare some change, ma'am?"

I am not prepared for this voice beside me. It is almost inaudible, easily brushed off as imagined. It comes from a homeless man sitting on the ground against a building, bundled in a knit mustard-colored hat and a green ski jacket. His curly hair looks knotted and matted. There is dirt in his clothes, on his face, and under his fingernails. As the wind whips the other way, it brings with it his smell, that familiar homeless smell, a combination of cigarette smoke, booze, and pee. His stench repels me, yet I am held captive by the contrast between him and us. We have a treasure hidden in the bank. We have each other. He has nothing. As night falls, we will be safe in our cozy apartment. Where will he retreat: in a shop doorway, under a graffitied bus stop facility, or under a tree in Golden Gate Park?

Slowly, I reach into my pocket. But Mom grabs my hand and pulls me away.

"His mother should have helped him more. And he should help her more," Mom says. "That's the problem with this country. No family loyalty. At work, you should hear what my coworkers say. When kids turn eighteen, their parents want them to leave home. When parents get old, their kids just dump them in a nursing home, *ka-chunk*, like a greasy, half-eaten Big Mac into the trash.

"You are surrounded by all these bad influences. I try to protect you from their contamination. Your papers say American, but your blood is Chinese. You inherit my genes. You eat my rice. You will mold to my shape, walk down the right path."

She doesn't mention that my father is Chinese too, but that once he brought us here, he was infected by these bad influences and left. She doesn't mention that half of my genes are his. As we make our way to the bus stop, I imagine the relentless sheet of wind sweeping me off my feet and carrying me away. Mom tries to hold on, but her brittle fingers break off. I see the look of horror in her eyes, her mouth forming a big ghastly O, her fingerless hand still reaching out to me. I see her disembodied fingers still digging into my arm, nails embedded in my flesh.

I then wrap my fingers around Mom's. Fortunately, they are still intact, though icy and purple from the cold. She and I both have chronically cold hands and feet. She hates having cold hands and never lets them leave her pockets when she goes out. She only took them out to hold on to me. Though my hands are cold too, I rub hers to warm them up. We rub each other's hands furiously, cold hands warming cold hands, as we wait for the Clement Street bus.

Chapter One

It is the first day of school, and my thighs are Jell-O-like and burning from all the stair climbing. That's what happens when you have first-period religion on the first floor, second-period French on the third floor, third-period AP government on the basement floor, and fourth-period calculus on the third floor. That's also what happens when you're tired from being on the second day of your menstrual cycle.

I step into my calculus classroom. Like all the other classrooms in this building, it has hard and shiny dark green floors, dingy white walls, black chalkboards, and a big clock on the wall, the kind that is in every classroom from kindergarten through high school. There are fewer than ten girls inside. Most students finish off senior year with only precalculus, so this doesn't surprise me. Everyone is seated in the back of the classroom or off to the sides, leaving a big hole front and center. The most convenient seat is right in front of Theresa Fong, who is sitting back and center. Theresa, the girl who got 1350 on her SAT, is the daughter of Mom's best friend, Nellie.

Whenever Mom compares me to Theresa, who is always superior, Auntie Nellie responds in kind, pointing out my good traits and describing how Theresa can't compare. When Mom compares Theresa's willowy frame to my more heavyset one, Auntie Nellie points out that at five four, I am tall for a Chinese person, unlike Theresa, who is only five feet tall. When Mom praises Theresa's modesty and obedience, Auntie Nellie praises my social skills and charm. For good measure, she adds that I will attract a husband faster for these reasons, so Mom won't have to worry. Then Mom argues that it is better to have a daughter who cleaves to your side for life than to put all your effort into one who will cleave to someone else and give you nothing in return. Mom and Auntie Nellie argue about this with the same intensity with which they argue about who gets to pay the dim sum bill.

The truth is I think that Auntie Nellie is just disagreeing with Mom out of Chinese modesty. Nellie sometimes puts down Theresa as a means of indirectly bragging about her. "Oh, my son is so lazy. Theresa got a five on her AP calculus exam. Ben only got a four. If my dense daughter can get a five, then Ben could have gotten a five if he had put in some effort." Then Nellie waits for Mom to praise Theresa's intelligence, which is the same as praising Nellie for being an amazing mother. But Mom never does that for me. The things she criticizes me for in public are the same things she criticizes me for in private.

If Theresa has already passed her calculus exam, then why is she here? Maybe she's volunteering as a teacher's assistant. There was talk about her doing that last year. Great. More ammunition for Mom.

Fortunately, I have my own defense system. In grade school I learned how to smile at Auntie Nellie but ignore Theresa whenever Mom bragged about Theresa's accomplishments. I learned to point out Theresa's small mistakes to send Nellie into a tirade criticizing her. By freshman year I learned how to pretend that I had plans with other friends so I couldn't hang out with Theresa. That only provided Nellie with more ammunition to point out that I had better social skills than Theresa.

Theresa sits with perfect, good-girl posture. Her long, thick black hair is pulled up with a ponytail holder, the kind with two transparent red cubes. My hair, in contrast, is so thin that those ponytail holders would slip right off. Mom has threatened to dye my brownish hair black so it can look more like Theresa's. Theresa doesn't look anything like Nellie, who is short but plump, even more so than Mom. Nellie's thin hair is frizz-permed to add volume. Another difference between Theresa and her mother is their fashion sense. Theresa wears quiet colors, like pastels, camel, and light gray. Nellie, on the other hand, wears neon jogging suits. You'd never lose her in a crowd. Theresa must take after her dad, who is often out of town on business.

As I approach my desk, Theresa moves her book bag so I can sit down without having to step over it.

See, Fei Ting, how thoughtful Theresa is, not like you, always thinking only of yourself. See how she steadies her grandmother as she walks, how she opens the door for her mother? You never do these things unless you're told.

I mentally swat at my mother's buzzing words and sit down

in a huff, keeping my back to Theresa. Theresa is nice only for show. No one can really be that good.

Then the teacher walks in. She's petite but she has a large presence. She's wearing a crinkled velvet royal blue top and black pants. As she approaches me, I hear the *cluck, cluck* of her heels and notice that she's wearing big high-heeled black platform boots. Her clothes look like they're straight out of the Haight Ashbury area. I start to feel nervous. This is the first teacher I've ever had who wears neither a habit nor khakis and a button-down shirt. This is also the first teacher I've ever had who looks under thirty. The royal blue of her top makes her blue eyes electric. They sparkle behind her black cat-eye glasses, which have small rhinestones embedded in the corners. Her long, straight black hair contrasts sharply with the radiant paleness of her skin. As she passes me, she leaves behind the faint fragrance of perfume and cigarettes.

The new teacher turns quickly and writes her name on the chalkboard: Ms. Taylor. Then she faces us. The school bell rings, accenting her turn.

"This is my name," she says, pointing towards the chalkboard. "Now let's get to know you. Starting with you," she says, gesturing to the student in the far corner. "Please state your name and what your goals are after you graduate from high school."

My mouth goes dry. I'm used to being invisible in class and standing out through my papers and exams. Frantically, I rehearse my own response. Most of the girls state the party line, that they want to go to college. A few know exactly what college they want to attend. One girl picks Mills College, a private women's college in Oakland. Another mentions Stanford. A few know what they want to major in and what careers they wish to pursue.

What astounds me is Ms. Taylor's ability to remember people. Each time we finish a row, Ms. Taylor repeats the names of everyone who has spoken. When someone mentions a specific field, she offers encouragement and suggestions for schools or internships. She seems to know everything.

Then it's my turn. "My name is Frances Ching, and my goal is to go to UC Berkeley and pursue a career in medicine." I make my voice calm, to mask my pounding heart and sweating hands.

"Excellent, Frances. Have you ever volunteered at a hospital?"

I shake my head.

"You might want to try that at some point, to have the experience of dealing with patients and being in a hospital setting."

Her advice makes sense, but it sounds as attractive as eating unseasoned seaweed on cold day-old rice. I am swamped with schoolwork. I don't have time to volunteer. Besides, I spend every day with Mom. I don't want to be around more sick people. Then I wonder if Ms. Taylor can hear my thoughts. I wonder if Mom can too.

Then Ms. Taylor turns to Theresa, the other straight-A student in the room.

"Uh . . . my name is Theresa, and after high school . . . um . . ."

If only Mom could see us now. I suppress the urge to smile.

Before I can savor this moment, however, I notice the expression on Theresa's face. Her eyes are round and wide. The faintest traces of tears are puddling along her lower lids. Her bottom lip is quivering. I want to whisper in her ear, *Say doctor. Say lawyer. Say business. Say Berkeley or Stanford or just plain college. Make up something vague.*

"Um . . ." And finally she says it: "I don't know."

What a horrible answer. Ms. Taylor pauses. I hold my breath.

"You know what, Theresa?" Ms. Taylor says. "That was the most courageous answer I've heard so far."

Theresa's jaw drops. So does mine.

"Did you know that most college freshmen go in as undeclared?" Ms. Taylor says to the class. "Many college seniors approach graduation not knowing what they want to do. This is normal. You're at a time in your lives of figuring out who you are. 'I don't know' is a good place to start. Theresa here demonstrated honesty and courage in her response. Good work, Theresa."

My response, which seemed smart and poised at the time, now seems tinny and hollow.

Ms. Taylor picks up her chalk again and writes *Speech*. That puzzles me. How does speech relate to taking the AP calculus exam, a totally silent endeavor?

"Okay. Why speech?" she asks, as if reading my thoughts. Her bright eyes shine with intensity. Everyone is silent, but Ms. Taylor remains undaunted. "Why is speech important?" she asks. Again, more silence, not even the sound of breathing. Ms. Taylor walks slowly from one end of the room to the other, the low *cluck, cluck* of her boots shattering the quiet as she eyes us one by one. Each of us is seared into her memory, where we can't hide.

"All right, then. Let's take another approach," she says. "What makes humans different from other animals?"

The only answers I can come up with are so obvious that they sound stupid. Humans walk on two legs, not four. We hold jobs and watch TV.

Then a memory comes to me from years ago. I was twelve then. It was a damp, gray day. Mom and I were at the zoo. We were surrounded by trash smells and animal smells, like wet fur and fresh urine. I was standing several yards from a polar bear and her cub. The bears were a dirty yellow, not snow white as I had expected. Mom was holding my hand. She shook it to get my attention. "Fei Ting," she said, "see all these animals, tigers, monkeys, bears, and seals? They nurse their young for only a year or two. In just a year or two, the babies grow up and the mothers abandon them, and that's that. But a human mother never turns her back on her baby. The baby eats up her mother's food and money for the next twenty years. But even then, their relationship doesn't die. Then mother and child switch roles, and the child cares for her mother."

"Frances?"

I nearly jump in my seat. My knees start shaking. A bead of sweat trickles down the gutter in my back. I reach my mental hand into the magic hat, grope desperately, and pull out . . . nothing. I decide to try Theresa's response.

"Um, I don't know."

"Yes, you do."

I shake my head.

"If you decide to share it, let us know." Then she turns her attention to the class once again. "Language, ladies," Ms. Taylor says to us. "Language is what separates humans from other animals. Language gives us the ability not only to talk about the present but to reflect on the past and plan for the future. We are also the only fiction-creating animal. Because of human language and human imagination, we can create and recreate our identities and our cultures. Through language we can exchange ideas. In so doing, we discover what is true for us and we can speak those truths."

Truths? How can "truth" be plural? Isn't there only one truth, like one true God?

"So, how is this important to us as women?" Ms. Taylor says.

Again, silence. I want to hear more and am annoyed by the pause.

"Language is power," says Ms. Taylor. "We as women have the power to define ourselves and persuade others, to change the ideas of our society and to pass that down for generations to come."

However unconventional this class may be, I feel excited. I have a feeling that this will be my favorite class this semester, if not my best class ever.

"You ladies are lucky," Ms. Taylor continues. "You're going to St. Elizabeth's, an elite all-girls school. Here you will be heard.

Here you have the chance to nurture and strengthen your own voice. That's why you're enrolled in this speech course. To develop your own unique, individual voices."

Speech course?

Ms. Taylor continues, listing and describing the different genres of speech and how we will cover each genre during the course of the class. Panicked, I reach for my computer printout schedule. First period, Theology, Sr. Mary Rose, room 102. Second period, French, Ms. Rochette, room 304. Third period, Advanced Placement Government, Mr. Robinson, room 12. Fourth period, Speech, Ms. Taylor, room 301. Fifth period, Advanced Placement English, Ms. Taylor again, room 302. Sixth period, Physics, Ms. Trent, room 204. Calculus isn't even on the schedule. I read my classes over, as if doing so will cause calculus to materialize. But it doesn't. I will have to talk to Ms. Costello and fix this.

I imagine having to force myself to pay attention in calculus class and do my homework, as I have for the last several years in other classes, while being deprived of this special feeling. To console myself, I separate the world of tomorrow, when I have to switch classes, from the world of today, when I am still enrolled.

The school bell blares. Usually, at the sound of the bell, the students make a mad stampede out the door, nearly leaving footprints on the teacher's back. But today everyone stays seated, entranced by Ms. Taylor's spell.

"This week, we will practice impromptu in class. Meanwhile,

for your homework, I want you to prepare your first original oratory speech." Then she goes on to explain what "original oratory" means.

Slowly, as if stunned, the girls gather their belongings and exit the classroom. As I turn to get my book bag, I notice Theresa standing behind me, her book bag hanging over her shoulder. I move aside to let her pass. She shakes her head and gestures for me to go first. I nod and gather my stuff.

Theresa smiles at Ms. Taylor and gives a small wave.

Ms. Taylor beams back. "See you tomorrow, Theresa. You too, Frances."

My heart turns sweet and sour, sweet because she wants me to come back and sour because I can't.

On the way out, I notice that Theresa is walking unusually close behind me. As we exit the room, Theresa whispers in my ear, "You have a stain on the back of your skirt."

Alarmed, I look behind me to see how bad it is.

"You can wash it off in the second-floor bathroom," she says. "I'll walk behind you so no one will see."

"Why not go to the third-floor bathroom?"

"Because it doesn't have the hot-air hand dryer."

I look at her like *So?*

"How will you dry off your skirt afterwards?" she says.

Together, we walk to the bathroom. I take slow, mincing steps, fearful that big steps will make it flow out faster. Theresa has to slow down so as not to step on my heels.

Once inside the bathroom, I drop my book bag to the floor

and turn my skirt to observe the damage. Sure enough, there's a bright red stain the size of a quarter. Though the busy plaid pattern of the skirt obscures the stain a little, it's still visible. I wonder when it happened, how many teachers and students saw it. And my AP government class is taught by a man. How humiliating.

I run the faucet and lift my skirt to it.

"You're going to get water all over yourself," Theresa says. "Go inside one of the stalls and take it off."

I do so. As I stand skirtless in the stall, changing my sanitary napkin, I hear Theresa squeezing a bottle, which makes no sense, because our soap dispensers don't make that sound. I feel a cold breeze run up my bare legs, and I start shivering.

Theresa didn't have to tell me about the stain. She could have let me walk around the rest of the day, even go home on a public bus, and let everyone see. That's what I probably would have done. Not only did she warn me, now she's cleaning it off for me.

I hear the faucet running and the rubbing of fabric between fingers. Then the faucet is turned off and the hand dryer is turned on. After a few minutes of that, Theresa hands me my skirt over the stall door. I take it and inspect where the spot was. It is spot free and perfectly dry. I put it back on, grateful and relieved.

"What were you cleaning it with?" I ask her afterwards.

Theresa pulls out a travel-size bottle of stain remover. "The same thing happened to me last year. I've always kept this in my book bag ever since, just in case."

We both burst out laughing. Our laughter echoes off the tile walls so it sounds like a group of us laughing.

"Now, whenever it's that time of month for me, I always check my skirt several times a day," Theresa says.

"Well, I'll be sure to check yours if you continue to check mine," I say.

"It's also why I sit up so straight, so it stays in the middle and doesn't go to the back."

We start laughing again. "That's strong motivation for good posture," I say.

As our laughter subsides, we pause in an awkward moment of silence. For the first time, I notice that Theresa has a bright smile that lights up her whole face. Her eyes form shiny black crescent moons, with a dimple forming a third crescent.

"You know," Theresa says, "I'm really embarrassed about saying 'I don't know' in class. That sounded so stupid."

"You shouldn't feel stupid," I say. "Didn't you hear what Ms. Taylor said, that your answer was courageous?"

"Yeah, courageously stupid. Your answer was smart. It was clear and strong, full of confidence. Even my mom notices that about you."

"Really?"

"Yeah. Whenever I'm around other people, she mentions that to me afterwards, that I should be more well spoken, like you. That's why she wanted me to take this course in the first place. But today I think I proved that I'm hopeless."

I wonder if Theresa has ever hated me in the same way that I've hated her. Then again, Theresa doesn't seem capable of hatred. Maybe *envy* is a better word.

"I think you're being too hard on yourself," I tell her. "Ms. Taylor is really impressed with you."

Theresa's face brightens up. "You think?"

"Yeah. She said so."

"You don't think she was just being nice?"

"She's not that type."

"Gosh! Wow! Thanks! That really makes me feel better."

I've always found Theresa's "gosh, gee willy" personality to be dorky and uncool. But today her "I don't know" feels honest and down to earth.

❦

The shiny white walls and hard green tables of the cafeteria seem to amplify the rowdy screaming from the other students. But Theresa and I have found a far-off corner where we can be private and hear each other. I brought two pastries from the Golden Phoenix—a baked bun filled with curried beef, and a steamed chicken bun with water chestnuts and chives. Theresa brought a *jong*, which is sticky rice, chicken, mushroom, and salted egg yolk wrapped in bamboo leaves.

"I'm so sick of these," Theresa says.

Though they taste great, I don't blame her. Because they take eight hours to boil, Auntie Nellie tends to make a lot at one time. Theresa has probably been eating these every day for the last week.

"Have you eaten all the ones Mom brought over?" she asks.

"No. We still have five in our freezer."

"She keeps making me eat these heavy lunches because she says I'm too skinny."

"You're lucky to be so thin," I say. "You can eat anything you want." I can hardly disguise the envy in my voice. Then I say what I could never before admit publicly. "I always wished I could be as thin as you."

"Your weight is fine," Theresa replies. "But at least weight is something you can change. I can't make myself taller by changing my diet or exercising."

"Take heart," I say. "At least you have beautiful hair."

"Oh, this." She carelessly tosses a glossy strand over her shoulder. "It's impossible to manage. There's so much of it."

"I'd be more than happy to trade mine for yours," I say. "When my hair is wet, you can see my scalp."

"Oh, it's not that bad. Actually, I think your hair has a nice color. Lots of Chinese are bleaching their hair to get it to look like yours."

I cut my buns in half and push a half of each towards her.

"Oh, no, I couldn't," Theresa says. "That's your lunch."

"It's okay."

"Okay, but only if you have half of mine." She borrows my plastic knife and cuts her *jong* in half. She slides the side with the egg yolk, the most expensive ingredient, towards me.

"You should keep the yolk for yourself," I say.

"No, I want you to have it."

I hesitate a little before accepting.

"Thanks for talking to me," she says.

"What do you mean?" The moment I say it, that fake feeling comes back.

"Well . . ." Theresa shifts in her seat uncomfortably. "Nothing."

"No. Tell me."

"Well . . . I always thought that you didn't like me."

I bristle a little at her comment, afraid that she has seen through me. "Don't be ridiculous," I say.

"I know. Sorry. I'm being stupid. I thought that you were stuck up because you never talked to me."

Her comment stings, but I fight to maintain my composure.

"But now I realize how wrong I was about you," Theresa says. "You're not only smart, but you're really nice too, a good friend. Probably you didn't talk to me much because I never talked to you. I think I just told myself that you were stuck up because I was jealous of your good qualities. I was being a jerk, and I'm sorry. Will you forgive me?"

"Of course," I say. "You didn't do anything wrong." I say this to her, but silently, I direct it towards myself.

I roll the egg yolk around with my plastic fork. It's bright orange, the color of the sun as it descends towards the horizon. I cut it in two and drop one part over Theresa's half *jong*. Theresa stabs her half yolk with her plastic fork and holds it up like a wineglass.

"Here's to a good speech class and a good senior year!" she says.

We click half yolks, pop them into our mouths at the same time, and laugh.

"I just told you why I'm taking speech," Theresa says. "How about you? Why did you enroll in this course?"

"Well . . . actually . . . I didn't."

Theresa looks at me quizzically. I explain my mix-up to her.

"No! Frances, what are you going to do?" Theresa says.

"Talk to Ms. Costello and get myself reenrolled in calculus, I guess," I say.

"*Because of affirmative action, it's going to be harder for you to get into a top school,*" Theresa says, mimicking Ms. Costello's nasally voice. "*Along with a high grade point average, you need to take practical, hard-core college-prep classes, like calculus and physics . . .*"

"*Not fluffy electives, like art and psychology,*" we mimic together in a singsongy fashion.

"I'm so disappointed," I say. "I was hoping we could be in this together."

"Yeah. Me too."

A couple of seconds pass. Then, simultaneously, we sigh. Then we laugh at our timing.

"Too bad you didn't take calculus last year," Theresa says. "Too bad you can't just stick with speech and not say anything to your mom."

"Yeah."

We linger there for a moment, both of us basking in wishful thinking.

Then the bell rings.

"Would you do me a favor and not say anything to your mom or my mom about this?" I say. "I just need some time to straighten this out."

Theresa nods. "In the meantime, you ought to fill out an appointment slip to see Ms. Costello," she says. "The deadline for switching classes is in two weeks, but you should do it now, on your way to English class, before you lose your nerve."

On the way to our next class, we pass the auditorium, and I peek through the doorway. The cavernous room, where we do our school plays, is dark except for one spotlight beaming down on the stage. I imagine myself standing there, several inches taller in both body and spirit. I am speaking to a large audience. I don't know what my words are just yet, but I imagine how it must feel to voice them, to give them life.

On my way to my English class, I tell Theresa to save me a seat, and make a reluctant detour towards Ms. Costello's office. I pick up an appointment slip and fill it out. Then I hold it over the slot in her message box. My hand is trembling slightly, my thumb and index finger pressed together, unable to let it go.

I pull my hand back, fold the paper into fourths, and slip it into my sweater pocket.

The deadline is still two weeks away. I'll get around to it. Just not today.

Chapter Two

In speech, we practice impromptu, expository speaking, and debate. I am so absorbed in the class that I almost forget about the wrinkled counseling appointment slip in my pocket. I promise myself that I will see Ms. Costello on the very last day to change classes. Unfortunately, I find out that I got the deadline wrong—one day too late.

So here I am in Ms. Costello's cream-colored office, sinking into the sofa as she sits across from me.

"Frances, you had two weeks to take care of this." Ms. Costello's eyes are wide with disbelief. "This is so unlike you. Why didn't you say something sooner?"

She's right. This is unlike me.

"It's stuff like this that makes me gray," she adds.

Her shoulder-length hair is almost completely white. I hate to think that I could cause someone that much stress.

"I'm sorry about the inconvenience," I say, "but is it possible to make an exception?"

"Normally, I would say yes," says Ms. Costello, "but I tried getting someone else in Ms. Thorton's class yesterday, and she nearly hit the roof. She's been complaining about overcrowded classes for years, and if I do this to her again, she'll probably quit. I'm sorry, but you should have taken care of this the first day of class, as soon as you found out."

It's not my fault that the computer made a mistake, I want to say, but inside I know she is right. I just stare at her, like a dog begging for table scraps, hoping she will pity me enough to make one last exception.

Ms. Costello stares into space, deep in thought. Then she says, "Maybe speech isn't such a bad idea after all. Calculus will put you at the front of the pack, but it isn't a college-prep requirement. Speech could also look good on your application, especially if you attend competitions and win." Ms. Costello flips through my file. "You did score higher on verbal than math on your last SAT. So maybe this is the area where you can shine. You can use your writing skills to create a winning speech. Of course, it would have looked better on your application had you started competing last year. . . ."

Then why didn't she tell me this last year?

"But you can still compete in at least one tournament before the application deadlines," Ms. Costello continues. "And if you win, even better!" She closes my file and nods, punctuating her conclusion.

In the meantime, I'm sandwiched between two bad decisions. If I compete, I'm indulging in extracurricular activities, which, in Mom's opinion, will only serve to distract me from my studies. If I don't compete, I will have neither speech nor calculus to brag about in my college application, which will hurt my chances of getting into Berkeley.

After my appointment with Ms. Costello, I enter speech class late. I spend the rest of class enduring the itch to tell Theresa what happened, while Theresa endures the itch to hear about it. It isn't until the bell rings that we are able to have a good scratch.

"Well, how did it go?" Theresa asks.

I summarize what happened and explain my dilemma. "What do you think I should do?" I ask her.

"Ms. Costello's right," Theresa says. "If you don't have calculus on your transcript, you'll need speech to have a shot at Berkeley."

"Maybe I can just get an A in speech but not compete," I say.

"But it only counts in your CV if you compete," Theresa says. "Otherwise, it's just another fluffy class."

"Ladies, before you leave," says Ms. Taylor, "remember that your original oratory speech is due tomorrow. Also, I'm leaving a sign-up sheet for joining the school speech team. I encourage you all to sign up."

Theresa and I look at each other. Quietly, we disappear into the small crowd of exiting students and slither out the door.

I am sitting at my desk at home, a used mahjong table, which faces the front window. Like a bad friend, the sun, which abandoned us all summer long, is deciding to come out and play now that we are deep in schoolwork. I stare at what I've come up with so far for my original oratory speech—a blank sheet of paper. For the last two weeks, I rationalized that I would be out of this class by now, so why work on the speech? Who knew I'd be stuck in the course?

I think about Ms. Taylor's words on the first day of class: *Language gives us the ability not only to talk about the present but to reflect on the past and to plan for the future. . . .* I like her message, but I don't know how or where to begin. It's like turning a circle of tape around and around and searching for where to start peeling.

I look at my watch. I've been sitting here for a half hour and my page is still blank. My eyes wander to the wall. There hangs a red Chinese calendar, which includes all the good luck things to do and the bad luck things to avoid for the day.

Right below the calendar is a white statue of Gwun Yum, the goddess of compassion and mercy. Next to her is a plastic Chinese-red ancestral shrine for Popo. Popo's large photo is black and white. She is wearing a traditional black high-collar blouse with frog buttons. She has chiseled cameo features and very high cheekbones. There is no mirth in her expression. Her giant black eyes are hollow and piercing. Her thin lips are pressed into a straight line. Her bobbed black hair is clipped back tight, so tight that it accentuates the harshness in the angles of her face. Had she been younger and less austere in the photo, she could have looked like a Chinese Greta Garbo.

Gong Gong, Mom's dad, passed away a few years before Popo, but his picture is not in the shrine. He was successful at his business, but every dime he earned went to his illegitimate family as Mom struggled to support her mother and siblings.

The smoke from the burning incense makes me woozy. The three oranges my mother left for her ancestors in the afterlife are starting to mold. I am tempted to remove the oranges, but I hesitate. When I was little, I learned about King Tut and the pyramids of Egypt. I placed four oranges in the shape of a pyramid at the shrine, thinking that would impress my mom. Instead, she slapped me and removed the fourth orange. It turned out that four is a bad luck number, because the word for it, "*sei,*" is pronounced exactly like the word for death, "*sei,*" only in a different tone. That confused me. They were dead anyway. But I guess to Mom, they aren't.

My grandmother's face in the ancestral shrine stares back at me, her eyebrows drawn in a frown. She looks as though she can read my intentions. What if Mom is right? What if our ancestors are still with us? The eyes and ears of the dead are scarier than those of the living. They are silent yet everywhere. There is no escape. I tell myself to stop being superstitious, but I can't prove my ancestors' absence any more than I can prove their presence. I only have this eerie sensation that I can't brush off.

If spirits really do exist, then Popo probably knows about my speech enrollment. She probably knows about the appointment slip in my pocket, the one I failed to submit on time. Maybe she is blocking me from writing this speech.

Panicked, I pick up the phone and call Theresa.

"*Wei?*" says Nellie.

"Auntie Nellie? It's me, Fei Ting," I say in broken Chinese.

"Oh, Fei Ting! Have you eaten?"

"Yes." Actually, I'm starved, but saying so would make it sound like my mom isn't feeding me. "Is Theresa home?"

"She is. What do you want to talk about?"

"Um . . . schoolwork." Technically, that's not a lie.

"Oh, so hardworking. Theresa! Hurry up! It's Fei Ting!"

Theresa takes the phone. "Hello?"

"Theresa, I'm stuck on my speech—"

"Hold on." There is a pause. It sounds like Theresa is moving to another part of the house. "Mom, stop following me. I need some privacy!" Theresa says in English.

"Privacy? What you need privacy for?" Nellie says back in English. "Keep secret from me?"

Theresa groans. Then I hear the door shut. "Sorry," she says to me.

I give silent thanks for Theresa's discretion. "I don't know if I can go through with this. I feel like Popo's watching me." I'm whispering, as if keeping this conversation out of Popo's earshot.

"Didn't your popo pass away?" Theresa is whispering too, as if Popo might hear her as well.

"Yes. That's what makes it worse. I feel her eyes in the photo watching me." As I listen to myself whisper, I hate how nuts I sound. A Chinese person would berate me for my sins and urge me to heed my guilt. Everyone else would laugh me off as superstitious. Only Theresa can stand in the middle and see both sides. "I almost want to cover her face with a towel so she can't see me," I say.

"No! That feels . . . sacrilegious." Theresa pauses for a moment. "I've got an idea. What's the sweetest treat you've got in the house?"

"Well . . ." I open the pink bakery box on our kitchen table. "There's *dan tat* and *bolo bao*." "*Dan tat*" means "custard tart," and "*bolo bao*," which translates as "pineapple bun," is just a plain bun with a crusty sugar topping that looks like the outside of a pineapple.

"Which is your favorite?"

"The *dan tat*."

"Offer that to the shrine."

"But that's the last one." I cringe at my own selfishness.

"Even better," says Theresa. "It's showing your sacrifice. As you offer it to her, explain that you did your best to straighten things out. Promise that you'll make amends. You will write your speech to praise your mother as an unsung hero. So you're turning a bad thing into a good thing."

I pick up a *dan tat* with one hand and the base of the rotary phone with the other as I hold the receiver between my ear and my shoulder. I walk to the shrine, reluctantly place the last custard tart in front of Popo, and make my promise. "It's done," I say to Theresa.

Suddenly, my mother walks in. She is carrying our takeout dinner in one hand and her purse and keys in the other. I immediately turn my back towards her and walk away from the shrine.

"Well, thanks for the help with the calculus homework," I say.

Theresa gasps. "Did your mom just come home?"

I hear Mom's footsteps behind me as she approaches the dining table. "Yes."

"Do you think she suspects anything?"

"No."

"We better get off the phone now."

"Okay. I'll see you tomorrow." I hang up the phone, a little too quickly. I deliberately slow down, to make myself look casual.

"Who was that on the phone?" Mom asks.

"Oh, it's Theresa."

Mom raises an eyebrow. "I thought you despised her."

"That's not true." Well, at least not anymore.

"I'm glad that you've finally swallowed your pride and allowed her to help you with your weaknesses."

I begin setting the table with our ivory chopsticks, porcelain bowls, and small dishes. Our chopsticks have our Chinese names on them, engraved and painted in red. Our dishes and bowls have hand-painted dragons. They are red with gold trim. In contrast to our beat-up furniture, our dining ware is probably pretty valuable, like our jewelry at the bank. Did that, too, come from our former life?

Even before I untie the plastic bag and open the Styrofoam container, I recognize the scent of *cha siu* (barbecued pork), *chow fun* (flat rice noodles), *gai lan* (Chinese broccoli), and steamed rice. But overriding those tantalizing aromas is the smell of *fu gwa*, bitter melon. As I open the containers, which say HAVE A NICE DAY! the steam covers my face, fogging up my glasses.

"Four dollars," my mother says triumphantly. She prides herself on her ability to get a good deal.

As we sit down to eat, I notice how tired Mom looks. She is hunched over her food, in too much pain to hold herself up. She's been awake since three thirty this morning, to work the five o'clock shift, and didn't leave work until five in the afternoon.

"Maybe you should lie down awhile before you eat," I say.

Mom waves me off. "This food costs money. We have to eat it while it's still hot." Then she smiles and pats me on the hand. "*Gwai nui*. You always look out for your mother."

The barbecued pork is red and shiny. The ends are slightly burned. That is the sweetest and crispiest part. Mom picks out the end pieces for me and the middle slices for herself. The *gai lan* glistens with oil and oyster sauce. Mom picks out the tender baby stalks for me while reserving the older, more fibrous stalks for herself. Mom's chopsticks look like the beak of a mother bird pecking at a food source to regurgitate for her young. As she gathers the *chow fun*, she gives me the only two shrimps in the whole container and the brownest rice noodles, the ones with the most soy sauce. Then she gives herself the whiter, blander noodles and hardly any of the meat.

"Mom, it's okay. Save some of the good ones for yourself," I say.

"It's okay, Fei Ting. Mommy always saves the best for you.

Just study hard. When you become a doctor, you will make lots of money and you can buy Mommy the best food."

But what if I don't get into Berkeley because I'm not taking calculus? What if I don't get into medical school? Then Mom could be eating the middle parts of *cha siu* and the toughest stalks of *gai lan* and living in this cramped apartment for the rest of her life.

As if reading my mind, Mom says, "If you were talking to Theresa about calculus, how come your textbook isn't on your desk?"

I look over at my desk. There is nothing on it except my pen and my blank speech. "I forgot my calculus book in my locker," I say. "I was calling Theresa to get the questions." Can Mom hear the lying in my voice? Can she hear my heart pounding?

Mom's chopsticks move on to the bitter melon with sliced beef. The shiny dark green crescents have eyelet patterns on the outside. The alkaline smell fills my mouth with a taste similar to that of an unripe persimmon. The cook has added sugar to this dish, but no sweetness can dull the bitter taste that lingers on the tongue, tainting everything else you eat. Because it's Mom's favorite, she collects a giant heap and deposits it on my plate. It lands with a small thump, like a pile of manure.

"Mom, why don't you keep the bitter melon for yourself?" I say. "After all, it's your favorite."

"You're rejecting the best dish. Stop fussing. Just eat."

"It's really bitter."

"If you eat bitterness all the time, you will get used to it. Then you will like it."

"But I don't want to. I don't like *fu gwa*."

Mom's face becomes dark and stormy. I've figured out too late that I've said the wrong thing.

"I've been up since three thirty this morning, and I worked twelve hours—*twelve hours*—to earn the money that bought this food," Mom says. "You think I *like* to go to work? I work for *you*." Her eyes are red, tears welling in them, as her voice escalates to a shriek. "You don't realize how lucky you are to have education and food anytime you want. When you bathe, you use so much shampoo and soap, twice as much as I do. When you eat chicken, you leave little traces of chicken and cartilage on the bone. And now you're wasting a whole container of good food. I could support another child with all that you waste."

And now I am wasting her money for my education.

"This weekend I'm working too. So now I'm working seven days a week. You know why?"

I assume that her question is rhetorical, so I don't answer.

"You know why?" She is interpreting my silence as disrespect.

"To pay for my tuition," I say, my voice barely a whisper.

"That's not all. I also have to pay for Princeton Review, because your SAT scores are so bad. Theresa got 1350. How could you only get 1050? Auntie Nellie said that Theresa took Princeton Review. She guaranteed that it will help you. Seven hundred dollars just to help you. Because you can't help yourself."

Reluctantly, I lift a clump of bitter melon with my chopsticks and force it into my mouth. I chew it just enough so I can swallow it. The chewing unleashes more bitterness, which bleeds and lodges itself into every taste bud. I continue until the pile of bitter melon on my plate is gone.

But my efforts are not enough to placate her. Mom flings her chopsticks onto her plate. "Now look what you've done," she says. "You've upset me so much that my stomach hurts even more, and now I can't eat." Mom takes her lunch container and starts piling the rest of the bitter melon into it. "Because you don't like it, I guess I will have to finish it."

Now I am left with tender stalks and barbecued pork ends for the rest of my dinner. But I've lost my hunger for them. Mom puts on her apron and rubber gloves.

"I can wash the dishes," I say.

"Go study and do your homework," Mom snaps, keeping her back to me. She turns on the hot water and begins scrubbing the dishes in angry, jerky movements.

I quietly open Mom's container and scoop the remainder of my dinner into it. Then I turn around to make sure she isn't watching. Her back looks twisted and hunched over, as if chewed up and spat out by the hardness of life. I wonder what her life would have been like had I never been born. Maybe she could have moved back to Hong Kong, where her family and friends are. Maybe she could have pursued a college education, so she wouldn't have had to slave away at her current job. Maybe she could have found another husband, a nice man, a rich man who could have given her all the nice things she deserves. But she gave up all those opportunities. For me.

Shortly after the dishes are done, Mom retires to the bedroom, and I am left alone in the living area. I open my *Bartlett's Familiar Quotations*, my source of inspiration when I write essays, and look up quotes from Confucius. Twenty minutes later, I've come up with the following list of quotes.

> In serving your father and mother, remonstrate with them gently. On seeing that they do not heed your suggestions, remain respectful and do not act contrary. Although concerned, voice no resentment.

> A person who for three years refrains from reforming the ways of his late father can be called a filial son.

> When your father and mother are alive, do not journey far, and when you do travel, be sure to have a specific destination.

> Children must know the age of their father and mother. On the one hand, it is a source of joy; on the other, of trepidation.

Then I read my last quote, a Chinese proverb.

> Vicious as a tigress can be, she never eats her own cubs.

Tigers and cubs . . . My mind drifts back to the zoo and what my mom said about the difference between animals and humans.

I begin my speech. As I write, I imagine delivering it in the school auditorium. Ms. Taylor is sitting in the front row, her stained-glass blue eyes glistening with pride. Hidden from my view in the back row are my mother and, next to her, the spirit of Popo. They are angry with me for defying their orders.

As I finish my speech, the whole audience stands up and applauds loudly. Their applause beats against my eardrums and vibrates the floor under my feet, like heavy raindrops in a downpour. As my mother sees the sea of hands clapping for me, she has tears in her eyes. She regrets being so hard on me. She sees that she was wrong to have hidden my talent from the rest of the world. She realizes that she has been wrong about me all along, that I am beautiful, smart, hardworking, and loyal, the best kind of daughter. She vows to her mother that she will never take me for granted again. She will never again need to compare me to someone else, because she knows now how lucky she is.

Even as this image fades from my mind's eye, the sound of clapping remains, fueling the enthusiasm in my heart, and I continue writing.

Chapter Three

The closest Princeton Review class is held at St. Augustine's College Prep in the Sunset District, so I have to take the bus from the Richmond District through Golden Gate Park to get there. St. Augustine's is the most prestigious—and most expensive—of the Catholic schools in San Francisco. In contrast, St. Elizabeth's is the least expensive. Traditionally, Catholic high schools have been either all girls or all boys. This year, however, as Catholic schools struggle to keep their enrollment up, some of the boys' schools are going coed. St. Augustine's is one of them, and many freshman girls have flocked there. Their parents want the St. Augustine name to help them to get into the Ivy League schools. The girls want to be the precious female minority in a large pool of cute, preppy boys.

Because it's the first day, because I've never been on the St. Augustine campus, and because I'm bad with directions, it takes me a while to find the right classroom. This reminds me of my confusion on the first day of speech class. What if I think I'm in a Princeton Review class and it turns out to be acting, painting, or underwater basket weaving? On the positive side, it could be calculus. Then I could kill two birds with one stone.

I pass by several classrooms and some flyers for the St.

Augustine fall dance before I finally find the correct room. I check the number on the door with my confirmation sheet several times just to make sure. I feel like I'm the last one here. Most of the seats are already taken up by the St. Augustine students. The majority of them are boys in crisp white shirts, navy pants, and matching ties and V-neck sweaters. The girls are wearing the same, except that they have on navy pleated skirts instead of pants. I am suddenly aware that I haven't shared a classroom with boys since the eighth grade. The very thought floods me with self-consciousness.

The instructor asks me to sign in. He is an older man with white hair and wears a polo shirt and checkered golf pants. He shakes my hand warmly and introduces himself as Mr. Engelman. Then he gives me my workbook materials for the class.

There are two empty seats at the back of the classroom. One is to the left and the other is two rows to the right. The seat on the right-hand side is next to a blond boy. He is tall and lean, with long limbs. He has a long face with rosy cheeks. The sunlight from the window catches on his straight, fine hair, making it glow like golden silk threads. He looks at me and smiles. His eyes are the color of arctic glaciers.

Quickly, I look away, my face hot and my heart pounding. I sagely choose the empty seat on the left. But another latecomer takes that seat before I can get to it. I reroute my path towards the seat next to the blond boy. I avoid looking at him the whole time.

As Mr. Engelman begins class, a group of three boys next to the blond boy starts acting up. The boy behind me, the ringleader, has big green eyes and curly brown hair. The boy behind the blond boy has curly dirty-blond hair. The boy behind the ringleader has shocking orange hair and a rash of freckles on his face. The three play a kicking game, seeing who can kick whom the most without getting caught by the teacher. They time this so that it happens only when Mr. Engelman is writing on the board. Every time the boy directly behind me kicks or gets kicked, my desk is jolted. I'm not going to absorb any information with all this going on. I turn and give them a dirty look, holding my index finger up to my lips. For a while, they are quiet. Relieved, I resume my note taking. A minute later, however, a crumpled ball of paper hits me on the back of the head. This is followed by quiet sniggers. I try to ignore them, but a minute later, another paper ball hits me and lands next to me on the floor.

To my surprise, the blond boy reaches down, picks the paper ball off the floor, and hurls it back at the troublemakers. It hits the ringleader in the face.

Unfortunately, that is the moment when Mr. Engelman turns towards the class.

"Collins," he says, staring daggers at the blond boy. He points to the door. The blond boy sighs and gathers his things. As he passes me, I give him an apologetic look. He answers that with a rueful smile. We lock gazes as he walks towards the open doorway, until he runs into the doorframe, missing the doorway by an inch. The blond boy grimaces, holding his face in his hands as he exits the room. The troublemakers behind me snigger.

Meanwhile, Mr. Engelman has resumed his instruction. He turns his back to us again to write something on the board. I continue staring at the doorway until another ball hits me in the back of the head.

⌘⌘⌘

During the bus ride home, I can't stop thinking about the boy named Collins. I mentally replay the way he smiled at me, the way he defended me against those dumb kids, and the way he slammed into the doorframe. I decide that I should reciprocate the sacrifice he made for me. That evening, I copy my notes for him in my neatest writing. My hand is so careful that it almost trembles.

My mind wanders. How will he react when I give him his notes? Will he smile again? Will he talk to me? I remember the flyers in the hallway for the St. Augustine fall dance. I imagine him asking me, *Are you going to the dance?*

Suddenly, the door jerks open. Mom has just come home from work.

I nearly jump out of my seat, as if I were caught burgling. Mom does her usual routine, tossing her purse onto the couch and the takeout into the microwave with a heaviness that matches her mood. Meanwhile, I try to act normal, even though my heart is pounding. Fortunately, she can't read my thoughts. Right after thinking this, I look down at my notes and realize that while copying the vocabulary list, I wrote "dance" instead of "abstinence," the word following "abstemious." Frantic, I cross it out before Mom can detect it with her eagle eyes. What would Collins think, seeing "dance" in the middle of his vocabulary list? I cross it out several more times, until it is nothing more than an opaque black rectangle on the page. Instead of obliterating my mistake, however, scratching it out seems to highlight it more, like giant arrows screaming *Mistake, mistake! Stupid!* I toss the whole page and start over.

I can see Mom's point about not going out with boys. They are distracting. I can see how they could threaten one's chances of acing courses and getting into a top college.

I return to Princeton Review the following afternoon with a typed, mistake-free copy of my notes in my hand. I scan the room for Collins and find him sitting in the same spot. The moment he sees me, his face lights up with a warm smile. On cue, my heart starts hammering. I walk towards him, my fingers trembling as they clutch the paper. Quietly, I lay the notes on his desk and assume my seat. He peruses them and smiles again.

The three troublemakers walk into the classroom. Great. I look at Collins. He cringes. But this time, Mr. Engelman clears his throat, gives the boys an authoritative look, and points to the side of the room opposite Collins and me. We exchange looks of relief.

During class, we keep our eyes on the board while my thoughts focus on his presence. I fight to divert my attention back to the teacher. I panic about my lack of self-control. My mother has paid hundreds of dollars for this class and I am throwing it away by not paying attention. As I think this, I wonder if this is how he feels too.

After class, I eagerly await his first move. Will he talk to me? Will he escort me to the bus stop?

Instead, he gathers his things and quickly exits the room, leaving me alone in the dust.

Did I just imagine the friendship between us? Did I make a fool of myself?

I suppress the pain in my chest. I tell myself that this is a lesson about losing control of my emotions. It's better to be hurt now than later, when it's too late. I vow to myself that this will be the last time I think of him. In fact, next time, I won't even sit near him. I'll pick a seat as far away from him as possible.

In speech class, we move on to thematic interpretation, and original prose and poetry. We listen to famous speeches, like Martin Luther King's "I have a dream" speech, analyzing why they are effective.

The bell rings in Ms. Taylor's class. As we gather our things, Ms. Taylor calls my name. Startled, Theresa and I turn around. Ms. Taylor is motioning for me to approach her. Theresa and I look at each other as if to say, *Why?*

"I'll wait for you outside," Theresa says.

I nod and slowly approach Ms. Taylor's desk. My armpits and hands are clammy. Have I done something wrong? I review the last couple of weeks and can't remember having caused any problems.

For almost a minute, Ms. Taylor is reading. I sneak a peek and realize that she is reading my original oratory speech.

My speech must be horrible. She must be calling me up to tell me that I got a D, or that I should do it over, or worse yet, that I am flunking out of the class. I thought I was doing well, but maybe I was wrong. I brace myself for the humiliation.

Finally, she looks up at me. Her face glows brightly, her eyes glistening with tears. "This is one of the most beautiful speeches I've ever read," she says.

Her words have penetrated my ears, but not the rest of me. I replay them in my mind, to make sure that I heard them correctly.

"The sign-up sheet for speech team has been up for almost a month. Why haven't you signed up?" she asks.

Usually, questions asked by adults are accusations disguised as questions, such as "Why are you so lazy and forgetful?" or "Do you realize how much trouble you are?" Or the adult already knows the answer to the question and is drilling me for the right response. In contrast, Ms. Taylor is posing a question because she doesn't know the answer and wants to find out.

"I don't know," I say.

"This speech has a lot of potential," Ms. Taylor says. "It would be a waste of talent if you didn't compete. I really think you can win."

I tense up at the word *waste*. When my mom uses it, it means I've done something bad and I'd better do things the opposite way. "Um, okay," I say.

"Great!" says Ms. Taylor. "I'll add your name to the list."

By "okay," I meant "Okay, I agree that it's a waste," not "Okay, I'll join." But I am paralyzed, unable to protest.

"The first tournament is coming up in a couple of weeks," says Ms. Taylor. "I'm anxious to start practice. Can you start today after school?"

I'm supposed to be at Princeton Review this afternoon.

"Could we do it tomorrow morning, before school?" I ask meekly.

"To be honest, I'm not much of a morning person," Ms. Taylor says. "The only reason I make it to first-period class is because I drink two strong cups of coffee before coming in to work. I feel I can give you my best later in the day. Will that work for you?"

Ms. Taylor is already going out of her way for me. How can I inconvenience her further? "Okay," I say.

"You sure?"

Reluctantly, I nod.

"Fantastic!" she says. "I've taken enough of your time. You'd better get some lunch before your next class. I'll see you at three."

I exit Ms. Taylor's classroom. Theresa is waiting for me outside.

"Well?" she says. She's shifting her weight back and forth, like she's about to pee in her pants.

Over lunch, I tell her what happened.

"Holy Moses!" says Theresa. "I really want you to do this speech thing, but ditching Princeton Review, that's a really expensive course. Your mom worked really hard to pay for it."

"But it's only one day!" I say. "Besides, this is a once-in-a-lifetime chance."

Theresa nods solemnly. She is now deep in thought, so much so that she has stopped chewing. Finally, she says, "Maybe you should just compete. In the big picture, you're still trying to get into Berkeley, only you're plotting a different route. Besides, you have your collateral." She is referring to my promise to Popo to write my speech about my mother. "When you go to your tournaments, you can tell your mom that you're studying with me, and I'll cover for you," Theresa says. "And you won't *really* be lying, because you will be studying with me. I've taken the Princeton Review. I can help you study for the SAT. That way, when"—she stops to correct herself—"*if* Auntie Gracie finds out, you can show her that you're really obeying her, just differently than she expected."

"Really?" I am stunned by Theresa's cleverness. I am also nervous about her selflessness. "No, I can't. That's too much work for you."

"No it's not," Theresa says. "The SAT is easy for me. Those tests aren't really about what you know or how smart you are. They're really about how well you can second-guess the test."

I am envious of Theresa's talents and irritated that she takes them for granted. The SAT makes my brain tired. I've done poorly on fill-in-the-bubble tests since grade school.

"You have a special talent, Frances," Theresa says. "It's not right to waste it."

I blush with pride. "That's what Ms. Taylor said too," I say.

Theresa's crescent-moon eyes are sparkling. "You know what?" she says. "I used to be envious of your talent, because I thought that it made you more important than me. But now I realize that my approach was wrong. I show my importance not by competing against your talent but by supporting it."

Once again, Theresa outshines me without trying. But this time, I bask in her light, just as she does in mine. Theresa is a true kindred spirit.

I imagine Collins waiting for me in class this afternoon, missing me, wondering where I am. I imagine him at home, copying his notes for me. He worries that I am avoiding him. A warm, sweet feeling pools in my chest.

Then I flash back to reality. I remind myself that he walked out of the classroom just yesterday without thanking me for the notes. This isn't someone who's going to notice that I'm missing. And it is probably for the best. I don't need this kind of distraction.

Chapter Four

Ms. Taylor's room, which is always warm in the afternoon sun, is made warmer by my nervousness. Ms. Taylor has drawn the old, mismatched curtains, rust colored on one side and olive green on the other, to keep the room cooler. My face and trunk flush hot, while my hands and feet feel cold, clammy, and purple, as if my trunk and extremities belong to two separate people.

Ms. Taylor is sitting near the back of the small classroom. She is wearing her usual black platform boots and matching pants and an emerald green velvet top. The shimmery top makes her eyes look bright green. With those emerald eyes and black rhinestone-studded cat-eye glasses, she looks like a cat or a sorceress.

I squint at Ms. Taylor's eyes. When she wears her blue blouse, her eyes look like sapphires. When she wears her purple blouse, they look like amethysts. No matter what color shirt I wear, my eyes are always dark brown. If Ms. Taylor's eyes keep changing with her outfit, then what is her true eye color?

Ms. Taylor nods at me and smiles. It is time for me to begin.

I have rehearsed this speech so many times that the words pour out of my mouth automatically. I am proud that my recitation is flawless, and I imagine that Ms. Taylor is too as I await her feedback.

"Frances, your writing is very eloquent and your argument is compelling," Ms. Taylor says. "However, I feel that you're going through the motions of reading your speech instead of being in the moment and meaning it. You know what I mean?"

I nod eagerly, hiding my confusion and disappointment.

"Okay. This time, slow down. Pause after each sentence and think about what it means."

I start over again, making a conscious effort to speak slowly.

"My mother's perseverance and hard work . . . are an example and inspiration to me."

As I recite my speech, I become aware that my sentences are excruciatingly long.

"After I graduate from high school, I hope to attend UC Berkeley. . . . Afterwards, I plan to attend medical school and become a doctor. . . . My medical knowledge will improve her health. . . . My future income will support her, so that she won't have to work and suffer anymore."

I'm not getting enough air into my lungs.

"When I feel tired or daunted by my quantity of school-work . . . I remember that my hardship can't be half as hard as my mother's and that someday . . . when my hard work pays off, so will hers."

I gulp for air after each sentence.

"Frances, are you okay?" Ms. Taylor is staring at me, her cat eyes wide with alarm.

My chest is heaving. Ms. Taylor's image becomes blurry, so I blink. To my surprise, tears run down my cheeks. My face turns hot from humiliation, as if I have just thrown up in public. I turn my face away to hide my alarming behavior.

"I'll get you some water," Ms. Taylor says. She leaves the room.

I sit down in one of the desks. Every limb is trembling violently. I recited my speech just fine at home. Why can't I do it here? The image of Popo's photo comes to mind. Maybe she has cursed me.

I need to withdraw from this competition. I have to sneak out and go to Princeton Review.

But I promised Ms. Taylor that I would rehearse today. And she's getting water for me. It would be rude of me to let her go to all that trouble only to come back and find me gone. Then I would never be able to face her again.

Ms. Taylor returns with a paper cup. The water is shockingly cold. As I swallow, it forms an icy stream down my throat and pools in my stomach.

"Good work today," Ms. Taylor says.

I cringe at her praise. She's just trying to be nice to me when all I've done is mess up.

"Let's call it a day," she says. "Need a ride home?"

Suddenly, I go from deflated to uplifted. Ms. Taylor wants me to ride in her car! I'm probably the only student at St. Elizabeth's who has received such an offer.

Ms. Taylor's car is a sky blue Beetle. Bugs are my favorite cars. They're round and cute looking, like ladybugs. Most cars today look like boxes on wheels. Too bad no one makes Beetles anymore. As I get inside, I notice that the seat sinks down pretty far under the pressure of my weight. If this car gets any older, we may sink right through the seats until our bottoms brush the ground. The interior has that old-car smell. I also notice the smell of Ms. Taylor's perfume and the odor of cigarettes.

On the dashboard is an open ashtray with two cigarette butts inside. Ms. Taylor smokes! How scandalous! I guess I've smelled it all along, but the scent didn't register. I imagine Ms. Taylor and me driving along the Great Highway next to Ocean Beach, each of us with a cigarette in hand, talking and laughing like old friends. Or better yet, Ms. Taylor and me sitting in a café, each with a cigarette in one hand and a cup of coffee in the other, talking and laughing.

Ms. Taylor quickly closes the ashtray. "I'm setting a bad example," she says. "You don't smoke, do you?"

"No." For the first time, I wish I did.

"Good. Don't start. I hate to be a hypocrite, but it's an impossible habit to break."

"Yeah. I know." Actually, I don't, but that sounded cool.

As Ms. Taylor drives down Turk Street past the University of San Francisco, I notice the rumbling and bouncing of the seat, the jerky back-and-forth motion of the car as Ms. Taylor shifts gears.

"Don't worry about the stage fright," Ms. Taylor says. "You'll always get the jitters, but you'll manage it better with practice."

Stage fright. She talks about it like it's something every public speaker has. Even if that's true, I doubt that every speaker has a mother breathing down her neck. Fortunately, we perfect and perform the same speech throughout the school year. If I had to reinvent my speech for each competition and overcome stage fright all year long, I would probably have a nervous breakdown.

As if reading my mind, Ms. Taylor asks, "Has your mother read your speech?"

"No."

"You really should share it with her. I bet she'd be proud. Parents aren't allowed to attend competitions in the state circuit, but maybe we can find another tournament for her to attend."

I force a pleasant smile.

"May I ask you a personal question?" Ms. Taylor says.

I tense at the request. "Sure."

"Is it ever too much pressure for you, living up to your mother's expectations?"

"No. I mean, I never thought about it before."

"Really? I mean, your decision to become a doctor, did your mom say, 'Frances, I want you to become a doctor,' or did you decide that on your own?"

"She feels that it would be the best thing for me," I say.

"Have you ever not wanted to become a doctor?" Ms. Taylor asks. "Or have you ever secretly wanted to do something else?"

"I never really thought about it," I say.

Ms. Taylor shrugs. "Okay. When I suggested volunteering at

a hospital on the first day of class, I really meant it. Just getting into med school requires tons of premed prerequisites during undergrad. Then it's another four to five years of med school, followed by another few years of residency. Volunteering in a hospital or working part-time in a doctor's office will either steer you elsewhere, or it will strengthen your resolve and help you through the hard times."

Ms. Costello has gone over this with me already. But hearing it from Ms. Taylor feels like a sinking stone in my chest. By the time I become a doctor, I'll be . . . thirty? I'll be over the hill by then. The thought of having to work as hard as I do now, or even harder, for the next thirteen years of my life makes me not want to go to college at all.

"So, are you applying to other colleges besides Berkeley?" Ms. Taylor asks.

"San Francisco State, just in case I don't get into Berkeley," I reply.

"You ought to apply to all the UCs, just to expand your options," Ms. Taylor says. "They're all on one application, so all you have to do is check off the other schools."

Only Berkeley is prestigious enough for Mom. It is also the only UC within commuter distance. I smile and nod, hoping that Ms. Taylor will change the subject.

"Have you ever thought about Scripps College?" Ms. Taylor says.

Because St. Elizabeth's is a private all-girls high school, it invites recruiters from various private women's colleges to speak to us about their schools. Scripps is definitely a St. Elizabeth's favorite, along with Mills, Smith, and Wellesley. "We can't afford to go to Scripps," I say.

"You could apply for scholarships and take out student loans. I did."

"It's too far away."

"Far away is a great opportunity to develop your sense of identity and independence."

A cold wave creeps through me. I sit on my hands to still their shaking.

"At first, I was really afraid to go away to college too, but I made new friends and started making my own decisions," says Ms. Taylor. "Trust me, a women's college is a very nurturing and empowering learning environment for a young woman. Actually, it was my experience at Scripps that inspired me to teach at an all-girls high school."

Could college actually be fun, unlike grade school and high school?

"What was it like there?" I ask.

"Well, it's a lot smaller than a UC or State, so it was more intimate," says Ms. Taylor. "I felt like a person, not a number. I really got to know the professors, and a couple of them became my mentors. They were the ones who got me fired up about literature and language and teaching. Also, I met my closest friends there. Before college, I had friends to hang out with but no one I could call a kindred spirit. It wasn't until college that I met people my age who got me. By the time I graduated, I had this big feeling inside, like I had accomplished so much and could accomplish so much more."

Wow. Currently, I have "friends" at school, people with whom I'm friendly, but I've never felt completely comfortable with them. Theresa is the only friend whose company I enjoy. Until now, I've perceived college as an extension of high school, only worse, with more students, more faculty, and more pressure. I imagine being at a college like Scripps, living among a community of Theresas, being taught by a whole faculty of Ms. Taylors. No one there would criticize me for my looks or for liking one thing and not another. I could pursue whatever inspired me. If such a college existed, I would go, not with head down, but with my arms wide open.

"Was your mom okay with your going away?" I ask.

"She was the one who suggested it in the first place," Ms. Taylor says. "She wanted me to have a good education, spread my wings and fly. My first month in college, I cried every day and called home asking to drop out or transfer. But Mom encouraged me to stick it out one semester. By the end of the semester, I loved it. I just needed time to discover that I could do it on my own."

"Wow. Your mom sounds pretty liberal."

"That's one way to look at it. You see, my dad was a real dud, and my mom realized that she didn't want me to walk the same path that she had, so she really pushed me in a different direction. That's what every mom wants for her kids, to do better than she had done. I'm sure your mom feels the same way."

That's exactly what my mom has said, yet her methods are so different from that of Ms. Taylor's mom. I wonder if Ms. Taylor's mom is one of a kind, or if there are other moms like her too.

"Where are you from originally?" I ask.

"North Carolina."

"Really?" She doesn't sound the least bit Southern. "Is it hard being away from your mom?"

"Not really. I mean, I miss her a lot, but we talk on the phone once a week, and I visit during holidays. In a way, distance doesn't matter. When you're close, distance can't tear you apart. Likewise, if you're not close, then living close by won't bring you together. At any rate, consider Scripps. I think it will be a good match for you. Either way, let me know if you need a letter of recommendation."

Suddenly, Ms. Taylor's car starts to lose control. It swerves back and forth, unable to stay within the lane.

"What's going on?" Ms. Taylor says as she grips the steering wheel.

I hear rumbling and crumbling sounds outside the car. Moments later, it is over. Ms. Taylor turns on the radio. A newscaster announces that there has been an earthquake.

Ms. Taylor swears under her breath. I'm too shaken to be shocked by her language. "Is your mom home?" she asks me.

"Yes," I reply. As I stare at the houses along Balboa Street, I remind myself that all the homes in our area are still standing, even if their brick facades have fallen into piles on the ground. There are no fires or explosions. As long as our building is still intact, my mother should be fine. But I can't be completely sure. Suddenly, I'm gripped with the fear that our apartment has collapsed and my mother is crushed under the rubble. I picture her smashed body in a pool of blood, her arms, legs, and head angled in unnatural positions.

Finally, we arrive at my apartment. To my relief, it looks more or less the same, still three stories, windows intact. As Ms. Taylor pulls into the driveway, I notice a white piece of paper stuck to the metal gate. I get out of Ms. Taylor's car and notice that my name is on the note. I open it. It is in Theresa's careful script. It reads:

> *Auntie Gracie is at our house. We're okay. Come over <u>without</u>*
> *Ms. Taylor.*

"What is it?" Ms. Taylor calls through her rolled-down window.

"My mom's at Theresa's house," I say.

"Great. Let's drive over."

"No. You've spent too much time on me already."

"I've spent an extra couple of hours. What's another few minutes?"

"Um, I need to walk. It's only a couple blocks."

"If something falls on you along the way, I'm going to feel responsible."

"You're not responsible," I insist. "I need the air. To clear my head. It's just a couple of blocks. I'll be fine."

"You sure?"

I nod and start walking away.

Ms. Taylor drives alongside me. I wish she would just drive away. I am nervous that Mom or Nellie will notice her from Nellie's front window. Ms. Taylor doesn't pull away until I reach Theresa's home. Before I can ring the doorbell, Auntie Nellie opens the door.

"Wah! Fei Ting! We've been so worried!"

Moments later, Theresa and Mom are hobbling down the stairs. Theresa is propping Mom up as she descends the steep, pink-carpeted steps. Mom is hunched over, clutching her abdomen. Once she reaches the foot of the stairs, she grabs my arms and weeps.

Then Nellie starts pushing us inside. "Don't stay outside! It's dangerous!" Even when Nellie is calm, she sounds like she is shouting. Now that she's excited, my ears are ringing. Theresa and Nellie take Mom by the arms and help her up the curving stairs. I follow closely. Once we're upstairs, Theresa and Nellie help Mom settle down at the dining table. I remain standing, unable to endure the luxury of sitting. To my surprise, the floors are clean. The only way I can tell that an earthquake has passed is by the open kitchen cabinets, which are half full. The rest of the dishes and bowls must have fallen and broken and been cleared away.

Nellie says, "Let's make tea."

"You can't use the gas stove, Mom," Theresa says.

"Oh." Then Nellie begins flipping the light switches on and off. "Hey! The lights don't work."

"The electricity's out," Theresa says.

"Oh. Then go find some candles."

"We can't use candles."

"Why not?"

"Because if there's gas in the room, they might cause an explosion."

"Then what do we use? It's getting dark!"

"Flashlights." Theresa's talking to her mother as if explaining things to a five-year-old.

Theresa leaves the room for a while. Meanwhile, Nellie finds a flashlight and begins flicking the on-off switch back and forth. "Hey, how can the earthquake affect this too?" she says.

Theresa comes back with new batteries. She takes the flashlight from Nellie, changes the batteries, and turns on the flashlight. It seems that without Theresa, Nellie could not survive in this world. I imagine myself in Theresa's shoes. I wouldn't have known not to turn on the stove. I probably would have lit a candle and blown my mom and me up.

"Look how smart Theresa is," Mom says. "She's really worth the rice you feed her."

"When the earth was shaking, I was so scared, I just started running around the room screaming," Nellie says. "Then Theresa grabbed me and pushed me under the dining table. Good thing too, because I probably would have gotten hurt from all the flying dishes."

Mom is probably wishing she and Nellie could trade daughters. And who could blame her? Theresa was there for Nellie during the quake. She was there for Mom when she needed comfort and protection. Where was I? Practicing for a speech competition behind my mother's back.

"Where did you go after school today?" Mom says to me.

"Princeton Review. Remember?" I try to spy Theresa from the corner of my eye, but she is looking at her lap.

"How come you weren't there when everyone else was leaving?" Mom says.

How did she know that I wasn't there?

"I tried to call Princeton Review, but the phone didn't work," Mom says. "Then I ran to Nellie's house, even as the ground was shaking, in case you were there, but you weren't. Then I made Nellie drive me and Theresa to Princeton Review. We waited outside the building and looked for you as everyone else left, but you weren't there. Nellie and I began asking the kids if they knew where you were, but no one did. Then, I found your teacher."

I stifle the urge to gasp.

"I asked him where you were. He said something like 'She's not with you?'"

Had Mr. Engelman said, "Frances wasn't here today," I would have been caught for sure. How much longer before my luck runs out? Maybe I should just surrender the truth and get my punishment over with.

"My heart nearly fell into my bowels," Mom says. "Then Theresa said that maybe you had left and were on your way home. Then I told Nellie to drive me home to find you, but

Theresa told me to stay at her house. She offered to walk to our apartment, risking her own life, to wait for you and bring you back. But Nellie and I were too scared for her, so she said she would leave you a note and come right back."

I picture Theresa sitting nervously in the backseat of Nellie's car, scared of what would happen once Mom and Nellie discovered that I wasn't at Princeton Review. She probably nearly peed in her pants when they ran into the teacher. It would have been so easy for her at that moment to give up and drop our charade. I watch Theresa from the corner of my eye. She is still looking at her lap.

"Why weren't you with your teacher? Why weren't you with the other kids?" Mom asks.

Theresa looks up at me, her eyes wide with alarm.

"Well," I say, "like Theresa said, I had already left. I was worried about you, so I rushed out the door."

"But how did you get home?"

"I just . . ." I can't say that I walked. It is too far. But would the bus still run in a time like this? "I just found a way," I say, aware of how lame I sound.

"Aiyah! Gracie!" Nellie fans the air in front of Mom's face, as if to slap some sense into her. "Who cares how she got home? The important thing is she's here! See what a good daughter she is? She risked her own life to return home and make sure you were okay!"

"Theresa is the true hero," Mom says. "Not only did she figure out how to get us all together, she helped sweep the floor of all the broken dishes and bowls. Right now my kitchen is littered with broken things. We better head home soon to clean up."

"No!" Nellie holds out both arms as if stopping an oncoming bus. "Stay with us tonight. You can go home tomorrow."

"I can't be a burden," Mom says.

"You're not a burden. We need you too. Daddy's in Hong Kong and Ben is at MIT, so we need the company." By "Daddy" Nellie means Theresa's dad, her husband.

That night we eat cold leftover *chow mein* and *chow fun* from Nellie's fridge. Mom and Nellie are stuffing themselves past the point of fullness. Even a dangerous crisis cannot erase their aversion to wasting food. Theresa warns everyone not to over-use the flashlight.

After dinner, Mom gets the guest bedroom and I get to sleep in Theresa's room. Minus the lack of street lighting, everything in Theresa's room looks the same. Her giant New Kids on the Block poster still hangs on the back of her door. Her rainbow comforter still drapes her full-size bed, and her stuffed Hello Kitty and Care Bears still sit on her pillows, like magic animals on clouds.

As Theresa and I get ready for bed, Theresa is quiet and does not look at me at all. She turns her back to me as she changes into her long white cotton nightgown. I change into Nellie's orange polyester pajamas with dark pink flowers. Her waistband sags around my hips. I wonder if Theresa is mad at me, but I lack the courage to find out for sure. All I can think is *mm ho yee see*. I don't know if there is a perfect English translation. It's what people say when they feel embarrassed about imposing, or when someone does them a big favor and they can't reciprocate.

Theresa crawls into bed and flips her rainbow comforter over her. I hesitate, unsure if she wants me near her. But Theresa stays on one side of the bed and says, "Aren't you getting in?" Relieved, I crawl in next to her.

As I look out the window, I expect to see the streetlights filter through the blinds, painting streaks on Theresa's white walls. Instead, all I see is pitch-black. I realize then that in the city, it's never really perfectly dark. We think it's black when, in fact, we can see our hands in front of our faces, and the shadows of light gray cast upon darker gray. In this cloak of darkness, I muster what little courage I have and turn to face Theresa. "Thanks," I say.

"It's okay," she replies.

"Sorry," I add. I choke back the urge to cry.

"It's okay," Theresa says. I immerse myself in the luxury of her forgiveness.

"This upcoming competition," Theresa says, "maybe you should think about quitting after that one. Or tell Auntie Gracie that you're competing in speech and sell her on it. I don't think I can take this anymore."

I wonder if that was why Theresa continued our lie, not so much to protect me but to protect my mother from heartbreak.

CARA CHOW

Chapter Five

The following day, Mom and I finally go back to our apartment. In the living room, our fifteen-inch television has tumbled facedown onto the floor, its glass splintered in every direction. The white Gwun Yum statue has also fallen and has broken in two. Now that it is broken, I can see that it is hollow inside. Popo's photo has also fallen facedown. There is shattered glass everywhere. Mom runs to the picture and picks it up. There is a big harsh diagonal scratch across Popo's face. The scratch pains me. It looks as if a knife has slashed her face. Mom is crouched over and kneeling as she clutches the photo, oblivious to the broken glass all around her.

"How do we remedy this, Fei Ting?" she says. "This is my only picture of her, no negatives, no copies."

I have no answer for her. Not putting it up isn't an option, but displaying the big scratch also seems offensive. Instead, I avoid the issue. "Don't move," I say. I get a broom and begin sweeping away the glass so she won't get hurt. Mom stays frozen like a large round boulder. The photo in her hands has become a part of the boulder, like a piece of quartz embedded in stone. Even her tears are frozen. They are vibrating just under her eyelids, but no sobs come forth. I continue sweeping around her in a circle, like a satellite revolving around the earth.

I turn over the broken television.

"I worked so hard to buy that TV," Mom says.

It is thirteen years old. It's black-and-white, even though everyone else has color. But to Mom, it's still money. She mourns every grain of rice that is not eaten. She cringes at every pair of panty hose that runs, scorning its owner for her carelessness. She stoops into gutters to pick up pennies, as if each penny were a nugget of gold. Quietly, I shuttle the TV away, to remove this assault from Mom's field of vision.

In the kitchen, our cabinets and drawers are all open. The porcelain bowls, plates, and cups, and ivory chopsticks have spilled onto the linoleum floor. After cleaning the living room, I begin stacking our dining ware, separating out the broken pieces. Once that is organized, I sweep those floors as well. Mom is still hunched over in the living room.

After cleaning up the kitchen, I proceed to the bathroom and then to the bedroom. As I clean, I notice how this work wears down the body and saps the spirit. It seems endless, relentless. I want to take a break, stop for today and continue tomorrow, but I can't. The punishment is cleansing, proof to Mom that I am not lazy or incompetent. I remind myself that this is how Mom must feel, day after day. No time for rest, no time for fun.

Once I am done with the bedroom, I go back to the living room to tend to Mom. I peel her hooked fingers from the photo frame, remove the remaining shards, and place it back on the mantelpiece in the shrine, ignoring the big streak across Popo's face. Then I help Mom up from the floor and draw her a hot bath.

We go over to Theresa and Nellie's for dinner, but afterwards, we return home. Mom's stomach is worse than ever. She is so hunched over that she is nearly crawling up the stairs to our apartment.

Once we're inside, I wrap Mom in blankets on the couch and make her a pot of loose-leaf oolong tea. Since we now have no television, I bring out my plastic childhood record player, another relic Mom has refused to throw away or donate. Under my desk, I find the stack of records Mom brought over from Hong Kong. She has Elvis; the Beatles; Peter, Paul and Mary; and several Canto-pop records from the sixties and seventies. I play one of the Canto-pop records. The music sounds like Western music with Cantonese lyrics. The singer's voice is smooth and sweet, not nasally as in the Peking operas. I sit next to Mom, and the two of us scan the room. There is a giant crack running from one corner of the ceiling to the other.

Mom heaves a deep, sad sigh. "Look at all these cracks," she says. "I can work so hard to make everything perfect, to put everything in order, yet in one moment, all that can be wrenched away from me. It is a mockery of my efforts. That is how cruel nature can be."

I smart with indignation. I just spent hours cleaning up, but all she can focus on is everything I can't fix, as if I haven't done anything at all.

Then Mom rises from the couch to survey the apartment. Immediately, I tense up. She will find some flaw with my cleaning. It will never measure up to her standards. But instead, Mom nods and smiles. "Good girl. The apartment looks so nice now, almost as if the earthquake had never struck."

This is the first time she has ever complimented me.

"As long as I have you, they can take everything away from me—my TV, my picture, my dishes, even my home!" Mom says. "To hell with them all! When you become a successful doctor, we can get all these things back!" She releases a big belch, as if punctuating her declaration. To an outsider, that would sound comic. But I know that passing gas is a sign that Mom's stomach is recovering. I can give back to her what others have taken away: money, health, and dignity. All this time I have seen her expectations as pressure, when really they were the sign that she believed in me.

Mom returns to the sagging couch and sighs. "I am so old and broken, Fei Ting, just like this apartment."

"That's not true," I say.

"Yes it is," she says. "I'm also getting fat."

"No you're not."

"You just don't notice, because you're around me every day. But I've had these pants for over twenty years and they don't fit me like they used to. Also, my hair is turning white."

"But your skin is so beautiful," I say. "Not one wrinkle in sight."

"You think so?" Mom says ruefully.

CARA CHOW

Never before has Mom cared about my opinion. In the past, she has always rushed past me in the race to get things done, arguing that I'm not competent enough to help. But this time, I get to show her that I, too, can take care of things. That is why she is talking to me in this new way, like a friend rather than a mother.

I will make sure that I am different too. My first competition will be my last. Once speech class is over, I will redirect my attention, with a more penetrating focus. I will right all the wrongs, wipe the slate clean.

I take my backpack to the bedroom and pull out my UC application. As I proofread it, I recall Ms. Taylor's advice to apply to all the UCs, to expand my options. I look at the list of schools: UC Davis, UC Berkeley, UC Santa Barbara, et cetera. Only Berkeley has an X next to it. Ms. Taylor's suggestion, if only a flicker of temptation, is now snuffed out, a charred match floating in a puddle of gutter water. I fold my application neatly, place it inside the envelope, and seal it. I walk my UC application and my San Francisco State application, which I filled out last week, to the mailbox down the street, risking being caught outdoors should an aftershock strike.

When I return to the apartment, Mom is hunched over in the kitchen, sorting through the trash. She lifts a porcelain bowl, the one with the red-and-gold dragons, from the trash bag. It is cracked and missing a huge piece. "This was a wedding present," Mom says. "This was the life we were supposed to have." Then she gasps and drops the half bowl onto the floor. It shatters. A bead of blood forms on Mom's thumb. I run to the bathroom to get the first-aid kit. Then I clean Mom's finger and bandage it.

"Those pieces are sharp. You shouldn't touch them," I say. I shuttle Mom off to the bedroom. Then I help her get into her pajamas and into bed.

Afterward, I begin to return to the kitchen, where Mom dropped the bowl, but I stop myself halfway. My bones ache. I've done enough today. I can always clean this up tomorrow. I return to the bedroom and climb into bed.

The next day, I wake up to the sounds of running water and clanging silverware and dishes. At first, between sleep and wake, I think I am dreaming, but as the haze of dreaminess fades away, the sharp sounds from the kitchen remain, sending a spark of alarm through me. We didn't cook last night. Why is Mom washing dishes?

After making my bed, I put on my slippers and walk to the kitchen. Mom is standing at the sink. Her arms move in a flurry. A collection of bowls and dishes is accumulating in an organized manner on the dish rack. Hot white steam rises from the sink and the dish rack, but it seems to emanate from her body rather than the hot water.

"Mom, why are you washing dishes?" I say.

"They all fell onto the floor during the quake," Mom says. Her consonants form jagged edges. "Don't you know that the floors are dirty? How can you put them back in the cupboards without washing them?" As she places each dish on top of the other, they make increasingly loud clanging sounds that further punctuate her fury.

"Why help at all if all you do is make things worse?" Mom says. She turns off the faucet and points to the floor. "Look." She crouches over a spot on the kitchen floor, still pointing. Her index finger shakes with rage. Puzzled, I bend over, my nose following her finger, which is just a few inches from my face. Next to the trash bag, porcelain pieces form a mosaic in a fine cloud of white porcelain dust. One of the pieces has a dragon's head on it.

"I couldn't find my slippers this morning, so I went to look for them," Mom says. "Then I decided to go to the kitchen to make tea, and now look!" Mom removes her right foot from her slipper and holds it up to my face. The ball of her foot is covered with a bandage. A large spot of blood is visible through the gauze.

Mom slips her foot back into her slipper and starts marching around the kitchen. "Then, afterwards, I walk around, and all I hear is crunch, crunch, crunch! There is porcelain everywhere!" Mom circles back to where I am kneeling and points again. "Tell me what you see," she says.

"That's the bowl that you dropped last night," I say.

"No! They're the pieces you forgot to clean up."

"But that's not true," I say. "The floor was clean before you dropped it. You inspected it last night and said that it was fine."

"I wouldn't overlook something as obvious as this."

I stare at her incredulously. She has always been the one to memorize phone numbers after seeing or hearing them once. She remembers people's birthdays and never forgets a promise made or broken. Can she possibly have forgotten that she cut her finger on this bowl and dropped it?

Or is she just pretending that she never dropped it so she can blame it on me?

I decide to test her. "You must have dropped the bowl," I say. "How else did you get the cut on your finger?" I point at the bandage on Mom's right thumb.

Mom ignores that last remark. "You're imagining things, Fei Ting. Stop twisting the truth and accept your shortcomings."

I start to wonder if I really did imagine the events of last night. Then I remember Ms. Taylor's words on the first day of school. *Language is power. We . . . have the power to . . . persuade others . . .*

Is this the power of language? I think of witches' spells, how the right words can change princes into frogs. To shake off Mom's spell, I focus on her bloody finger. I remind myself that had she not touched the bowl, that wound wouldn't be there. But I keep that knowledge inside, where it is safe.

"You can't do anything right," Mom continues. "Follow me."

She marches into the bathroom. Assuming a posture of deference, shoulders slumped and head bowed, I follow. Mom points at my bath towel. It is lemon yellow, a glaring contrast to the pink and maroon tiles. As far as I can tell, it is arranged just as she likes it, folded longways, then draped over the towel bar.

"You can't even hang your towels properly," Mom says.

I squint at my towel, looking for the flaw. Seeing my confusion, Mom points at the edges.

"It's crooked!"

Then I see it. It is crooked. By about ten degrees.

"*Mo no! Mo yong!*" she says. That means "brainless" and "useless." She says this as she drills her index finger into my temple, as if tattooing these labels onto my head. "Fix it now," Mom says.

Carefully, I lean over to adjust my towel. I make it perfectly aligned. Then, on a whim, I position my back to her so that she can't see my towel and I adjust it ten degrees in the opposite direction. I hold my breath, waiting for her reaction.

Mom scrutinizes my towel. Then she says, "This is how you should do it from now on. You should be able to do this on your own without my reminding you."

"Yes, Mommy," I say, looking at the floor.

Mom exits the bathroom and returns to the kitchen to wash dishes. I wait another second before letting a smile erupt on my lips. Then I take Mom's towel, which is lemon yellow, just like mine, and adjust it exactly the same as mine, ten degrees off center. After all, that's exactly how she wants it done. I wait the rest of the day to see if she notices. She doesn't.

That night, in bed, while Mom is snoring softly on the bottom bunk, I lie on the top with my eyes wide open. One word keeps echoing in my mind.

Liar. My mother is a liar.

Why should I feel guilty about lying when she does it too? What have I gotten all these years in return for playing things straight? Nothing.

I envision myself at a fork in the road. One prong leads to Berkeley, then med school, then residency, then working and living with my mother for the rest of my life. The other road leads to speech, then Scripps, then . . . I can't see the rest. I can only see my arms spreading, like wings taking flight.

Regardless of the cost, I must go ahead with speech and protect it with whatever means necessary. I will apply to Scripps, Ms. Taylor's school, a school far away from here. From now on, it's me against Mom, warfare with words. Mom is the superpower. I am the guerilla fighter.

The flames of the day have calmed down to an ashy gray and orange. But that's when the coals are the hottest. I blow on the orange in my heart. It warms me until I drift off to sleep.

Chapter Six

Ironically, just as I strengthen my resolve to pursue speech and Scripps, Mom decides to change her schedule, making it more difficult for me to cover my tracks. She gets home before I do now, and she sits at the window every day, waiting for me to step off the bus or out of Nellie's car. I end up staying over at Theresa's a lot just to ease the claustrophobia at home. But then Mom calls me at Theresa's just to make sure that I'm there, so that I'm not missing again should another natural disaster strike.

During speech rehearsals, Theresa hangs out at the library after school, to make it look like we are doing academic research together. As we plan for the competition, Theresa and I figure that since Mom works overtime on Saturdays and my tournament is on a Saturday, getting to the tournament should be a slam dunk.

However, on the night before the competition, Mom has other ideas.

"Fei Ting," she says during dinner, "Mommy has a surprise for you. I have taken tomorrow off from work. We can have dim sum, look at jewelry, even buy a new TV."

I cringe at the saccharine quality of her voice. She has never taken a day off, not when she was sick, not even when I was sick. What has gotten into her?

"I already promised Theresa that I would spend Saturday with her," I say.

"That's okay. The four of us can eat and shop together."

"But we're doing school stuff, research for an English term paper."

"But Nellie said that you did that last weekend."

"Well, one day isn't enough," I say. "It's a big paper. Also, some of the periodicals I needed were checked out. I'm hoping that they're available tomorrow."

"Can't you do that next weekend?"

"It's very urgent. Our outlines are due this week."

Mom's voice changes from saccharine to caustic. "Why didn't you take care of that this week? Now look what you've done. You've made me miss a whole day of work and lose money for nothing."

My eyes say, *Well, you should have told me about this ahead of time so I could have altered my plans, instead of springing this on me at the last minute.* But my mouth says nothing.

"I know what you're thinking," Mom says. "I spend all this money to educate you, and now you think you're so smart." She nods slowly, her eyes skewering me. "Ah-hah, I can see how smart you think you are, smarter than your own mother. I need your permission to make changes. Your schedule prevails."

"That's not true," I say.

"The next time you place your studies over me, just remember where your education comes from," Mom says. "You have what you have only because I choose to give it to you."

Mom begins clearing the dishes from the table. "You better study now," she says. "Do what is most important to you. Your servant mother will clean up after you."

I leave the table hurriedly, as if the dishes were covered with worms.

Once I am in the bedroom, I close the door, shaking. I am glad that no one at school knows about my life at home. No one at the competition will know either. I am glad that I have speech, a place where I can be courageous and strong.

All night long, Mom tosses and turns violently in the bottom bunk. My bed rocks back and forth with each turn. Because I've upset her, she can't sleep. And if she can't sleep, then she won't let me sleep either. She wants me to know how much I am making her suffer. I've heard that sleep deprivation is a common form of torture for POWs, that the exhaustion can wear soldiers down and make them divulge any military secret. I can see now why this might be true.

As Mom tosses and turns, I stay as still as possible, afraid to give away that I am awake and that her strategy is working. After several hours, I quietly press the night-glow button on my watch and look at the time. It is 3:57 a.m. I am tempted to cave in, to apologize and give up on the competition, just to make her happy. Just as I'm about to open my mouth to say sorry, she becomes silent. She has fallen asleep. Relieved, I allow my body to relax and move a little. It is stiff from holding the same position for so many hours.

But as her breathing deepens to a soft snore, I am wide awake, my eyes like bright lights shining on the ceiling. I wish I could toss and turn to wake her up now, see how she likes it. But I'm afraid of provoking her and reigniting the whole battle.

⤜⤐⤑⤐⤑⤐⤑⤞

When my alarm goes off the next morning, I check below me. Mom is still asleep. I tiptoe down the ladder and towards the bathroom. I am sticky and oily from last night. I should be exhausted, having had no sleep at all, but sparks of excitement keep me awake. I scrub briskly in the bathtub, as if washing off Mom's accusations.

As I pump up my layered bangs with Aqua Net and a hair dryer, I review my plan. Theresa will pick me up at seven thirty and drive me to school. There I will meet Ms. Taylor and the rest of the team to carpool at eight to Cupertino, where the competition is. Ms. Taylor is borrowing someone's van to transport us all. While I'm competing, Theresa will study and do research at the library or hang out somewhere, anywhere but Clement Street, Irving Street, or Chinatown, where she might be spotted by Mom or Nellie. Then, once we get back to school, Theresa will pick me up and drive me back home.

I put on the clothes I prepared yesterday, black tights and a pressed white long-sleeved shirt. I pull up a pair of jeans over my tights. I packed a black sheath skirt in my backpack yesterday, to put on in place of my jeans as soon as I get to school. I picked black because it is supposed to be a slimming color; I hoped it would hide my pouch and my thunder thighs.

As I step into the kitchen, I look forward to a decadent breakfast of toasted Eggo waffles, but Mom is already there. She has not forgotten about last night. I can tell by the sticky, heavy static in the air. I ignore her, hoping to avoid more fighting. I pick up a banana and head to the bedroom, pretending to be busy with school stuff.

Minutes later, Theresa honks her horn. The sound of it startles me, even though I've been expecting her. I rush to the door with my backpack.

"You're not even going to say 'Good-bye, Mommy'?" Mom asks.

"Bye," I say. To soften her mood, I add, "Have a nice day."

But her reaction is the opposite of what I intended. "That's *it*?" Theresa's horn honks again. "Is that how little respect you show your mother?" Mom says.

I can't tell what she wants from me, so I guess. "Bye, Mommy," I say.

"How can you be so cold?" Her sentences are broken up with sobs. "I went through all this trouble just to take this day off. For you! But you don't care."

As inconspicuously as possible, I eye my watch. It's 7:38.

"See, even now, I'm crying, begging for you to care, and all you do is look at the time," she says.

"I have to go now," I say. "I'm running really late."

"The library's open all day," she says. "So what if you miss an hour?"

An hour? She's going to do this for an hour? The doorbell buzzes. Theresa has gotten out of her car and is trying to reach me at the gate.

"Theresa's waiting outside," I say. Perhaps the mention of Theresa will pull on Mom's guilt strings.

"Let her wait," Mom says coldly. So much for guilt strings.

"I'm sorry about the mix-up," I say. "Let's spend some time tomorrow, to make up for today."

"I'm busy tomorrow. I have to clean the apartment, wash your clothes, pay your bills, and make your dinner."

"Can't you do those things today, so you'll be free tomorrow?"

"I can't. You've upset me so much that I'm too sick to move."

At first, I am frustrated and confused. I can't convince her to reason with me. Then it dawns on me: being unreasonable is her way of winning. No matter what I say, she will turn it against me to keep me from leaving. I will have to either placate her by giving up on the speech tournament or do the unthinkable: ignore her outbursts and walk out the door.

Our doorbell buzzes again. This is my last chance.

"Well, if you're not feeling well, then maybe you should rest," I say. "You wouldn't be well enough to go out with me anyway."

I am surprised by my own cleverness. Mom stares at me in shock. Before she has a chance to recover and reload her ammunition, I rush out the door.

At the bottom of the stairs, Theresa is clutching the gate and looking at me through the spaces between the metal bars.

"What took you so long?" Theresa says as we get into Nellie's car.

"Sorry," I say.

Though Mom's fit cost me a good ten minutes already, Theresa has no intention of making up for lost time. She refuses to exceed the speed limit, even by a mile an hour. She leaves twice the necessary distance between her and the car in front and makes complete stops at every stop sign, looking to the left, then to the right before proceeding.

At 7:59, Theresa pulls up in front of St. Elizabeth's. I wait for her to say good-bye so I can jet out of the car. Instead, she looks at her lap. I am antsy with impatience.

"I'm sorry I got mad," she said.

"That's okay," I say. I am eager to end this conversation so I can leave.

Then Theresa pulls a bright green pendant from underneath her blouse. It is hanging on a long red string around her neck. The pendant bears the image of Gwun Yum, the goddess of mercy and compassion. In most Chinese households, Gwun Yum is a more popular deity than the Buddha and second only to the three fat old men who represent happiness, prosperity, and longevity.

"My great-grandmother gave this to me right before she passed away," Theresa says. "She said that Gwun Yum would guide and protect me." She takes off the necklace and puts it on me. She tucks the pendant under my blouse, carefully positioning it over my heart.

My impatience has fallen to the soles of my shoes. The pendant is warm against my sternum from Theresa's body heat. I want to thank her, but I'm afraid that I might lose control and cry. I've got a big day ahead and must maintain my composure. I nod thanks to Theresa, avoiding her face. Slowly, I step out of the car.

After spending nearly four years at St. Elizabeth's, I forget how large other high schools are. I belong to a class of ninety-six girls. How many seniors will commence at this school, two thousand?

Ms. Taylor, my teammates, and I are standing on the playground, awaiting our room assignments. We're a pretty small group. There are only three speakers on the St. Elizabeth's team: me, Salome Sanchez, and Diana Chandler. We're an oddly matched trio. Salome has dark spiked hair streaked with red, blue, and blond. She wears heavy makeup, a nose ring, and a gold crucifix necklace. Diana is the star dancer in the dance department. She is tall and extremely thin, with long arms and legs that seem to have no joints. She looks like a dancer even when she's not dancing. When she raises her hand in class, she looks like a swan lifting its wing. She sits tall and straight, as though a string were attached to her head, pulling her up.

Secretly, I think Diana Chandler is the most beautiful girl in the school. I envy her Grace Kelly poise, her clear, translucent skin, her cloud of dark brown hair, and her willowy figure. My only consolation is that Diana is the weakest speaker on the team, whereas I am the strongest. Also, I have better grades.

"Listen up, ladies," says Ms. Taylor. She motions for the three of us to huddle. "Competition is about comparing people, judging who is the best. According to those rules, whoever wins is successful, and everyone else loses.

"But I want you to think about success differently. Winning is part effort and part luck. What judges think, how well other competitors do, that's luck. Talent, that's also luck. Some people are born with more and some with less. Luck is totally out of your control.

"What is under your control is your effort. You have all worked hard for this competition. You have all made significant improvements over the last couple of months. It takes incredible courage to speak in public and to speak your truth. You should all be proud and hold your heads up high.

"You've done the work; now it's time to reap the rewards. Reward time isn't after the competition, when they hand out trophies. Reward time is now. It's the thrill of competing, the opportunity to show them what you've got. Relish this time. Don't worry about how other people are doing. Focus on what you're doing. If you're doing your best, if you're having fun, then you're a success."

I detect the faintest odor of cigarettes on Ms. Taylor's clothes. For someone who is confident that we're all winners, she is smoking like someone who's nervous for us.

The room assignments are posted. I am number three out of a group of five speakers. I'm disappointed. The last spot is the best spot, because the final speaker gets to leave the lasting impression on the judge. The first spot is the second luckiest, because you get the freshest ear. Being in the middle is the worst, because you are easily forgotten. I am careful not to show my frustration, because Ms. Taylor hates whiners. Instead, I wish Salome and Diana good luck, I assume my speech pose—straight spine and shoulders back—and I walk confidently to my room.

It is a typical classroom, similar to Ms. Taylor's. Yellow sunlight filters through the windows. Seated in the middle of the room is the judge. She looks like a cross between a cookie-baking grandmother and an absentminded professor. She wears round metal-framed glasses. Her half-inch-thick lenses protrude from their frames, making the frames look like tongs holding ice cubes. Her curly salt-and-pepper hair pokes out in all directions. Her body is lean and frail, and her mannerisms are nervous and fidgety. She smiles kindly at me as I walk in. I pick a seat behind her and off to the side and sit down.

I discover quickly that a side seat is a good seat. From this vantage point I can scope out my competition. A girl with brown skin and thick, wavy black hair walks in, then a white girl with straight brown hair. They both pick inconspicuous seats at the opposite side of the room. Then a tall, freckled girl with curly red hair enters. She sits way in the back, behind the judge. Then the fifth competitor walks in. He is tall, lean, and blond and wears a dark suit and a long black coat. He looks at me. His eyes are like arctic glaciers.

It's Collins.

Chapter Seven

My heart starts pounding. As he approaches, I look away, pretending not to recognize him. He sits down one row behind me and two seats over. I wish I could make myself invisible or disappear.

The judge asks the first speaker to begin. It is the girl with the wavy black hair. She is giving a speech about apartheid. A paragraph into her speech, she begins to lose track of where she is. She does this frequently, as if she hasn't spent enough time rehearsing. I'm irritated. If she hasn't prepared, why should she waste our time like this? Then it occurs to me that in a competition, her disadvantage is my advantage. So I sit back and watch her unravel.

The brown-haired girl is next. Her speech is about education. Oddly, she too starts losing track of where she is in her speech. She begins by stuttering here and there. I don't know whether to feel confused or glad. Then she says a few sentences, then stops, then tries to begin again. After the second time of starting and stopping, she seems to forget how her sentence is supposed to end and then tries to backtrack. Soon she can no longer remember where she was in the speech at all. I notice that her eyes keep traveling to the same spot just before she makes each mistake. Her mouth is frozen open, but no words come out. She seems mesmerized, her eyes transfixed on the same spot in the back of the room.

I look to see what she is staring at. Sitting at the back is the red-haired girl. Her chin is resting on her palm. She has the most bored expression on her face. She rolls her eyes, then crosses them. I look at the brown-haired girl. Tears well in her eyes. Her bottom lip is quivering.

It was no coincidence that the first girl also faltered. That red-haired girl probably sabotaged her too.

Suddenly, I no longer see the brown-haired girl as my opponent. She has become an ally, a fellow good guy against the bad guy sitting in the back. I try to hide the horror on my face. Not that she would notice. She isn't looking at me. She is still staring at the red-haired girl.

The brown-haired girl has been silent for several seconds. Why isn't the judge saying anything? Doesn't she notice what's going on? I turn to look at her. Half the time, she is looking at the brown-haired girl and nodding encouragingly. When she is not watching the girl, she is buried in her notes and scribbling furiously. She is so focused on what she is doing that she has tuned everything—and everyone—else out.

Does Collins notice what's going on? I steal a glance in his direction. He is cringing, as though watching a car accident in slow motion.

Finally, the brown-haired girl runs out of the room. I can

hear her clamoring footsteps and the faint sounds of choked sobs echoing down the hallway.

The judge looks puzzled and concerned. "Uh . . . speaker number three?" she says.

As I walk towards the front of the room, I realize that no rehearsal is ever enough to prepare you for the real thing. As I recited my speech at school, all my classmates smiled and nodded in encouragement. Ms. Taylor never coached us on how to deal with mean-spirited saboteurs.

The cool breeze from the hallway licks my cheek, beckoning me to follow the brown-haired girl out of this room and out of this competition. I'll never have to see these people again, so what does it matter?

Then I realize that that's not true. I'll have to see Collins again. I would have to die a thousand humiliations each time I went to Princeton Review. And I would have to explain my cowardice to Ms. Taylor. She would be so disappointed in me. All that time spent after school would have been a complete waste.

I have no choice but to face the red-haired girl. I close the door, symbolizing my decision. I make my way to my battleground at the front of the room. This is an impossible task. How can I conquer the red-haired girl when two others have failed?

"Now, no need to feel nervous," says the judge. "Just do your best."

Easy for you to say, I want to tell her. *Why don't you try looking behind you?*

CARA CHOW

I try to recall the first line of my speech, but I only hear my heart pounding. I try to visualize the first line, but all I see is the red-haired girl rolling her eyes. My mind races like a hamster in a wheel, running faster and faster and getting nowhere, unable to escape the redhead and the ticking clock.

My thoughts are interrupted by the brief sound of a chair scraping the floor. It's Collins. His elbows are resting on his desk and his hands are folded in front of his mouth. He nods at me, so slowly, so subtly, that it is detectible only to me. *Come on. You can do it*, his eyes say. My frantic thoughts quiet down. I take a deep breath and begin.

"Recently, in *Newsweek*, there was an article titled 'Asian American Whiz Kids,'" I recite. I direct my words to Collins. If I can maintain eye contact with him, I won't have to look at the red-haired girl.

"The article noted the high success rate of Asians in academics," I continue. "It posed the question of why Asians are so successful. Is it genetics or is it due to social factors? Or are nonimmigrant students merely doing less well than their predecessors? Have they grown complacent? I would argue that the success rate of Asians in academics does not stem from superior genetics, but rather from a set of values that includes education and loyalty to family."

As I continue reciting, Collins exhales a sigh of relief. He smiles triumphantly, as if to say, *You did it!* I remember Ms. Taylor's advice to connect with everyone in the room, especially the judge. I peel my gaze away from Collins and direct it towards the judge, who is smiling and nodding. Eventually, I venture to look at the girl with the black hair, the first speaker.

Several minutes later, in a moment of lapsed concentration, I notice that the red-haired girl is laying on the facial expressions. She even adds a facial tic for good measure. At first, I try pushing her face out of my mind, but I soon discover that thinking *Don't think about her* is like telling myself not to think about pink elephants. It's like that old Chinese saying: The more afraid you are of stepping on doggy doo, the more likely you are to step on it.

I look at Collins. His eyes narrow. *Don't let her win.*

So instead of avoiding the red-haired girl, I decide to step on her. Step on her and twist my foot into her, smooshing her into the ground.

"In the pursuit of individualism and focus on the self, they have lost focus on their families and feel no obligation to reciprocate their parents' financial and emotional investment," I say. "As a result, they become complacent." I pierce the red-haired girl with dagger eyes, emphasizing the word *complacent.*

I walk closer to the red-haired girl and maintain eye contact with her as I continue. "Their energies become diffused, even stagnated. This is true not only of American teens but of American society. We are currently the richest and most powerful country in the world. Meanwhile, Japan is creating better technology, and European countries are planning to consolidate their economies. At the top, where life is comfortable, where else can America go but down?" I say this to her as if this is all her fault.

Just minutes ago, I was intimidated by this girl. But she was stronger than I was only because I believed her to be. The other two girls confirmed this belief. But now I am towering over her. Her tactics haven't changed, but they no longer have power over me.

Finally, I conclude my speech. "When President Bush speaks about the thousand points of light, I think about my mother and others like her, who make up the backbone of our families and the foundation of our country. Thanks to them, our future is still bright."

Before bowing my head, I steal a glance at Collins. He gives me a subtle thumbs-up. I return his gesture with a small smile and go back to my seat.

"Speaker four," says the judge. She looks relieved that at least one speaker in her group didn't bomb.

The red-haired girl is speaker number four. How should I pay her back? Should I make faces? I might get caught. Perhaps I don't need to pay her back. I just did by giving a good performance. So I'm going to do the most powerful thing: nothing, the greatest insult of all. As she speaks, I gaze at her pleasantly. Her speech topic is why prostitution should be legal. I suppress the urge to laugh but only halfheartedly, so I end up grinning and looking like I'm trying not to grin. She tries to stand up tall, as I did, but she keeps her face high, so high that she is literally looking down her nose at us. Her voice is serious and haughty.

I sneak a look at Collins. He smirks. *She's not that great,* his eyes say. I nod in agreement. As she finishes and walks back to her seat, I smile to myself. He's right. Her speech wasn't half as good as mine.

Finally, it is Collins's turn. His speech is about the pitfalls of compassionate conservatism. To my surprise, he is not the same boy who walked into a doorframe just days ago. He emanates poise and confidence. His voice sounds half formal and half conversational, neither amateurish nor too rehearsed. His hand gestures look natural, perfectly punctuating every point. He navigates the floor like he owns it. He is doing everything Ms. Taylor has taught us to do. His speech is organized and succinct, yet caring and not clinical. Though I have never competed before, I know instinctively that this guy is a champion. I, Frances Ching, first-time competitor, big speech fish in a small school pond, am no threat to his dominance.

After his speech, he walks back to his seat. As he passes, I give a humble thumbs-up. He smiles. After we are dismissed, I hesitate for a moment before leaving. If I linger a bit, maybe he will talk to me. Then I remember my resolve to control my emotions, and I rush out of the room.

I place second in my first round. The confidence I gain from my first round helps me through the subsequent rounds. Diana is cut before the semifinal round, and Salome is cut after semifinals.

Only I among the students in our speech class get to go to the final round. Ms. Taylor is ecstatic. She tells me that this is an amazing feat for a first-timer. Salome and Diana have to sit around and wait until I'm done. Understandably, Salome is less than ecstatic. Strangely, Diana seems perfectly happy to wait. I do not see Collins again until the final round.

He walks quietly behind me as we head to the competition room. As I reach for the doorknob, he reaches over me and opens the door for me. My face flushes hot. I nod, acknowledging his gesture as I step through the doorway. Once again, I pick a seat off to the side. I wait to see how he will react. He picks the seat right next to me. This time, he is speaker two and I am speaker four. As he speaks, I give him nods of encouragement—not that he needs them—and he does the same for me when I speak. As I deliver my speech, I find myself emulating some of his gestures and his tone. My delivery feels more natural and confident. Like Collins, I am assuming a different persona, somebody stronger and more confident. Throughout the round, I feel tingly excitement from my chest all the way to my fingers and toes. All five of us are very good, and fortunately, no one here is a saboteur. I rationalize that I shouldn't feel bad if I place last, considering my competition.

After the last round, I walk very slowly to the door so that Collins can stay right behind me. I reach for the doorknob in slow motion, waiting for his reaction. He reaches over me to open the door. Our hands brush. His skin is soft and warm. The fine hairs on the back of his hand tickle my skin. A lightning bolt of excitement runs up my arm. I step in front of him and walk down the hallway in slow, even strides, aware that he is following and watching my every move.

By the time we get outside, the orange sun is low in the sky. I look behind me. He is gone.

I squash my disappointment and cross an outdoor area to join my team. It is then that I see him again. He is standing a few yards away, leaning casually against a wall, smiling and chatting with his teammates. Speakers from other teams greet him as they walk by. If all these other people can just walk right up to him and say hello, then why shouldn't I? With my heart in my throat, I take a step towards him.

Then Diana approaches him. She stands much closer to him than the others. She leans into him and kisses him on the cheek. Collins returns her affection, giving her a soft peck . . . on the lips. Slowly, it dawns on me. They know each other. Very well.

Quickly, I turn away and walk towards Salome and Ms. Taylor. My chest hurts, but I don't know why.

Ms. Taylor, Salome, and I make our way to the gymnasium for the awards ceremony. I haven't been inside a gymnasium since grade school. In high school, we are required to take one year of PE, but Ms. Costello waived the requirement for me to make room for all the college-prep courses. The shiny floor feels waxy under my soles. The painted lines bring back the old days of torture in grade-school PE, in which I got hit in the head with many a dodge ball and lost many a basketball while attempting to dribble, sometimes to the wrong basket, because I was so directionally confused. At the center of the gym is a podium next to a long table with the three trophies—large, medium, and small—and several ribbons with medals. The wall behind the trophies sports a painting of the school's mascot, a roaring tiger with big white fangs. We are sitting among the other teams and their coaches. The chaos of the conversations around us bounces off the walls, enveloping us like a hive of bees.

One of the coaches seated in the bleachers waves at us. "Hey, Shannon," he calls out. He is a friendly-looking heavyset man with thin strawberry blond hair, a ruddy complexion, and glasses. He wears a polo shirt and khakis.

Ms. Taylor waves back. "Rodger!"

She introduces Salome and me to the coach, whose name is Mr. McCormick.

"I'm missing one of my kids," says Mr. McCormick. "Have you seen Derek Collins?"

Derek Collins? All this time, I've thought that Collins was his first name.

"No, sorry," Ms. Taylor says. "In fact, I'm missing one of mine too. Where can they be?"

Salome looks at me and rolls her eyes. "Adults can be so blind," she mutters. Another pang hits my chest.

"Beats me. I'd hate to see one of my guys miss his own awards ceremony," Mr. McCormick says. "Hey, I saved you guys some seats." He bows and makes a circular gesture with his arm, like a musketeer, at the empty bleacher in front of him.

No, no, no! I don't want to sit near Derek Collins. I especially don't want to sit near Derek and Diana together. I look at Ms. Taylor, hoping to sway her response, but she doesn't notice me at all.

"How chivalrous of you," Ms. Taylor says, curtsying.

Ms. Taylor climbs up to the bleacher in front of Mr. McCormick and gestures for us to follow. Salome sits next to her. Reluctantly, I follow and sit next to Salome.

Moments later, Derek finally arrives—with Diana. They aren't touching this time, but they are standing too close to each other to look like acquaintances. I fight to keep a pleasant and casual demeanor as they approach. As Derek climbs up the bleachers, I scoot over to let him pass. He climbs over me, and his coat brushes against my arm. The warm scent of his fabric softener fills my nose. Diana follows him and sits next to me.

Soon after, the ceremony begins. I try to ignore him and pay attention to what's going on. The emcee announces the honorable mentions. Soon all the ribbons are gone. The emcee pauses, then announces the third-place winner. My breath stops in anticipation.

"Frances Ching!"

I hear that name as if it were someone else's, but Ms. Taylor's jubilant voice plus the nudges of Salome and Diana jolt me back to reality. Mr. McCormick pats me on the shoulder with his bear-paw hands. "Great job, Frances," he says enthusiastically.

As I turn to thank him, I see Derek next to him, giving me his quiet smile and thumbs-up. Against my will, my heart flutters again. I smile and quickly turn away. As I walk to the podium, I pass by the red-haired girl and smirk. She pretends not to see me. I shake the emcee's hand as I receive my trophy. It is big and brassy but lighter than it appears. I stand there with the honorable mentions, looking into the sea of faces on the bleachers. People are looking at me. And they're applauding. It seems as if the whole world is noticing me for the first time.

The only person missing is my mother. For a moment, the applause of the audience seems hollow, like the light, brassy trophy I am carrying. But then I see Ms. Taylor in the bleachers. Whereas others are sitting, she is standing, giving me an ovation. She is applauding, not politely at her waist or chest, but up and out, as if giving me an offering. She's nodding at me, as if to say, *You've done it!* The brightness in her eyes fills the vacuum in my heart until I can no longer remember why it was there in the first place.

The emcee announces the second-place winner, the girl who spoke about the feminist movement during my third round. Then he announces the first-place winner: "Derek Collins!"

Derek shakes hands with Mr. McCormick. His teammates either pat him on the back or shake his hand. Derek walks towards the podium with a long, confidant stride, only to trip over his own feet halfway to his trophy. If I had done that, I would have died of humiliation, but Derek only blushes and smiles sheepishly. He shakes the emcee's hand, accepts his trophy, and makes fun of his own clumsiness, pretending to trip again, stopping his fall, and feigning relief at saving his trophy. The audience laughs and applauds more loudly. Derek bows dramatically. He then holds his trophy up to his coach and team, as if to say, *I couldn't do this without you.*

It's time for the winners to congratulate one another. I immediately begin congratulating all the other winners. When I can't avoid Derek any longer, I turn to congratulate him. Derek approaches me with his giant trophy and shakes my hand. "Congratulations," he says. His voice is professional, without any hint of our alliance from the final round, the first round, or even Princeton Review. Gone is his usual warmth and humor.

As we walk to Ms. Taylor's rental van in the crisp, dry night air, I clutch my trophy, reminding myself that this is what I came here for. *This* is real. Derek's feelings for me are not. Diana can have her Derek. I have something better, something longer lasting. As I reach for the van door, a painful yellow streak of electricity zaps my fingers. The shock almost causes me to drop my trophy. I remember the electrical sensation of Derek's hand brushing mine. I squash this memory as I force the door open. No shock this time. I will never be caught off guard again.

By the time we get back into the city, it is nearly nine o'clock. As Ms. Taylor drops us off at St. Elizabeth's, she says, "Frances, wait. I have something for you." She reaches into her briefcase

CARA CHOW

and hands me a large envelope. She winks at me. "Now go home and flash that trophy of yours to your mom."

If only she knew.

Theresa is parked nearby. She is eyeing her rearview mirror nervously for cops and meter maids, because she is waiting in a no-parking zone. I hurry to her car and get inside. Once she sees my trophy, she forgets about the parking police and begins jumping up and down in her seat and clapping. "I knew you could do it!" she says.

Then I remember the Gwun Yum pendant and place it back on her. "Thanks," I say.

As we head home, I open the envelope Ms. Taylor gave to me. Inside the envelope are an application for Scripps College and two sealed letters of recommendation, one for Scripps and one for Berkeley.

"What's that?" Theresa asks.

"Oh . . . just a copy of my speech." I'm not ready to burden her with this yet, especially after all she has done for me.

Theresa looks confused but quickly dismisses it. With all the stress she has had to endure, she probably doesn't have the energy to question me. I will tell her about Scripps later, when the time is right.

Theresa parks in a spot on a quiet street a few blocks away from my apartment so I can change back into my jeans. Though it is dark, she covers my lap with my jacket as I change. Then we continue home. As we near my apartment, I know that it is time to hide my trophy, but I hesitate. All this work I did, all this accomplishment, and Mom will never know. All I have to do is leave it on my lap in plain view, let its shiny surface reflect the streetlight into our apartment window, into Mom's line of sight. Our whole secret would be destroyed and, along with it, Mom's image of me as brainless and useless. I continue to eye my trophy, daring it to shine into our living room, daring Mom to see it.

"Quick, put it in your backpack," Theresa says.

I do as she says. But I can't hide my trophy in my backpack forever. Where on earth will I hide it once I get inside? "Can you hide it for me? In your house?" I ask.

"*My* house?"

I nod. "Our apartment is so small. There's no place for me to hide it. At least your place is bigger. There are more potential hiding places."

Theresa squirms in her seat. "Oh . . . okay. I guess I can find someplace."

I take the trophy out of my backpack and hand it to her. She places it in the backseat and covers it with her sweater before I open the door to leave.

As I approach the metal gate to my apartment, I feel as though I am returning to prison. With each step I take up the stairwell, the fire and spirit in me that defeated the red-haired girl threaten to diminish to a distant memory. Only the thought of my shiny trophy gives me the courage to open the door and face what is behind it.

Though it is nearly dark outside, there are no lights on in the apartment. At first, I think that maybe Mom is out. I turn on the light and find Mom lying on the couch under a blanket. Her face looks haggard, like a dirty, wrung-out rag. She probably has not moved from that couch all day, not even to turn on the light, get food or water, or use the bathroom.

"I rested. Just like you told me to. I hope you're happy," she says.

I continue walking towards the bedroom.

"Of course, if you hadn't broken my heart, I wouldn't need to rest in the first place," she adds just before I close the door.

I remind myself that I have a trophy now. Mom can't take that away from me. After coming this far, I can't give up. I open my backpack. Ms. Taylor's envelope is inside. I pull out the Scripps application. I am not a helpless prisoner anymore. Like a secret agent, I am plotting my escape.

Chapter Eight

I spend the rest of the weekend enduring my mother's hot screaming and cold silence. The following Monday, during homeroom, Mr. Daniels announces my speech win over the PA system. My homeroom teacher, Sister Pam, congratulates me, and the whole room claps for me. During speech class, the support I get is even more enthusiastic. It reminds me that there are people out there who appreciate me, even if Mom does not.

At the end of speech class, I tell Theresa that I must meet with Ms. Taylor. "College stuff," I explain with a dismissive wave of my hand. Theresa nods. She assumes that I am referring to my application to Berkeley, and I don't correct her.

After the other students have left the room, Ms. Taylor goes over the different kinds of financial aid with me. There are grants and loans. You have to pay back the latter with interest. I ask what interest is, and Ms. Taylor explains that I'll need to pay back more than I borrowed. That's how the lender makes money. This concept also applies to buying a car or a house. It even applies to bank accounts and retirement accounts.

"Think of it this way," Ms. Taylor says. "*Interest* is why it's in the lender's best *interest* to lend."

"That's very interesting," I say, joking.

Ms. Taylor hands me the financial-aid form for Scripps. Because grants and loans are based on financial need, she explains, I will have to get my mother to fill out and sign the portion of the application that asks about family income.

My heart falls to my stomach. There is no way that I can get my mother to fill this out. Does this mean that Scripps is out of my reach?

Then Ms. Taylor explains about scholarships. These can come from the school or corporations or organizations. Though some are based on financial need, many others are based only on merit. Ms. Taylor hands me a book listing the various corporations and organizations that offer scholarships.

I quietly decide to focus on the merit-based scholarships.

I spend the last ten minutes of lunch break wolfing down my pork bun in the cafeteria while Theresa goes over my Princeton Review homework.

"Now that you've finished your speech competition, you won't have to miss any more Princeton Review," Theresa says.

The mention of Princeton Review brings back the memory of Derek Collins pecking Diana Chandler on the lips.

"What's wrong?" Theresa asks.

"Oh, nothing." I shrug and paste on a smile.

Theresa looks skeptical. I look away.

"You can tell me," she coaxes. "Maybe I can help. Are you worried about your next SAT?"

"No." I then divulge the whole Derek saga, from my first day of Princeton Review, to the showdown with the red-haired girl, to his inexplicable cold shoulder right after the competition.

"But why is he getting you so down?" Theresa asks, looking genuinely puzzled.

"I just told you," I say, totally annoyed. "He acted like he was my friend, and then he turns around and acts like he doesn't even know me."

"But he's just an acquaintance," says Theresa. "It's not like he's your best friend or your boyfriend." Though Theresa means no harm, that last part stings.

"But it's . . . it's disrespectful." My voice cracks. Against my will, tears well up in my eyes.

Theresa's eyes widen. "Do you . . . Do you *like* him?"

My tears spill over. I wipe them away with my napkin. Theresa offers me a tissue.

"Maybe he likes you but more like a friend," she says.

"Then why did he ignore me?" I ask. "Friends don't do that."

Theresa thinks this over. "Maybe he didn't want the others to know that you were friends," she says.

"But why?" I ask. Is he embarrassed to be associated with me? Am I that dorky? I want to ask Theresa this, but I'm afraid to consider the possibility.

"Maybe he secretly likes you back but can't express it because he's with Diana," Theresa says.

I give her a skeptical look.

"All the times he was friendly towards you, like during Princeton Review and during speech rounds, she wasn't around," Theresa points out. "But once she showed up, he acted aloof. Also, when he is friendly towards you, he does it in a covert way, with secret smiles and gestures. Why would he do that unless he had something to hide?"

She does have a point.

"There's only one way to know for sure," Theresa says. "Observe it scientifically. See how he acts towards you in class this afternoon. Then see how he acts the next time others are around."

"Kind of like an experiment," I say, admiring Theresa's social acumen.

"Well, more like a correlational study," Theresa says. "Technically, it's not an experiment, because you can't control all the variables."

I return to St. Augustine's with a mission to be a better scientist. Instead of observing mice in a cage, I am observing humans in their natural habitat. I catch the early bus this time so that I can get there before Derek does. I'm manipulating a variable. If I get there first, Derek must choose whether to sit next to me or in some seat farther away. At first, I sit in my usual seat. Then it occurs to me that if Derek sits next to me, it could mean that he wants to be near me or that he is just sitting in his favorite seat out of habit. So I move to a seat a couple of rows over.

Ten minutes later, Derek enters the room. He walks to his seat and then looks surprised to find that I am two seats over. He walks to the back of the classroom and proceeds up the row next to mine. I pretend not to notice, making myself busy organizing things in my backpack. When I am done, Derek is in the seat to my left. There is something on my desk. It's a copy of the notes from the classes—three total—that I missed while practicing with Ms. Taylor prior to the competition. The notes are typed. On top of the notes is a folded sheet of paper. I unfold it and find a note written in jagged, slanted blue ink.

Why a different seat today?

I run my fingers over Derek's words as if reading Braille. He presses hard into the paper when he writes. I fold the paper over and write:

Wanted a change. P.S. Thanks for the notes.

Unlike Derek's handwriting, mine is light, small, and round. I fold the paper again, and when Mr. Engelman turns to face the board, I slip it onto Derek's desk. Derek opens it and reads. A faint smile appears on his lips. He refolds the paper, writes something on it, and folds it again. Several minutes later, when

CARA CHOW

Mr. Engelman's back is turned to us again, Derek slips it back to me. I open it.

You're welcome. ☺

Below that is a phone number. Then, below that, it reads:

(In case you have q's or need more notes.)

I fold his note and write my phone number on it before folding it one more time. I wait for Mr. Engelman to turn to the board again before passing it back to Derek. He opens the note, reads it, and chuckles. What's so funny? He writes something in his notebook; then he writes something on the paper. He folds it again and returns the note. It says:

You forgot to copy my # down.

I blush. I passed his number back to him. How stupid!

Mr. Engelman finishes writing on the board and turns to face us again. We both look down and stifle a laugh.

After class, we gather our things and walk out together. As we proceed down the hallway, a friend of Derek's approaches him. He has shiny black hair, fair skin, and silver-framed glasses. He looks Chinese. He's as lean as Derek but several inches shorter.

"Hey, dude, where've you been?" he says to Derek. "I've been looking all over for you."

Immediately, Derek turns from me and starts walking away with his friend. The two tease each other as they walk down the hallway. My first impulse is to feel hurt. Then I remember Theresa's interpretation of his actions. At the bus stop, I pull out the sheet of paper that we passed between us, now folded into sixteenths. I open the note, read our dialogue backwards, and mentally re-create every facial expression. If what Theresa says is true, then his turning away from me is actually a good sign. He wouldn't mind introducing me to his friend if he didn't have feelings to hide.

A strong gust of wind threatens to blow the paper out of my hand, but I cling to it. I run my cold fingers over Derek's handwriting, as if they can read something that my eyes missed.

Derek and I sit next to each other for the duration of Princeton Review. We don't say much to each other. Our communication consists mostly of charged smiles, nods, and waves. The following day, I report every smile, nod, and wave to Theresa, who patiently shares my enthusiasm, though the news is almost the same every time.

On the last day of Princeton Review, Theresa points out that I probably won't see Derek again until the next speech tournament, which will be in December. Even then, our interactions won't be the same, especially if Diana continues competing. Usually, I'm in a rush after class to gather my things so I can catch the earliest bus home. Tonight, however, I take my time getting ready. Derek seems to do the same. After I've packed my last item, I pause, hoping that Derek will offer to walk me to the bus stop. But he says nothing. Defeated, I'm about to leave when he says, "How are you getting home?"

"I'm taking the bus," I reply. "Why?"

"It's dark out." He says this with disapproval, though it has been dark after class for the last few weeks. "Need a ride?"

I picture Derek explaining to his mother why she should go out of her way to chauffeur me. "It's too much trouble," I say.

"I don't mind."

My heart starts pounding. "Okay. Thanks."

As I follow him outside, I marvel that after a month of knowing each other, we are finally having a real conversation. I am also marveling that he is walking beside me. He isn't hiding his friendship with me from the world. It's chilly outside but not cold enough to justify how much I am shivering. I expect him to wait at the curb for his mom, but instead, he leads me to a small black BMW sports car in the campus parking lot. The license plate says COLLINS 3. He opens the passenger door and waits.

My jaw drops. "Uh . . . you're driving?" I ask.

"How else am I supposed to get you home?" he asks, obviously puzzled by my question.

Dumbfounded, I get inside. Derek's car has that new-car smell. The dash is still shiny. Derek closes the passenger door and gets in on the other side. As he tosses his book bag towards the backseat, the warm scent of fabric softener once again fills my nose.

"How did you get such a nice car?" I ask.

"My dad bought it for my sixteenth birthday," he replies. "So, where do you live?"

"Thirty-second and Balboa."

Derek pulls out of the parking lot. His car is much quieter and smoother than Ms. Taylor's, even quieter and smoother than Nellie's. Instead of heading towards Golden Gate Park, which is the shortest way, Derek heads towards the ocean. Unlike Theresa, whose driving style is very cautious, Derek drives about five miles over the speed limit. The whole time, I am stunned that I am sitting in this luxury vehicle. I am even more stunned that Derek is driving it in such a matter-of-fact manner.

We proceed north along the Great Highway. To our left, the waves from the ocean are glowing white under the streetlights.

"How come you're going this way?" I ask.

"I like this route," he says. "I like the view. Is that okay?"

"Yeah, it's great," I say eagerly.

"There's a really good restaurant up the hill called the Seacliffe. You can look out the window while you eat, and it feels like you're hovering over the ocean. But you probably already know that."

I nod, though I had no idea there was a restaurant there at all. The closest I have come to the ocean is about 42nd Avenue, where there are Chinese shops and restaurants.

"We should go sometime," Derek says.

My heart skips a beat. Then I sternly remind myself of what happened the last time I let myself misconstrue his friendliness for something more meaningful.

"Thanks," I say, changing the subject. "Not just for the ride, but also for helping me out at the competition."

"I didn't do much," Derek says. "Ultimately, it was you who defeated Sally Meehan. Actually, I've never seen anyone overcome her tactics as well as you did."

"How about you?" I say, oozing with admiration, against my will. "She doesn't faze you at all."

Derek turns right onto Balboa. Our weight shifts backwards, because the hill is steep. Suddenly, it occurs to me that Mom is probably home. What if she is looking out the window when Derek pulls up? Besides, I don't want Derek to see where I live. He probably lives in a mansion. How would he feel about my dingy apartment? I watch the street signs as we pass them: 46th Avenue, 45th, 43rd, and so on. With each passing street, we get closer and closer.

As we approach 34th, I say, "Can you drop me off here?"

"Here? But this is Thirty-fourth. I thought you lived on Thirty-second."

"I know, but I need to get out here."

"Why?"

"Because." As if that could explain everything.

Though Derek is confused, he pulls over. As I open the car door, Derek says, "Wait. Are you going to the dance tomorrow?"

Dance. That word takes me back to when I copied my notes for him. The words *dance* and *abstinence* flash before my eyes.

"I'm planning on being there," Derek says. "It'd be nice to see you." The light inside the car illuminates our faces.

"It'd be nice to see you and Diana," I say, emphasizing "Diana."

"Well, actually . . . Diana and I aren't together anymore."

"Oh. I'm sorry to hear that." I look away so that he can't see my face.

"It's okay. I mean, it's for the best." Derek tries to look sad, but he can't quite pull it off. "So . . . can you make it?"

I want to jump up and say yes, but immediately, my mother's voice booms between my ears. *No distractions . . . No socializing or running around with boys.*

"Well, I don't know," I say. "I'll have to see."

Derek's face falls. "Oh. Okay. Well . . . it was nice having class with you. I guess I'll see you at the next speech tournament." He keeps his eyes on the steering wheel as he says this.

I reluctantly step out of the car and walk towards my apartment. I listen for the sound of Derek's car pulling away, but all I hear is his engine humming. It fills me with a pained happiness. He's lingering to watch me for just a few seconds more.

As I approach my apartment, I look up at my second-story window. Fortunately, the blinds are down. But just as I think that, my mother yanks them up in one brisk motion. Her black silhouette is outlined by the light from the kitchen. Though I can't see her face, I can feel her hawk eyes peering down at me. Can she see Derek too?

Nervously, I look behind me. Derek's car is gone. Breathing a sigh of relief, I hurry to the security gate like a mouse running for cover.

After dinner, I explain to Mom that I have an exam tomorrow and that I need Theresa's help.

"She helps you all the time with calculus," Mom complains. "Why can't you figure it out on your own? Why are you so slow?"

I slump my shoulders, presenting the image of a very stupid person. Then I grab my backpack and hurry to Theresa's. Nellie greets me, offers me what is left of their dinner, and calls Theresa to the kitchen. Then she continues to the living room to catch up on her Chinese soaps.

"You're a genius!" I say to Theresa. Then I give her the latest Derek Report. When I get to the part where he asks me about the dance, Theresa interrupts.

"Why didn't you say yes?" she asks. "He was clearly planning to ask you to go with him."

I sigh. "My mom won't let me go out with boys."

"What if you go stag?" Theresa suggests. "Then, technically, you won't be going with him."

"She won't let me do anything social, especially if there's a remote threat of interacting with boys," I say. "If I don't go to this dance, I'll miss my only chance." I pause, waiting for Theresa to offer a suggestion. But she just passively accepts that I can't go.

"Mom lets me hang out with you, though," I say, hinting.

"But how will hanging out with me help with going to the dance?"

I give her a knowing look. Slowly, Theresa's face registers understanding—and alarm.

"W-Wait a minute," she says. "I thought we agreed not to lie anymore."

"We talked about *speech*," I reply. "We never mentioned *dances*."

Theresa opens her mouth to argue.

"I'm not asking you to lie," I say. "I'll be the one lying. You don't have to say anything."

"But—"

"*Please?*" I say.

Theresa sighs. "The dance is tomorrow. How do we get tickets?"

Chapter Nine

Theresa and I figure out that we can get tickets at the door for a slightly higher price than they were selling for earlier. However, that presents another problem: I have no money to pay for my ticket. Unlike Theresa, I don't get an allowance.

We decide that our alibi is that we're going to the movies. And if we're going to see a movie, then I'll need money from Mom. That is why I am bugging Mom right before bedtime, when she is tired and grouchy, for permission to be out tomorrow night.

Mom is wearing her orange-and-brown pajamas. They are so old that she might have been wearing them back in Hong Kong, before I was born. Her contacts are out and her glasses are on. Those too look old, like from the sixties. Actually, come to think of it, they look similar to Ms. Taylor's black cat-eye glasses, minus the rhinestones. I always thought they looked dorky on Mom, but on Ms. Taylor they look cool. Mom is in the bathroom, brushing her teeth. She is brushing so aggressively that the flesh under her upper arms is jiggling.

"Theresa's invited me to go to the movies with her tomorrow night," I say.

Mom continues brushing, as if I have said nothing at all.

"There's this movie she really wants to see," I continue.

Mom spits and starts gargling.

"She's done so much for me," I say. "I really don't want to say no to her."

More gargling. At least she's not yelling. Maybe she is considering my request.

"Why can't you see the movie on Saturday or Sunday?" Mom asks. "Then you wouldn't have to be out at night. That's safer. You could also see a matinee. That's cheaper."

I didn't think of that. What to do?

"They're offering a special double feature, so it's two for one," I reply, "even cheaper per movie than a matinee."

"What are you seeing?"

The Little Mermaid." Theresa showed me a review, because she really wants us to see this film. I read the review, which included a synopsis, in case Mom quizzes me about it later.

Mom is silent as she flosses. Her floss makes clicking sounds every time it passes between her teeth. Finally, Mom says, "What time is the movie?"

I suppress the urge to dance with glee. "Seven o'clock."

Mom wipes her mouth and goes to her purse. She pulls money out of her wallet and hands it to me. It is twice the amount of one movie ticket.

"Treat Theresa," Mom says. "Tell her it's from me, to thank her for spending time teaching you."

"Thank you," I say. "I'm sure she'll appreciate it."

"Don't think I don't know that it's really for you," she says.

"You wouldn't have the nerve to ask me unless it was associated with her."

I try to hide any trace of alarm. But underneath my calm demeanor, I wonder, how much does she know?

Since I'm paying for the dance, Theresa decides to pay for our makeup, which we buy at the drugstore on the way to the dance. We buy only one set for the two of us, since we probably won't have the opportunity to wear this stuff again unless we sneak off to another illicit school dance.

St. Augustine's fall dance is held in the gymnasium. The music is so loud that we can hear it halfway down the block. Since the theme is autumn and Halloween, the gymnasium is decorated with fall-colored leaves and jack-o'-lanterns. We bypass the coat check and head straight to the bathroom, which smells like pee, used sanitary napkins, and Aqua Net hairspray. The bass outside is so loud that it rattles the door. I am wearing a red sweaterdress with a low waist and a tube skirt. As I scrutinize myself in the mirror, I notice that all the other girls are wearing darker colors, like navy blue and black.

"Do you think my outfit is too bright?" I ask Theresa.

"No. Red looks really good on you," Theresa says. "How about me? Does this look okay?"

Theresa is wearing a lavender-and-white-lace sailor dress with an empire waist.

"It's very pretty," I say. It really is pretty, but it's probably more appropriate for a wedding than a school dance. It also makes her look twelve instead of seventeen. I wonder if my dress really is too bright, if Theresa is trying to spare my feelings as well.

I inspect my face in the mirror. I've been struggling with my complexion for the last two years. I get the occasional red swollen pimple, the kind that hurts when you touch it, but most of the time, I just have a plethora of tiny bumps, the kind that don't show up on photos but that you can see close-up. As luck would have it, I have two swollen red bumps today, one on my chin and the other on my forehead. Maybe I'm being punished for disobeying my mother.

We pull out a plastic bag filled with foundation, powder, a blemish stick, eye shadow, eyeliner, mascara, and lipstick, all still unopened.

"How exactly do you put this stuff on?" I ask Theresa.

Theresa flips the foundation over and examines the back of the packaging. "Follow the directions, I guess," she says.

We start with the foundation, taking turns pouring it on our fingertips and smearing it on our faces. Then we inspect ourselves in the mirror. Somehow, it just doesn't look like in the commercials. In the commercials, the ladies' faces look like porcelain—white, smooth, and flawless. On us, the foundation looks peachy and pasty, especially on me, because I caked it on to cover up my acne.

"It didn't look this orange on the color chart," I say.

"Maybe we need to blend it in better," Theresa says.

We both try blending it in more, but that doesn't seem to help. I can't see my real skin color, but I can still see my acne. With the blemish stick, I begin burying my pimples. Then we take turns applying the powder. Fortunately, the powder works wonders for my oily, shiny skin, though I still think the color is a bit too orange.

Now it's time for the eye shadow. We try our best to imitate the picture on the back of the packaging, doing the eye shadow version of painting by numbers. Then we move on to the eyeliner, lipstick, and mascara.

We examine ourselves in the mirror. Do we really look prettier now? We look at each other, shrug, and exit the bathroom.

I scan the gymnasium for Derek. This is particularly challenging, considering that the room is dark except for the dozen spots of red, white, and blue light that orbit the dance floor. The occasional epileptic strobe light is not much help either. The bass is vibrating in my sternum, making it hard to breathe. Am I the only one who thinks this music is too loud? I check to see Theresa's reaction. She is trying to smile for me, but clearly she's not having any more fun than I am. Though this is called a dance, there isn't really much dancing going on here. About a dozen people are on the dance floor, but most are standing in the periphery in small single-sex groups. These groups rarely intermingle. The couples on the dance floor are probably couples that came in together. I recognize a few girls from our school but, alas, no Derek.

"I don't see him," I say to Theresa.

"What?" her lips mouth.

I lean towards Theresa's ear. "Do you see him?" I yell.

"What?"

I point to the bathroom and she follows me there.

Once we're inside, I say, "Maybe he's not coming after all."

"Maybe he's running late," Theresa says. "Or maybe he's out there but we just didn't see him." She rubs her ears. "I can hardly hear myself talk. I think I'm going deaf."

"This was a waste of time," I say. "We should just go."

"It would be a shame if we left now and he showed up five minutes later," Theresa says. "We may as well give a hundred percent effort. That way, if we fail, it's not because we didn't try our best."

When Ms. Taylor says this, I feel inspired. When Theresa says it, I feel annoyed.

Nonetheless, she has a point, so we march out into the cannon fire of dance music for one last-ditch attempt. We look around for another fifteen minutes but, still, no Derek. Theresa and I look at each other, shake our heads, and go back to the bathroom.

"If he's not here by now, he's not coming at all," I say.

I thought we had this connection, Derek and I. Now I am wondering if that was just a figment of my imagination. Only Theresa knows about my foolishness, yet I feel as if the whole world can see my folly. I don't want to go home defeated.

"You know what we should do?" I say.

"Go home?" Theresa says, her face lighting up.

"No. We should forget about stupid Derek and ask some other guys to dance."

Theresa's face falls.

"We each ask one boy to dance," I say. "Then we go home. We never have to attend another dance again. Deal?"

"I have a better idea. What if you ask a boy to dance and I go hide out and wait for you to finish?"

"But I need your help!"

"I'll cheer for you from the sidelines."

"But that's not the same! We have to be in it together."

Theresa groans.

"Come on," I say. "Just one song."

Theresa sighs. "Fine. Just this once."

With half bravery and half trepidation, we march arm in arm back out to the gymnasium. The music has gone from rap and hip-hop to slow. The DJ announces that this is the last song for the night. More couples are gravitating towards the dance floor.

"Okay. Last dance, last chance," I say. "I'll go left and you go right. Afterwards, we'll meet back at this spot and report back to each other on how it went."

Theresa nods. We let go of each other and forge ahead. I scan the clusters of boys. Who would be a good candidate? Definitely no tall, slender blonds. I don't want any posttraumatic stress. He can't be too cute and popular looking because I need a fair chance of success, but he can't be too unattractive either, because I'll have to dance with him.

The first guy I see is tall and lean, with dark skin and giant black doe eyes. One lock of his shiny jet-black hair curls lazily over his forehead. He smiles at a friend, revealing a perfect set of white teeth.

Out of my league. Pass.

The second boy I see has frizzy brown hair, thick glasses, and sweaty, oily skin that is peppered with acne. His bulging figure makes his striped T-shirt and cords look two sizes too small. His belly is protruding over his waistband. As he laughs with his friends, he looks like he's wheezing and snorting.

The thought of him holding me close makes me shudder. Pass.

I see other guys, but their bodies are turned away from me and they are half enshrouded in darkness. The song is halfway finished. I begin to panic. I must choose someone fast.

There's a boy just a few feet ahead of me. He could be Chinese. He has thick, straight jet-black hair. He is wearing a polo shirt and khakis. He wears black-framed glasses that would look nerdy on someone else, but on him they look artsy and intellectual. Though he's standing with a couple of friends, he's not conversing with them. He's gazing at the dance floor, looking alone and lost.

Bingo. Here's my chance.

I march over to him. "Excuse me?" I say.

He doesn't hear me. I tap him on the shoulder. "Excuse me," I shout. "Wanna dance?"

He hesitates. His eyes travel from my face down to my feet,

then up to my face again. "No thanks," he says. His friends are staring at me.

I back away a few steps. Then I quickly retreat to the designated meeting spot. I half expect to see Theresa waiting there for me, panicked and desperate, relieved to see me at last. She would tell me that she lost her nerve and couldn't go through with it. Then I would tell her my story and she'd comfort me, saying that at least I had the courage to try. Or better yet, she would share a story similar to mine, and we would commiserate about how awful boys are and how we don't want to have anything to do with them ever again.

But Theresa isn't there. Where could she be? I scan the periphery, expecting her to be wandering around, looking for a boy to ask. But she's nowhere to be seen. After searching the periphery twice, I reluctantly search the dance floor. Then I see her towards the front. The orbiting lights make the white parts of her dress glow. She is swaying awkwardly with a boy who is a few inches taller and somewhat stocky. He's wearing wire-rimmed glasses, a collared shirt, a V-neck sweater, and khakis. As they turn, I get a look at his round baby face. He's Asian, probably Chinese. And he's gazing at her and smiling. Though I can't see her face, I know that she is gazing and smiling back at him.

Theresa got someone and I didn't.

They bump into another couple and take a few steps to the side to give them berth. As they move, I see the couple behind them.

It's Derek and Diana.

Diana is resting her head on Derek's shoulder. Derek's arms are cradling Diana's slender waist.

The song ends and the lights come on. Derek looks up. That's when he sees me. We lock gazes for a moment as both our faces register shock. Before he can say or do anything, I race out of the gymnasium into the cold night air.

I wait for Theresa outside as a herd of students exits the school. I'm worried that Theresa won't know where to find me, but I refuse to go back in there and see Derek again. Twenty minutes later, when most of the students have left, I see Theresa emerging from the front door with her dance partner.

"Frances!" She sounds frantic. "I was worried sick looking all over for you. I thought that we were supposed to meet at our spot. Why weren't you there?"

Her new friend is standing right behind her. I'm not about to explain my situation in front of him. "Sorry," I say. I eye the boy behind her suspiciously. Theresa turns to him.

"Oh, this is Frances," Theresa says. "Frances, this is Alfred."

"Nice to meet you, Frances," Alfred says.

I nod curtly and then ignore him. I wish he would just go away.

Instead, he says, "I'll walk you to your car."

"Oh! How nice," Theresa says.

The three of us walk for a couple of blocks. Theresa and Alfred chitchat all the way while I tune out their conversation. When we finally reach Nellie's car, Alfred and Theresa pause

CARA CHOW

and smile awkwardly at each other. Meanwhile, I stand there, arms crossed and foot tapping on the pavement.

"Well, it was really nice meeting you," Theresa says.

"Same here," Alfred replies.

They continue staring at each other, smiling. I clear my throat.

"Um . . . I guess we'd better get going," Theresa says. She reluctantly turns away from Alfred to put her keys in the car door. Alfred's eyes dart nervously between Theresa and me, like he wants to say something to Theresa but can't because I'm there.

"Wait," Alfred says. "I was wondering . . ." He glances at me and then seems to decide to pretend that I'm not there. "I was wondering if you wanted to go to the Winterball with me."

"Oh! I'd like that."

"Great! I can call you later so we can talk about it more."

"That'd be great!"

"Well, um, do you have a pen and paper?" Alfred asks.

"Uh . . ." Theresa fumbles through her purse and pulls out a Hello Kitty pen and matching pocket notebook. Alfred takes the pen, writes on the notebook, and hands everything back to Theresa. "Great! Thanks!" Theresa says.

"Oh, um, could you . . . ?" Alfred makes a writing-on-paper motion with his hands.

"Oh! That's right." Theresa writes her number on a separate sheet and tears it out for Alfred. I wish they would just hurry this up so I can go home.

"Okay. Well . . . I'll call you," Alfred says.

Theresa's face glows. "Great!" She looks open and eager, ignorant of all the disappointment and humiliation that might await her.

Alfred smiles and waves. Theresa does the same. The two of them look so cute I could just puke. Then he walks away, and we get in the car.

"If you hadn't twisted my arm, I would have never had the nerve to approach him," Theresa says. "Thanks!"

I remain silent.

"So how did it go with you?" she asks.

My face must say it all. Her smile fades. "Oh, I'm sorry."

"Derek was there. With Diana." I leave out the part about the boy who refused me. It's too humiliating.

"Diana? But I thought . . ."

I wave her off with my hand. "Let's just go home."

We drive in silence back to my apartment. I never thought that Theresa would get a boy before me. Not that she's ugly, but she isn't prettier than I am either. At least, I didn't think so. On top of that, she's not bold like me. She's a mouse, timid and nervous. She doesn't command an audience. I had thought that if we failed together, I wouldn't have to feel alone. But now that she scored a dance invitation, it only makes me look like an even bigger loser.

Theresa drops me off at my apartment. Our second-story window is dark. I hope that this time Mom really will be asleep and not just lying in wait. The chances of that are high, since it is past eleven. I open the door slowly. Inside, it is silent. I tiptoe to the bathroom and turn on the light.

"So. How was *The Little Mermaid?*"

My heart jumps to my throat as I spin around. Mom is standing in the doorway.

"It was good," I say, fighting to keep my voice calm.

"Hm. What is the movie about?" Her voice is like silk. It makes me nervous.

"It's about this mermaid who wants to explore the human world, but her father forbids her to venture beyond the mermaid world," I say. "But she ventures out anyway and falls in love with a prince."

"Hm, I see. So, what happens after that?"

"The sea witch offers to transform her tail into a pair of legs in exchange for her voice. The mermaid must make the prince fall in love with her or else the sea witch gets to own her." With each sentence, I find myself talking faster and faster.

"So, how does it end?"

I know that Mom doesn't care about the movie. Where is she going with this?

"She eventually succeeds in making the prince fall in love with her," I say. "She gets her voice back and they marry and live happily ever after."

"That's nice," Mom says. "Just remember, it is only a fairy tale. In real life, by venturing outside to get this prince, the mermaid would have lost her prince, her voice, and her life."

I shiver.

Mom's eyes travel down and up my body. It reminds me of the boy at the dance who said, "No thanks." "You're really dressed up just to go see a mermaid," she says.

"Oh . . . well, we just felt like dressing up, that's all."

"Hm. I see."

Mom pauses. In the silence, I can hear my heart thumping.

"Derek called," she says.

I stifle the urge to gasp.

I had almost forgotten that I had given him my number. Stupid! What was I thinking? And yet he wouldn't call unless he cared about me, right? Maybe going to the dance wasn't a fruitless endeavor after all. Maybe I can find a way to call him back later. Maybe I can use Theresa's phone. All I have to do is get through my punishment. If he cares, it will be worth it.

I brace myself for the sharp slap, followed by the shrill screaming. The sooner we can get this over with, the better. But Mom just stands there, looking at me, her eyes cool and mocking. The seconds stretch to minutes as my anticipation frays. Why hasn't she exploded? Could it be that she's not upset? Maybe she won't wring me out after all. I give myself permission to exhale.

"This Derek said that he wasn't going to the dance," Mom says. "He didn't want you to look for him."

How can that be? He was there. I saw him.

Mom doesn't miss the confusion on my face. "Was he there?" she asks.

"Yes."

"Did he ask you to dance?"

"No."

"Did any other boys ask you to dance?"

"No."

"You know why? Three reasons. Your acne, your weight, and all that makeup on your face, which makes you look cheap." Her lips curl into a smile. "When I tell you not to socialize with boys, it is for your benefit," Mom says. "I only do it to spare your feelings. But if you want to find out for yourself, what can I say? If you want to go, I am powerless to stop you. So be my guest." And with that, she walks away.

My whole body burns with humiliation. My chest aches as it did after the speech competition, only worse. I think about the overweight boy, the one I decided not to ask. Then I think about the boy who looked me up and down and said no. He probably saw me the way I saw the overweight boy. Does Derek see me that way too? I close the door and look at myself in the mirror. Under the harsh bathroom light, my makeup does look garish.

Frantically, I begin scrubbing my face with soap and water, splashing everywhere. I scrub and scrub until my pimples bleed. Then I tiptoe to my backpack, which is leaning against my desk, and pull out the folded note passed between Derek and me. I see my number, then his. I rip up the paper, watching our conversation fragment and separate, over and over again, until I can no longer figure out how to piece it back together. I don't throw the pieces away. Mom might find them. Instead, I shove them into the front pocket of my backpack.

The next day, I walk them to the outside trash receptacle on the corner of my block. I hold the loose pieces like a handful of hair, watching the cold, whipping wind knock the fringes to and fro. Little by little, I watch the pieces fall through my fingers.

Chapter Ten

In the days that follow, Theresa does not mention Alfred. Neither do I. I don't want any reminders of the dance debacle. I don't want to listen to Theresa gush about Alfred while I mourn Derek. Perhaps she has forgotten about him. Then we can go back to how things were before, just the two of us, as if this never happened.

Meanwhile, I redirect my attention to my scholarship applications. I apply to one of the scholarships offered by Scripps. I also comb through Ms. Taylor's book, pick out every scholarship I could possibly qualify for, and apply to every single one.

A week later, we get our report cards. Theresa and I are sipping hot cocoa during our midmorning break. We are both nervous about what we got, especially me, so we agreed not to open our report cards until we could do it together.

"The Winterball is coming up in five weeks," Theresa says out of the blue.

I cringe and hope that she didn't see. "That's plenty of time," I say.

"I'm wondering if I should call him."

"You mean, he hasn't called already?" I try to sound surprised, but my voice ends up sounding overly dramatic.

"No." Theresa sighs. "Maybe he lost my number. If I called him, that would solve the problem."

"But what if you call him, only to find out that he didn't like you as much as you thought? Or what if he did like you but changed his mind?" I say.

"We seemed to connect really well," Theresa says doubtfully.

"I thought the same about me and Derek, and look what happened," I say. "The moral of the story is that men are fickle. I just don't want you to be disappointed like me."

"But if he's not interested in me, wouldn't it be better if I knew for sure instead of having to guess?" Theresa says.

I am irritated by Theresa's logic. "If he doesn't call you, then that's all you need to know," I insist. "Don't humiliate yourself by calling him. If he wants you, then he should make the first move."

Theresa sighs again. We finish up our cocoa. Now it's report card time. I have Theresa's report card and she has mine.

"Ready?" I say.

"Ready."

We open each other's report cards. My biggest fear is getting a B and ruining my 4.5 grade point average. Mom would kill me if that happened.

"What did I get?" Theresa asks.

"Mostly As. A-minuses in speech and English. How about me?"

"All As, with A-minuses in government and physics." Good. That means I got an A in speech. It would be embarrassing not to do better than Theresa in speech when I'm the one who's been in competition.

Suddenly, Theresa's face falls.

"What is it?" I ask.

"Speech is on your report card."

"Yeah. So?"

Then it hits me. Our moms have to sign our report cards. My report card shows that I took speech and not calculus.

"What are you going to do?" Theresa asks.

I wish I knew. I stare at the signature portion of Theresa's report card. I visualize my mother's handwriting on the thick black line. I spell out her name with my eyes. Then I trace the sharp, slanted letters with my fingers. Slowly, an idea comes to mind.

At the end of speech class, I approach Ms. Taylor's desk. Theresa waits for me at the doorway. Ms. Taylor pulls out my college application for Scripps.

"Looks good. I think this is a winner," she says.

I nod and take the application. It feels good to have Ms. Taylor's stamp of approval. I hadn't planned on asking her to review it, but when she offered, I was more than happy to accept.

"Have you filled out your financial-aid form?" she asks.

I nod, even though it is still sitting in my folder, totally blank. "I applied for scholarships too," I add. At least that part is true.

"And one more thing." Ms. Taylor beckons to Theresa. "This is for you too." Theresa approaches. I quickly hide my application in my folder. Ms. Taylor pulls out a few papers stapled together. "The Chinese American Association is sponsoring its first speech tournament," she tells us. "Now, here are the challenges. It's not like the state-sponsored tournaments, where you compete in groups of five for several rounds. All the competitors are herded on a stage like cows, and each speaker goes one after another, so you're out of luck if you're number thirteen out of fifteen. You only get one chance to speak, so there's no second chance if you have a bad round. And the competition is Friday."

"*This* Friday?" I say.

"Sorry about the late notice, but I just got this information this morning," Ms. Taylor says. "Now here's the good news. Because this is only for competitors of Chinese descent, the competition pool will be different. You won't have to compete against all the Derek Collinses, so your chances of winning are higher."

I wince at his name. Then it dawns on me that she has a point. This could be my only guaranteed Derek-free competition.

"Also, unlike the state-sponsored competitions, winners get money as well as a trophy," Ms. Taylor continues. "The first-place winner gets five hundred dollars; the second-place winner gets two hundred fifty dollars; and the third-place winner gets one hundred twenty-five dollars. And this will be pretty high profile in the Chinese American community. Finally, this is the association's first speech event. Wouldn't you like to say you were a part of history? It'll also look good on your application." Ms. Taylor winks at me.

"Oh, and one more advantage," Ms. Taylor adds. "Unlike the state tournaments, family members are allowed to attend. So you can invite your family!"

Great. Just what I need.

Theresa starts shifting her weight from one foot to the other.

"Don't look so nervous, Theresa," Ms. Taylor says. "There is no reason why you can't do this and have fun."

"I appreciate the offer, but I'm more interested in just speaking in class, to improve my communication skills," Theresa says. "I don't want to be in the spotlight."

"Well, I'm leaving the door open in case you change your mind," Ms. Taylor says to Theresa. Then she turns to me. "I'm closing your door before you have a chance to sneak out." She smiles mischievously at me and winks again.

Theresa looks at me as if to say, *Tell her no!* I pretend not to notice. I walk out the door with Theresa.

Once we reach the hallway, Theresa starts walking faster, so fast that even I, with my longer legs, can't keep up with her.

"It wasn't my fault," I say.

Theresa rushes down two flights of stairs, not looking at me at all. I'm out of breath, but I manage to stay on her heels.

"I didn't say that I would do it. She just assumed," I add.

We reach the locker room. Theresa opens her combination lock, her fingers furious.

"How can I say no to her? She's counting on me," I say.

Theresa wrenches her locker door open. She hangs her head and sighs.

"But *you* are also counting on *me* to keep this a secret," she says. "And I was counting on you to stop. My dad is a member of the Chinese American Association. Do you realize how much harder it will be to hide this competition than it was to hide the first one? It will be in the Chinese newspaper. It will be on Channel Twenty-six." Channel 26 is the Chinese TV station.

"I said no to make it easier for you to say no," Theresa says. "If you didn't get to compete and I did, you would feel bad. Also, my mom would attend. So would Auntie Gracie. Ms. Taylor would talk to them about you and blow your cover."

I picture Theresa, the tongue-tied introvert, competing in a speech contest. "Did you really want to compete in the CAA tournament?" I ask.

"At first, I wasn't interested in competing at all," she says. "But then I saw how well you did and how that changed you. You look taller now, brighter somehow. It made me think that maybe I had made a mistake by not taking any risks."

"Well, you shouldn't deny yourself just so I don't feel bad," I say.

Theresa changes her books and retrieves her lunch. "Never

mind," she says. "I'd probably just make a fool out of myself anyway."

"That's not true," I say. "Maybe we can both compete. Maybe we can find a way not to let our moms know."

Theresa looks at me incredulously.

"I can't back down now," I say. "Not after everything Ms. Taylor has done for me."

"Are you really doing this for Ms. Taylor or are you doing it for yourself?" Theresa says.

My face flushes hot. "I can't believe it," I say. "You're my best friend and you're calling me selfish. Fine. Do you want me to tell Ms. Taylor to count me out? If so, just tell me and I'll do it."

Our stares form crossed swords prepared for battle. Finally, Theresa looks down. "I don't want to talk about this anymore," she says with a tone of resignation. She closes her locker. I follow her to the cafeteria, smiling inside over my victory.

To my relief and good fortune, Theresa is not the type to hold grudges. Before long, she is back to her cheerful self. We have a truce. I will compete. Theresa will not mention what I'm up to, but she won't lie for me either. Theresa will compete, but she won't invite Nellie to attend. We haven't figured out how we will compete without our mothers finding out, but we still have a few days.

We are supposed to leave for Nellie's house for dinner soon.

I am sitting at my desk. Mom is in the bathroom. I have before me the current report card and a report card from last year. The two lie side by side. On top of them is a sheet of white scratch paper with *Gracie Ching* written in cursive on it over and over. I hold the sheet of paper up to Mom's signature on the old report card. The second to the last *Gracie Ching* is close but not exactly like Mom's signature. It looks too shaky. I practice writing my mother's name a few more times. Then, with quick strokes, I write my mother's signature on the new report card with a blue ballpoint pen.

The phone rings, almost causing me to smear my forgery. I hide the report card in my backpack before picking up the receiver.

"Frances." It's Theresa.

"We'll be leaving soon," I say.

"That's not why I'm calling," Theresa says. "My mom found the trophy."

I gasp. Quickly, I look behind me to make sure Mom is out of earshot.

"I hid it in my closet in my suitcase," Theresa says. "Mom decided that we're going to spend Christmas with Dad in Hong Kong this year. If I had known about that, I would've hidden the trophy somewhere else. Anyway, she went into my suitcase this afternoon to see if it was big enough for all our stuff.

"At first, she thought it was mine. I probably should have said nothing, but I couldn't bear taking credit for your accomplishment. So I ended up telling her it was yours. She doesn't know that you're in speech class. She only knows that you competed and won. I said that you want to surprise Auntie Gracie. I made her promise not to spill the beans and spoil your fun."

Mom walks into the living room. She has her coat on and is clutching her purse and a fishnet bag of oranges.

"Okay," I say. "We'll be over soon. Bye." I hang up.

"If you weren't so busy chatting on the phone, we'd be there by now," Mom says.

I put on my jacket, swing my backpack over my shoulder, and follow Mom to the door.

"Why didn't you offer to help your mother carry the oranges?" Mom says.

"Sorry." I take the oranges from Mom.

"I shouldn't have to ask you. You should have thought of it on your own."

"Sorry," I repeat as I follow Mom down the stairs.

Nellie's kitchen and dining room, which were dingy white before the quake, have now been painted cotton-candy pink. It doesn't quite go with the lacquered dark-wood credenza, dining table, and chairs, but Nellie is thrilled about it. The four of us are sitting down to dinner. Though we eat here often, I never get used to the crinkly plastic seat covers, which are supposed to protect the embroidered white cushions. A tablecloth made of a similar plastic covers the dining table. Come to think of it, everything in this house is protected that way. The couch is covered with plastic too. Even the remote controls are covered with cling wrap. The idea is to cover everything so it will last longer but to keep the covers clear so that everyone can see what nice things you have. I'm surprised that they don't have a plastic covering for their carpet. Then again, there are plastic runners going down the hallway.

Nellie is like the plastic seat covers, which by covering the flashy seats are all the more obvious. As she hands me my bowl of rice, she nudges me, winks, and gives me the thumbs-up. Her back is to Mom, but her body visibly jiggles with enthusiasm, giving her away. Throughout dinner, she smiles brightly at me every chance she gets. I think she enjoys feeling like one of the girls, hiding this big secret from the grown-ups. I try to avoid eye contact with her, but that's like trying to ignore a pink elephant in the room. So far, Mom hasn't said anything, but it's only a matter of time. After dinner, Nellie and Theresa serve the sliced navel oranges that Mom and I brought over.

"Theresa is such a talented cook and so helpful too," Mom says.

"She's useful for something," Nellie says.

"Much more useful than my daughter," Mom says as she chomps through her orange slice. "She never helps at all around the kitchen, can't cook a single thing."

I boil with indignation. Every time I've offered to help, she has shooed me away, and now she is accusing me of not helping.

"Practice makes perfect," Nellie says in English. Then she says to me in Chinese, "Just keep following your mommy and don't worry, you'll be a great cook."

"What's the point?" Mom says. "She only fills her head with book smarts, but she has no practical talent."

"She has more talent than you realize, right, Fei Ting?" Nellie smiles at me and waggles her eyebrows up and down. "One day, she might surprise you."

Theresa and I shrink a few inches into our seats, but Mom doesn't seem to notice.

"If I let her in the kitchen, she'd probably start a fire and burn the place down," Mom says. "That's why I want her to be a doctor, because she probably wouldn't be good at anything else and she's not pretty. Who would want to marry someone like that?"

"She might have trouble finding a husband, not because she's too stupid but because she's too smart," Nellie insists. "Most men can't handle a woman who is more accomplished than he is. Right, Fei Ting?" Again she beams at me. This is too much. The sad thing is she genuinely believes that she's being subtle.

Quickly, Theresa gathers the dishes and leaves the room. She nearly trips over her own feet. Once in the kitchen, she turns on the faucet and begins washing the dishes.

"Wah, so helpful!" Mom says. Then she turns to me. "See what a good daughter Theresa is? Follow her example and you will be *dai sek.*" "*Dai sek*" means "lovable," or "deserving of love."

"The truth is Theresa can learn a lot from Fei Ting." Nellie winks at me again. Then she changes the subject. "How did Fei Ting do on her report card?" she asks Mom.

My heart jumps to my throat.

"What report card?" Mom looks puzzled.

"Gracie! Are you getting absentminded like me?" Nellie says. "Report cards came in two days ago, remember?" Clearly, Mom does not remember. "My Theresa went down from an A to an A-minus in English. How did Fei Ting do?"

Mom looks at me. I look at my lap. That subtle mistake gives me away instantly.

"I don't know," Mom says. "How did you do, Fei Ting?"

"I did okay," I say. I hear Theresa turn off the water in the kitchen.

"She's so modest, always hiding her accomplishments from others," Nellie says.

"Either that or she is hiding how much she didn't accomplish," Mom says.

Without warning, Mom walks to the couch in the living area, where my backpack is. She picks up my backpack and unzips it. After some fumbling, she takes out the report card and opens it. Nellie walks over to Mom and peeks over her shoulder.

"All As!" Nellie cheers.

Nellie is just scanning the letter grades. But Mom's eyes are examining every detail. "What's speech?" she asks. "And where's calculus?" She flips over the report card, in case calculus is written on the back. But there is no calculus back there, just her forged signature at the bottom. Mom blinks for a moment, confused, like maybe she indeed signed the card and has gone senile. For confirmation, she looks at me. The expression on my face answers her question.

Mom walks towards me. Her right hand, which is still holding the report card, swings at me and whips me across the face. The report card makes the sound of thunder against my ear. My neck cracks as my head turns from the impact. A second later, my cheek stings and grows hot, swollen, and tingly. I resist the urge to rub my cheek. That will only make her hit me harder.

Through the kitchen doorway, I see that Theresa's head is bowed, and her eyes are glued to the sink. In contrast, Nellie's eyes widen with alarm, like two spotlights. Her clownish smiling lips morph into an O of surprise at Mom's reaction.

"Gracie! Don't be so hard on Fei Ting!" she cries. "Wait here." She waddles to Theresa's room. Moments later, she returns, holding my trophy. "Look. She won this at a speech competition." The brassy trophy catches the light, and for a split second, I am blinded by its brightness.

Nellie hands the trophy to Mom, who is once again confused. Nellie is hoping that my success will soften Mom's anger. I am hoping so too. But my hopes prove futile. As Mom scrutinizes the trophy, I can almost see the images in her mind flashing behind her eyes like a slide show, documenting every moment I was not home and not accounted for. With each passing second, her frozen expression thaws, giving way to a steely stare.

"So all this time you've been working so hard on calculus, hah?" Mom says. Venom drips from the word *calculus*. "To win this award, you must have put in a lot of time practicing. Is this why you weren't at Princeton Review on the day of the earthquake? How many other classes did you miss?"

I don't answer, hoping that her question is rhetorical.

"How many!" My ears pop from the shrillness of her voice.

One thing I should know by now: if I answer her questions, she'll be angry that I gave the wrong answer, but if I don't answer, she'll be mad that I ignored the question.

"Two," I say.

Then she lunges towards me. Instinctively, I crouch down and shield my body with my arms as Mom beats me with the trophy.

"Put your arms down! Stand up straight!" Mom screams. But I'm unable to will myself to bring my arms down. Though the trophy is hollow and made of plastic, its sharpness and hardness penetrate my elbows, forearms, and hands.

That's when Nellie races to Mom and grabs her arms. "Stop, Gracie! It's okay!"

"No, it's not okay!"

"She's just a girl. She might get hurt," Nellie pleads.

"Hurt? I want her to die!"

"That's enough, Gracie."

"No! It's never enough!"

The trophy hovers an inch this way and an inch that way as Nellie and Gracie struggle back and forth.

"Tell Mommy you're sorry," Nellie says to me. "Hurry, beg for her forgiveness."

"I'm sorry," I say.

"Beg more. Kneel," Nellie says.

I get down on my knees. Though my legs are shaking, I fight to keep my back straight. A slouchy posture would only incense Mom more. "I'm sorry," I say. "I was wrong to lie."

"See how sorry she is?" Nellie says to Mom. "She's on her knees, worshipping you. How can you hit a child who is this sorry? I'm begging you as your sister to stop."

Finally, Mom's grip on the trophy relaxes, and Nellie snatches it from her hands. Mom gazes down at me. "Do you really mean it?"

Nellie peers at me from behind Mom and nods her head.

"Yes," I say, pretending not to see Nellie.

"Then say it," Mom says.

Didn't I just say it? What else does she want me to say? I look to Nellie for suggestions, but she keeps nodding encouragingly, which offers me no answers.

"I . . . shouldn't have lied. I apologize." Maybe "apologize" will sound more satisfying than "sorry."

"Say 'I'm sorry, Mommy,'" Mom says.

"I'm sorry, Mommy."

"And what do you deserve?" Mom says.

What's the right answer? I deserve nothing? I deserve to be punished? One wrong move and we could revert back to the beating. "Um . . ."

"Do you deserve to be yelled at?" Mom says, prompting me.

"Yes," I say.

"Do you deserve to be beaten?"

"Yes."

"Yes, what?"

"Yes, Mommy."

"And do I deserve a daughter like you?"

If I say no, would she interpret that as meaning that she deserves better or that she deserves worse?

"Do I deserve better?" Mom says.

"Yes," I say, eager to get this over with. Then I correct myself. "Yes, Mommy."

Mom looks satisfied. "Just remember," she says, "you can improve yourself and make yourself into the daughter I deserve."

"Good, good, good." Nellie rushes to me to help me off my knees. "Everything is okay now. Mommy isn't mad anymore. Right, Mommy?"

Mom ignores Nellie. "I have to wake up at three a.m.," she says. "Because of Fei Ting, my stomach hurts, and I won't be able to sleep at all. Then I'll be tired and upset all day tomorrow as I work."

"Well, we shouldn't keep you from sleeping," Nellie says with forced cheerfulness.

Nellie drives us home. Then she and Theresa walk Mom and me up the stairs. As soon as Mom and I enter our apartment, Nellie and Theresa turn to go.

I walk with them to the gate, as if I could follow them home. I want to beg them to stay awhile longer. I'm afraid of what Mom will do once they're gone. But I don't dare ask them to stay, not after what they've been through. Just by intervening as much as she did, Nellie already crossed the line. The proper thing to do would have been to mind her own business and not interfere, even agree with Mom and side against me. By trying to stop Mom from beating me, Nellie insinuated that Mom's choice was wrong. That is the worst offense of all, to accuse a parent of being wrong. The parents must always be right; otherwise they lose face. And by losing face, they lose their authority in the family.

Before closing the gate behind her, Nellie grabs my hand and squeezes it. "She didn't mean it," she whispers. "It's because she loves you so much that she gets this upset. So be good and don't upset her anymore." Nellie points to her heart. "I know that inside, you're a good girl." I watch Nellie and Theresa disappear into their car and down the street. I am left alone, weak and unprotected.

When I return to our apartment, Mom makes her way into the bedroom. "Ingrate," she mutters as she slams the door behind her. How many times I've wished that I had my own room. Now I will have to spend the whole night just a few feet above her body, where her anger and judgments reside, as if she is a fire and I am a roast pig being turned on a skewer above the flames.

I stand outside the door, afraid to enter the bedroom, while my toes turn to ice on the linoleum floor. After about fifteen minutes, when my feet have grown numb, I tentatively open the door. Mom is snoring softly. Thank goodness. I carefully climb up the ladder to the top bunk, trying not to make a noise. A couple of times, I cause a creak and break out in sweat, afraid that Mom will wake up and hit me all over again. Fortunately, she doesn't wake and I make it to bed safely. I pull the blankets up to my face and feel their softness against my lips.

After losing Derek, I consoled myself with speech. I vowed to hold on to it with all my might. But now it seems that even that is slipping from my grasp, in spite of my best efforts. How foolish I was to think that I could outsmart Mom. It is like swimming against a riptide, climbing out of quicksand, or hanging on to a pole in the midst of a hurricane. You can fight nature for only so long before you are swallowed by it.

Chapter Eleven

It is the day after my mother beat me with my trophy. I slow my steps as I approach the locker room. Theresa always gets there before I do. Normally, this is our meeting spot, where we gossip and chat before class. But after being beaten by my mother right in front of her, I can barely face her.

Theresa is quietly placing her books into her bag. Her movements seem particularly somber.

"Hi," I say, trying to sound normal, as I turn my combination lock.

"Hi." She waits for me as I unload my books. "Are you okay?" she asks.

"Yeah. Are you okay?"

"Yeah. Mom gave me a real tongue-lashing last night. She almost didn't let me compete this Friday. She was afraid that speech was causing me to go evil. But once she blew off some steam, she changed her mind. At least I didn't get hit or anything."

Then Theresa asks the inevitable question. "What are you going to do about this Friday?"

I know what I must do—even if Ms. Taylor hates me for it.

After speech class, I approach Ms. Taylor. I tell her about how I ended up in her class by mistake, about how I loved it and couldn't leave. I tell her about my mother's plans for me and about how I had hidden speech from her, how that blew up in my face last night, and how that precludes my involvement in this Friday's competition. I leave out that I ditched Princeton Review to rehearse with her. I also leave out that Mom beat me with my trophy.

I brace myself for Ms. Taylor's reaction. Will she be angry, hurt, disgusted? I've never seen her upset before and am frightened of what that might be like.

Ms. Taylor blinks a few times. Then she takes a slow, deep breath. "Well, that's dedication," she says, more to herself than to me. I can't tell if she is referring to my dedication to speech or my dedication to my mother.

"It was wrong of me not to tell you sooner. I accept whatever consequences come my way," I blurt out.

"Don't be so hard on yourself, Frances," Ms. Taylor says.

"If you decide to kick me out or flunk me or report me to the principal, I totally understand," I say.

Ms. Taylor waves away my proposed punishments with her hand. "Don't worry about any of that," she says. "I'm not upset. I can see why you did what you did. I feel honored that you trust me enough to tell me the truth."

She's not mad at me? What has gotten into her?

"Honesty is the best policy, but keep your actions in perspective. There are worse offenses," Ms. Taylor says. She places her warm, gentle hand on my back. She's silent, deep in thought, for about a minute. Finally, she turns to me and says, "It seems a shame not to compete, after how hard you've worked. Just come and rehearse anyway."

"But—"

"I'll talk to your mother. She has your best interest at heart. If she doesn't approve of speech, then it's because she doesn't understand its value. It's perfectly natural for people to fear what they don't understand. I'm positive she'll turn around once I explain what you're doing."

I have a vague suspicion that despite Ms. Taylor's good intentions, her intervention may make things worse instead of better.

"Don't worry, Frances. Everything's going to be all right." Ms. Taylor squeezes my forearm as a gesture of reassurance. She doesn't realize that she is squeezing my bruises from last night, bruises that I have hidden underneath my sweater sleeves. I fight the urge to wince as tears flood my eyes.

All afternoon, I can't concentrate on my studies. I keep expecting Ms. Taylor to call. But she doesn't. By five o'clock, I start to suspect that maybe she has changed her mind. I am simultaneously relieved and disappointed.

Then, at 5:07, the doorbell rings. I run to the window. It's Ms. Taylor. I buzz her up the stairs. Assuming that it is Theresa,

Mom opens the door. Instead of Theresa, she sees Ms. Taylor smiling back at her, right hand extended for a shake. I stand behind Mom, peering over her shoulder.

"Hi, I'm Shannon Taylor, Frances's teacher. I wanted to talk to you about Frances. Do you have a moment? May I come in?"

Afraid of appearing rude to a teacher, Mom lets Ms. Taylor in. As the two shake hands, I notice for the first time how young Ms. Taylor looks. Next to me and my classmates, she looks grown up, poised, and in control. In contrast, next to Mom, she looks eccentric and naïve, with her rhinestone cat-eye glasses, violet velvet shirt, and black boots.

"Very nice to meet you," Mom says, her voice and smile saccharine.

"Oh, it's an honor to finally meet you in person," gushes Ms. Taylor. "How well students do is often a reflection of parental support, and Frances is such a stellar student."

She's hitting all the right targets. Maybe this won't go as badly as I think.

"Would you like something to eat, some tea?" Mom says.

"No thanks. I just ate." Ms. Taylor looks at me. I shake my head ever so slightly. "But tea would be lovely," she adds.

I show Ms. Taylor to the couch. Then I join Mom in the kitchen to prepare the tea as she cuts oranges. She pulls out the *long jeng cha*, her most expensive tea, used only when special guests come over. She sprinkles the wrinkled dried leaves and pours boiling water into her special clay teapot from Li Hing in eastern China. As the tea brews, Mom gets out the egg roll cookies and lays them on a fancy plate. We bring the food and tea to Ms. Taylor and sit on hard fold-out chairs. Mom pours Ms. Taylor's tea first.

"Wow, that smells amazing!" Ms. Taylor says.

"It's a special tea from Hong Kong. One bag costs a hundred dollars," Mom says. I'm embarrassed that Mom would flaunt how much she spends on a guest.

"Oh! I'm so honored that you're sharing this with me. Thank you." Ms. Taylor inhales the steam and takes a tentative sip. "Mm, it's so fragrant."

"Be careful," Mom says. "If you drink it too fast, you might burn yourself." Mom emphasizes the word *burn* and stares at Ms. Taylor in a way that sends chills up my spine.

Our couch is so old that Ms. Taylor is sinking in it. Her bottom is probably half a foot off the floor. When Nellie sits in it, she looks like Humpty Dumpty in an egg crate, but Ms. Taylor is so petite that she looks like she's being swallowed.

"First, I have to take responsibility for Frances's involvement in speech," Ms. Taylor says. "Frances meant to attend calculus class and ended up in my class by mistake. She was too polite to walk out in the middle of class, and silly me, I just added her to my list of students. I didn't even think to check with her or her counselor.

"But you know, I must confess that even had I known that she wasn't supposed to be in my class, I wouldn't have wanted her to leave, because she has such a special gift. Her writing skills are excellent, and she has stage presence, charisma. Her delivery style has that perfect balance between sophistication and authenticity."

I look down at the floor, pleased and embarrassed by her glowing praise.

"Straight As and high SATs are a dime a dozen these days," Ms. Taylor continues. "What really sets one student apart from another is her extracurricular activities. Colleges aren't just interested in bookworms. They want to know if the student is well rounded. Speech definitely wins brownie points in the area of extracurricular activities. Without it, Frances's chances of getting into Berkeley would not be as strong, even if she had taken calculus."

Mom lets out a small gasp. "Really?"

"I'm serious. Anyway, I'm here tonight to invite you to attend Frances's next competition."

Mom startles at Ms. Taylor's invitation.

"Again, I have to take responsibility," Ms. Taylor says. "Frances really respects your authority, and she told me that she had to withdraw from this contest, but I told her to stick it out. I want you to see what she can do, Mrs. Ching. If you just saw her, you would feel so proud." Ms. Taylor's eyes are glistening with emotion. "This is no ordinary competition. It's the Chinese American Association's first ever speech tournament. Frances has the opportunity to make history."

"Really?" Mom says again, quietly.

"Yes. And do you know who's going to be on the judging panel?"

"Who?"

"Wendy Tokuda, Emerald Yeh, and David Louie, just to name a few."

Mom watches the news and recognizes the names of these TV journalists. She has fallen under Ms. Taylor's spell—I hope.

"Imagine how that would look on her curriculum vitae. Wouldn't it be a shame if she had to miss it? Wouldn't it be a shame if *you* had to miss it?" Ms. Taylor pauses, letting Mom soak this up. "Theresa's competing too. It would definitely be a shame if Frances couldn't join her."

That pretty much clinches the win. If Theresa got an opportunity that I didn't get, Mom would never be able to live it down.

"Anyway, I have to go now, but can I count on you to be there with Frances tomorrow?" Ms. Taylor's bright eyes shine on Mom like a spotlight.

Mom smiles sweetly. "Of course."

"Excellent." Ms. Taylor rises and holds out her hand. Mom shakes it. "Again, it is such a pleasure meeting you." Mom nods and bows slightly. Taking that to be a cultural gesture, Ms. Taylor bows too. Responding to Ms. Taylor's gesture, Mom bows lower, and Ms. Taylor does the same, still clutching Mom's hand. Once past the doorway, Ms. Taylor bows one last time and departs.

As Mom closes the door, she mutters, "Idiot. She thinks we're Japanese."

My heart falls. Does that mean that Mom was lying to Ms. Taylor, that I can't compete?

"Look at how she dresses," Mom says. "Those showy glasses, that hippie shirt, those giant, punky boots. What kind of teacher is that? That's someone who doesn't take herself seriously. If she doesn't take herself seriously, how can her students take school seriously?"

What she is saying about Ms. Taylor is untrue and unfair. But Mom is relentless. "And her manners, so nicey-nicey, so fake. She barely even drank my tea. How wasteful, not to finish a hundred-dollar tea. And she didn't even eat my oranges, after I went through all the trouble slicing them."

Ms. Taylor probably took Mom's words and actions at face value. She's probably driving home right now, thinking that the meeting went well, not realizing all the trash Mom is talking about her.

"I sensed all along that something in you had changed. Now I know where the source of that change lies. You're so foolish, lying to me to follow her. How you squander your trust. But she's not on your side, Fei Ting."

A chilly fear runs down my spine. At the same time, I feel impatient. Am I competing or not?

"But she has a point," Mom says. "I believe she was telling the truth about the benefits of this speech thing you're doing. I know of the Chinese American Association. Nellie's husband is a member. It would be good for you to attend. You don't realize it now, but this woman is using you. But that's okay. We can use her back. We'll go tomorrow. That will make us even."

I fight to contain my excitement. I get to compete tomorrow!

"Hopefully, she's not exaggerating your talent and you won't make a fool of yourself," Mom adds. "And if you don't get into Berkeley, you'll have yourself and her to blame."

Her last sentence punctures some of my enthusiasm. Speaking in front of Mom will be harder than speaking in front of strangers. What if I totally mess up? It will provide her with endless ammunition for humiliating me.

But I can't think about that now. I have a chance to compete. I must rise to the occasion.

Chapter Twelve

Nellie is driving Theresa, Mom, and me. I'm wearing what has become my speech uniform: black flats, black tights, a black sheath skirt, and a white button-down long-sleeved blouse. Theresa is wearing a similar outfit, only hers has white tights and a brown pleated skirt. Mom is wearing her respectable work clothes: camel slacks and a lavender cardigan sweater. Nellie is wearing her favorite outfit: a hot pink jogging suit with black jaguar patterns. Her over-permed hair looks like an Afro.

Nellie drops us off to search for parking. Theresa, Mom, and I step out into the whipping night wind and then into the Chinese American Association Building on Stockton Street in Chinatown. It's a big, heavy-looking building with two big doors out front. Mom struggles to open one, and Theresa has to help her.

The inside of the building reminds me of a large church. It is austere, with a high ceiling and yellow chandelier lighting. There are rows of metal fold-out chairs facing the stage, with an aisle down the middle. In front of the chairs is a long metal fold-out table, where the judges are seated. It's hard to recognize them from behind, but as they turn their heads to speak to each other, I can tell they're Emerald Yeh and Wendy Tokuda.

Off to the side are TV cameras from Channel 26 and journalists with cameras from the Chinese newspaper. The sight of famous people and cameras causes a lump to form in my already constricted throat. Mom notices them too. A sparkle flickers in her eyes. On an adjacent table are the large, medium, and small trophies, indicating first, second, and third place respectively.

Several feet in front of the judging panel is the stage. It's huge, elevated so that climbing onto it would be impossible. There are twelve chairs forming a half circle. This will be different from the state tournaments, where we can sit back in anonymity until it is time for us to compete. Like Ms. Taylor said, we'll be herded in like cows, then lined up like prisoners for the firing squad. Theresa and I look at each other and simultaneously swallow.

"Mrs. Ching." Ms. Taylor is waving and walking towards us. She is all in black, black blouse and blazer to match her black pants, platform boots, and glasses. She looks businesslike, with an artsy edge. She reaches for Mom's hand with her winners smile and says, "I'm so happy that you made it."

Mom smiles back. "Thank you for inviting me." Though Mom is smiling, instead of happiness, all I see are teeth. "I must thank you for all you've done for Frances."

"That's very kind, but honestly, Frances's accomplishments have more to do with Frances than with me," Ms. Taylor says. Then she turns to Theresa. "Where are your parents?"

"My dad's out of town on business, and Mom is looking for parking," Theresa says.

"Well, let's go backstage to prepare," Ms. Taylor says to Theresa and me. Mom begins to follow us, but Ms. Taylor stops her. "You can sit in any of those chairs," she says to Mom. "The competition will be starting in about twenty minutes." Ms. Taylor smiles graciously to soften her words. Mom nods, but in her eyes, I detect the slightest glare. As the three of us walk backstage, I can feel my mother behind us, her hot eyes boring into my back as we abandon her.

In the room behind the stage, Ms. Taylor is doing her pre-competition huddle with Theresa and me. I am familiar with her speech about inner versus outer success, but this time, she adds something new.

"I know it's hard, but try to forget that your mothers are out there." Ms. Taylor notices the skeptical looks on our faces. "Okay, think of it this way. Even if you totally bomb, they won't love you any less. They're your mothers. They love you unconditionally. That means for who you are, not what you do."

That's the first time I've ever heard the idea of unconditional love outside the context of religion. In theology class, I always hear about God's love, about his loving us even though we're sinners. But the idea that real live parents could be unconditionally loving is completely foreign. Often Mom and other Chinese parents say "dai sek." "Dai sek" describes children who are polite or affectionate, who excel in school, who serve their parents before themselves at banquets, or who send money back home. How can anyone be loved not for what they do but for who they are? Isn't who you are defined by what you do?

The lights in the room dim and brighten. This is our signal to line up for the cattle call. Theresa is assigned to be speaker number ten out of twelve. The only assignment worse than number ten is mine, number eleven.

Ms. Taylor leaves with the other coaches to sit in the audience as the competitors form a single line in reverse speaking order. The speaker in front of me is probably the tallest Chinese person I have ever seen. He is well over six feet tall. My eyes come up only to the shoulder blade portion of his argyle sweater. His hands remind me of baseball mitts. His coarse, straight hair sticks out in all directions. We march onto the stage to our chairs. Theresa and I sit as Ms. Taylor told us to, with our ankles crossed and knees together. Onstage, one must sit discreetly when wearing a skirt. Within minutes, my inner thighs are trembling from fatigue.

As I watch and listen to the speeches, I can't help feeling a growing sense of smugness. As Ms. Taylor said, there are no Derek Collinses here. None of my competitors has my writing skills or stage presence. A couple even have Cantonese or Taiwanese accents. No one else here could make the semifinal cut in a mainstream competition. Not only can I place, I can probably win by a landslide. Finally, Mom won't be able to compare me to someone else and say that that person is better than me.

Before I know it, it is Theresa's turn. Theresa takes mincing steps towards the front of the stage. She bows her head, then looks out at the audience and begins. Her voice is quiet and shaky at first, as if she is fearful of taking up space in the room. Then, gradually, she picks up momentum. Her body becomes less crouched and more open, even taller. Her voice becomes less mouselike and more audible. She stutters less. At the end, I can sense that she's smiling, even though her back is towards me. Then she bows her head again, signaling the end of her speech. Applause follows.

Suddenly, I hear shrill whistling from the back of the audience. Nellie is standing up alone in the sea of seated people, clapping and cheering one moment and whistling through her fingers the next. "Good job! Good job, Theresa!" she screams as she jumps up and down. With all her whistling and screaming, her hot pink attire seems only appropriate. My first reaction is embarrassment. Here Theresa is trying to make a good impression, and her mother is ruining it with her unrefined public behavior. I look at Theresa to exchange commiserating glances. But instead of being embarrassed, Theresa looks pleased. She locks gazes with her mom and smiles. Then she smiles at me as she walks to her chair and sits down.

Now it is my turn to begin. I stand up and take my position. I look out at the audience and remember my long-ago fantasy about speaking onstage. Strangely, this moment echoes my daydream. I am onstage. In the audience, Ms. Taylor is sitting in the front, and Mom and Nellie are in the back.

Then my thoughts dart back to my first speech competition, when Derek helped me. I picture him nodding at me, encouraging me to go on. This gives me confidence, and I begin.

"Recently, in Newsweek, there was an article titled 'Asian American Whiz Kids.' The article noted the high success rate of Asians in academics. It posed the question of why Asians are so successful. Is it genetics or is it due to social factors? Or are nonimmigrant students merely doing less well than their predecessors? Have they grown complacent? I would argue that the success rate of Asians in academics does not stem from superior genetics, but rather from a set of values that includes education and loyalty to family.

"Probably the best example to illustrate this is my own family. When I was three, my family left a comfortable life in Hong Kong to come to America. Britain would return Hong Kong back to China in 1997, and my mother wanted me to grow up in the land of opportunity and democracy.

"A few years later, my mother was forced to raise me alone. We were in a foreign country, with no money, no job, and no family to help us. For my mother, the easy way out would have been to return to Hong Kong. But she was determined to give her only child a better life. So she worked four part-time jobs, serving cocktails, proctoring tests, and filing for law firms, while taking evening ESL classes. Eventually, when her English skills improved, she got a job working full-time as a bank teller. She believed that I could get a better education in a private school, and she wanted to save for college, so she worked her way up to customer service representative and worked overtime and sometimes double time in order to afford the tuition."

Suddenly, everything I am saying about my mother feels much more real, even though I've said the same words many times. For a moment, I get choked up. I take a deep breath and continue.

> *"She has stayed at the same job for the last fifteen years, giving her best in spite of poor health, unforgiving customers, unreasonable managers, meager raises, and increased workloads due to mergers and layoffs. Every day she misses her family and friends in Hong Kong, but she never visits and she seldom calls. Any dollar spent on airfare or the phone bill would be a dollar siphoned from my tuition. My mother endures these hardships because she believes in my education. She always said that education was the most important thing. It is the key to greater wisdom. It is also the key to achieving the American Dream.*
>
> *"This is why she pushes me to strive for greater goals and never to rest on my laurels. This is why she emphasizes focusing on academics and forgoing the distractions of after-school jobs and dating. This is why she insists on doing all the housework, though she is exhausted every day after work, leaving me more time to study and do my best."*

How is my mother reacting to what I am saying about her? Is she moved? I want to sneak a peek at her face, but I'm too afraid.

> *"My mother's perseverance and hard work are an example and inspiration to me,"* I continue. *"After I graduate from high school, I hope to attend a top university."*

I almost say "UC Berkeley," which is what I had written before applying to Scripps, but fortunately, I catch myself in time.

"*Afterwards, I plan to attend medical school and become a doctor. My medical knowledge will improve her health. My future income will support her, so she won't have to work and suffer anymore. When I feel tired or daunted by my quantity of schoolwork, I remember that my hardship can't be half as hard as my mother's and that someday, when my hard work pays off, so will hers.*

"*I suspect that how my mother and I feel may be how other Asian immigrant families feel as well. Why do we think this way? Where do these values come from? Much of our sensibilities about family and education come from Confucianism. Confucius taught that the remedy for social chaos was for each individual to live a virtuous life and to follow the moral 'dao,' or way. His instructions on what constituted moral behavior were based on relationships between emperor and subject, father and son, husband and wife, elder brother and younger brother, and elder friend and younger friend. The former had to provide just leadership and good example. In return, the latter had to respect and obey the former and never usurp his authority. In so doing, members of society could maintain harmony with each other and with the heavens.*

"*Most American teens would find these expectations to be oppressive. In the pursuit of individualism and focus on the self, they have lost focus on their families and feel no obligation to reciprocate their parents' financial and emotional investment. They care more about their peers' opinions than their parents'. Parents defer to their* children instead of the other way around, so they don't discipline or push them. Nothing is denied to them. As a result, they become complacent. Their energies become diffused, even stagnated. This is true not only of American teens but of American society. We are currently the richest and most powerful country in the world. Meanwhile, Japan is creating better technology, and European countries are planning to consolidate their economies. At the top, where life is comfortable, where else can America go but down?

"Fortunately, America is still the land of opportunity, not only for those who have been here for generations but also for new-comers. With other cultures come other ideas, newer and better ways of doing things. The drive, talents, and success of immigrants should not be seen as a threat but rather as a source of inspiration. We represent the changing face of America, a new horizon that recedes as we reach further and further towards progress.

"But our success should not be measured only by test scores, college attendance, or annual income. My mother would not be seen by most as successful. She is not featured in Forbes or Fortune. But where would the suited figures on the covers be without workers like her? Where would our heroes be had they not had parents to guide them? When President Bush speaks about the thousand points of light, I think about my mother and others like her, who make up the backbone of our families and the foundation of our country. Thanks to them, our future is still bright."

Then I bow my head, as Ms. Taylor taught me, signaling the end of my speech. With my eyes closed, I feel the rumbling of applause, which builds to a loud crescendo. I open my eyes and see everyone looking up at me, their hands coming together enthusiastically. Then I look at Ms. Taylor. She nods at me as she claps, as if to say, *You did it.* I smile back with pride.

Then I look at my mother. She has a strange look in her eyes. Her hands are coming together much more slowly than the others'. Unlike Nellie, she isn't standing or cheering. Did she like my speech or did she hate it? Is she proud or disappointed?

The last speaker gets up from his chair. The way he walks reminds me of a tree that may fall over. I expect his speech to be as awkward as his gait until he begins speaking. His voice is deep and sonorous. I can see him singing bass in an opera. His speech is about Asian stereotypes and the lack of Asian American representation in sports and the media. This topic will appeal to the judges, who are Asian Americans in the media. To make matters worse, his speech is well written, and he is confident and likeable. To further seal my doom, he is the final speaker, the one who will leave the judges with the lasting impression. *Stutter, trip over your lines,* I think.

Just as I think this, he stops. A long pause ensues as he struggles to remember his next sentence. I notice the slightest tremor in his knees. He makes a couple of false starts, stuttering a little, before finding his way and continuing.

Suddenly, I remember the brown-haired girl in my first competition. I remember Sally Meehan and her eye rolling. I flush hot with shame, as if everyone in the audience can hear my thoughts.

The last speaker finishes his speech without further problems. Afterwards, all the speakers assemble with the coaches in the back room. Ms. Taylor embraces Theresa. "Look at what you've done. I knew you could do it," she says to Theresa. Then she wraps an arm around me. "Excellent as always, but this time I felt an extra oomph in your delivery. You definitely got 'em hooked." I am glad that she's pleased, but if I did so great, how come I don't get a hug too?

We wait for what feels like a half hour. What's taking the judges so long? Finally, the lights dim and brighten again, and we assemble back at our seats onstage for the awards assembly. The trophy table has been moved onto the stage. The vice president of the Chinese American Association is standing behind the podium, and his assistant is standing behind the trophies.

"Third place," the VP announces, "Tiffany Haffner!"

I look at Tiffany, the first speaker. She has Asian features but hazel eyes, light brown hair, and freckles. It never occurred to me that someone who's half could count as Chinese.

"Second place . . ."

It will be either me or the last speaker. I brace myself, just in case it is me.

"Stewart Chan!"

I breathe a sigh of relief. Stewart Chan walks over to the VP like a man on stilts.

"And first place . . ."

Suddenly, I am gripped with fear. What if I'm wrong? What if it's not me? What if I win nothing?

"Frances Ching!" In a daze, I stand up and take my trophy and check. I barely feel the VP's hand as it squeezes mine. I am acutely conscious of people looking at me, of the applauding judges and audience members, of the video cameras and flashes from the Chinese TV and newspaper journalists. As I shake the VP's hand, the flashes from the cameras blind me. All I can see are spots. Tiffany and Stewart stand on either side of me. We all hold our trophies as more flashes of light blind us. After the photos are taken, we congratulate each other. Stewart shakes my hand vigorously.

"I really liked your speech," he says with a big smile. "It made me think about things in a different way."

"Thanks," I mumble, averting my gaze. Quickly, I excuse myself and join Theresa, Nellie, Ms. Taylor, and Mom, who are just a few feet from the stage.

"Congratulations, Fei Ting! I knew you would win!" says Nellie. She is patting my shoulder so enthusiastically that it hurts.

"Me too," Theresa chimes in. She is sincerely happy, even though she didn't win anything. In fact, she seems happier than I am. How can that be?

Then I recall Nellie's reaction, her cheering and jumping up and down, when Theresa finished her speech. My mother, in contrast, was stone still, except for her arms, which clapped as if they were too heavy. If you judged only by appearances, it would seem that Theresa had won instead of me.

I wrote that speech for my mother. I sang her praises publicly, in front of her. But she wasn't even listening.

"Theresa, how do you feel about competing in your first tournament?" Ms. Taylor asks.

"It was fun," Theresa replies.

I know Ms. Taylor is happy for me, but I wish she would talk to me first instead of Theresa. I did better than Theresa. Why is she getting most of the attention?

"Frances," Ms. Taylor says, "I think some people want to meet you."

I turn around and see Emerald Yeh and Wendy Tokuda.

"Congratulations," says Emerald Yeh.

"Great job," says Wendy Tokuda. I shake both of their hands. I reciprocate their smiles, but mine never spreads farther than my mouth.

On the way home, Nellie says, "After listening to Fei Ting's speech, I can see why she keeps winning. She has real potential." The Chinese word for *potential* is *"teen choi." "Teen"* means "sky" or "heaven." To have potential is to have a gift from the heavens.

"That tree of a boy would have won if he hadn't messed up in the middle," Mom replies. I flinch at her remark. I am grateful for the cloak of darkness. I don't have to mold my face into a look of happiness or nonchalance.

I was happier winning third place in the previous tournament than I am winning first place in this tournament—even though this is being covered by journalists, and even though I am shaking the hands of Emerald Yeh and Wendy Tokuda. I try to figure out why, but no answer comes to mind.

CARA CHOW

Chapter Thirteen

The next morning, Mom and I go to Tai's Bakery. On the way out the door, Mom picks up the *Independent*, the free local newspaper, from the doorstep and tosses it in the trash. As we approach the glass door, I notice a few seniors enjoying buns and tea at the square tables against the mirrored wall. Under the morning sunlight, the hard black-and-white-checked floor looks old and scratched up. As we walk in, Mrs. Tai greets us.

"Congratulations, Gracie!" she says.

Mom stares at her, a blank expression on her face.

Mrs. Tai holds up the *Gum San Bo*, the local Chinese-language newspaper. On the front page is a picture of me, the vice president of the CAA, Stewart Chan, and Tiffany Haffner. "What a smart girl!" Mrs. Tai says. Mom takes the paper from Mrs. Tai and begins reading. I peek over her shoulder, but I can't make out anything except for "one," "and," and "but." Once Mom is done reading, she hands the paper back to Mrs. Tai. Mom holds it with a certain reverence, as if that floppy piece of paper were embroidered silk. "Thank you, Older Sister," Mom says.

Mrs. Tai pushes the paper back to Mom. "I got an extra copy for you, in case you don't already have one," she says.

Mr. Tai walks in from the back with a hot new batch of buns.

He is wearing his usual white undershirt and worn brown slacks. The steamy, sweet scent of fresh baked pastries fills the air. "Hey, you think she's in the *Independent?*" he asks Mrs. Tai. Mrs. Tai walks to the back room. Moments later she returns, waving another newspaper. She hands it to Mom. A similar photo sits right above a very short article, this one written in English.

"I'm assuming you already have this one," Mrs. Tai says.

Mom pauses, obviously remembering how carelessly she threw it away just moments ago. "Of course," she says, recovering her composure.

Mr. and Mrs. Tai give us the usual, a dozen *gai mei bao*, but this time, Mr. Tai adds a couple of extra buns.

Mom says, "That's too many."

"On us. As a congratulations present," Mr. Tai says.

"No, no, no, no," Mom says, pushing the pink box back towards Mr. Tai.

But Mr. Tai pushes it back towards Mom. "You're one of our best customers. We want you to have it." Then he winks at me.

Mom rushes home from the bakery. I almost have to jog to keep up with her. Once home, she digs through the trash to find the *Independent*. I fight to contain my glee. There is a large wet spot on the paper left over from a used tea bag.

Then the phone rings. Mom picks it up. It's Nellie. I can hear her talking loudly in excited tones through the receiver, though it's against Mom's ear. "What? Are you kidding me?" Mom says. "Now? Can we run over and catch it? It will probably be on again on the six o'clock news, won't it?"

Wow, I'm on television! Ms. Taylor made a big deal out of this tournament, but I thought she was just exaggerating. Mom tenses her shoulders, frustrated over missing my televised appearance. "Okay," Mom says. Then she hangs up.

"What is it?" I ask. I pretend not to know because I want to hear her say it.

"You were on the Channel Twenty-six news," she says. "Fei Ting, you were on TV."

After breakfast, Mom takes me on more errands. We go to the produce market, just down the street from the Tais' bakery. The outside smells of oranges, apples, and cabbage. The inside smells like beef jerky and dried cuttlefish. Lynn, the shopkeeper, smiles at me as she rings Mom up. "I heard from Mrs. Tai about Fei Ting's win," she says to Mom. "What a smart girl."

"Oh, good at school things. I'll be lucky if she ever learns to be good at anything practical," Mom says. A part of me cringes at the deflection of Lynn's compliment. Then I look closely at Mom's face. She has the faintest blush of pride.

Then we proceed to the butcher's, just two doors down. Unlike the produce place, which is painted green, this place is painted red, matching the *cha siu* coloring on the barbecued pork. In the display window are three crispy fried ducks hanging by their necks and a whole roast pig. The entire place smells of duck, pig, and grease.

As Mr. Lai chops up the pork for Mom, she looks at him expectantly. She is waiting for him to mention my win.

Unfortunately, she is unlikely to get any recognition from him. Mr. Lai has always been a curmudgeon. The only reasons his business is so successful are that his meat is tasty, his prices are low, and he is the only butcher in the area.

But like a glutton for rejection, Mom keeps waiting, hoping. Finally, she can stand it no longer. "Mr. Lai," Mom says, "do you know that Fei Ting won an award?"

Mr. Lai pauses for a moment, focused on his cutting, before he says, "Oh, really." He doesn't even attempt to feign interest.

"Yes," Mom says. "First place"—a splatter of pork juice hits her in the face; she blinks and wipes the drop of grease from her cheek—"in a speech contest." Still no response from Mr. Lai. "It was sponsored by the Chinese American Association." Her voice sounds tentative, just like when she talks to my teachers.

Mr. Lai wraps the pork in pink paper and tapes it closed. "That's two fifty," he says.

"Okay," Mom says. Her head is bowed. Quietly, submissively, Mom pays Mr. Lai and takes her bundle.

"Mr. Lai is mean," she says to me as we walk home together. She carries the meat as I carry the vegetables and pastries. "His heart is like a rock. He must have kids too. He should know what a big deal this is."

Then Mom stops walking. "You know what?" she says. "Maybe his kids are losers. Maybe they smoke and don't study. That's why he didn't compliment you. Because he's jealous." A slow smile creeps up on her face. "Maybe his kids went bad because he's a bad father. Look how mean he is to people out-side. Imagine how mean he must be at home. I feel sorry for his kids. I feel sorry for his wife." Her smile widens with triumph. "Serves him right. Don't feel bad, Fei Ting. We don't need him. I'll take the bus to Clement Street if I have to. I'm not going to spend another dime at his greasy shop."

I am totally moved by her show of support. For the first time, she is 100 percent on my side. We continue walking—no, make that marching—home.

Once we reach our apartment and load up the fridge, Mom takes the two articles. She goes into the coat closet, which, despite its skinny shape, holds more stuff than someone else's twice-as-big closet because of Mom's organizing ability. She pulls out two picture frames and sits at my desk, carefully arranging the articles so that they are centered in the frames. She is meticulous about this, moving each article a couple of millimeters this way and that, her shoulders tense and fingers slightly trembling, as she strains for the perfect position. When she is satisfied, she hangs them side by side on the wall facing Popo's picture. She is careful to keep them lower on the wall than the picture, out of respect for Popo.

"There," Mom says. "Now she can see them too."

Mom fixes the articles with a penetrating stare. "When Ms. Taylor talked about your talents, she wasn't exaggerating," she said. "She had done the right thing by tricking you into joining speech. You're a genius, like Mozart. I was wrong to force you to go to medical school," Mom says.

I want to cry at her words. After all those years of pressure, this admission is more than I could ever hope for.

"Clearly, your talent lies in speaking," Mom continues. "I saw all those TV journalists looking at you. You can be like them. It's like being a movie star, only more professional. You're not beautiful like a movie star, but with your speaking talent, you can be like Wendy Tokuda, or even better. You can be the next Connie Chung!"

A TV journalist? That seems as foreign to me as becoming a doctor. The idea is embarrassing, me with my marshmallow body on television, talking about issues that I have no knowledge of or interest in. But Mom can see this very clearly, so clearly that I can almost see it reflected in her eyes.

We arrive at Nellie's for dinner at five thirty, just to make sure that we don't miss the six o'clock news. Nellie and Theresa are making fish soup; steamed rock cod with soy sauce and green onion; *dou miu*, a type of sprout; and Chinese broccoli. All my favorites. Nellie is tailoring the menu for me. I sit at her kitchen table and watch her and Theresa cook. My two articles are tacked to Nellie's corkboard above the telephone, next to her coupons and Chinese takeout menus.

Mom is going through the *Chronicle* and the *Examiner* to look for additional articles featuring my win. Channel 26 is blaring in the living room. When Mom is through, she throws both papers onto the floor. "And they call themselves newspapers," she says, enunciating "newspapers" as if she is spitting on them. "Well, they will never make a customer out of me."

"Me neither," Nellie chimes in.

Again I am touched by their support, but I'm slightly worried too. It's not like I'm the president. If we stopped doing business with everyone who didn't acknowledge my win, we might end up very isolated indeed.

"Do you think we should watch the American news too?" Mom asks. "What if they feature Fei Ting?"

"I could bring in the other TV," Nellie offers.

"But which channel should we watch, seven, four, or five?" Mom says.

"Maybe we should tape them, just for keepsakes," Theresa suggests.

Before long, we are sitting down to dinner with three televisions turned on. The little kitchen TV is playing CBS. The medium-size bedroom TV has been moved to the living area and is playing ABC. The large living room TV is playing Channel 26. That one is playing the loudest. All three are hooked up to VCRs. This attention on me is slightly nerve-racking. I want to be featured on the news, but I dread seeing myself looking ugly or stupid.

Towards the end of the Chinese news, a clip appears, showing the inside of the CAA building. We see Emerald Yeh, Wendy Tokuda, and David Louie on the screen.

"Turn it up!" Mom screams. Theresa does so. The TV shows

me shaking the VP's hand. Then it cuts to a shot of the VP standing next to me, Stewart, and Tiffany, each holding a trophy, very similar to the photo of us in the newspaper articles. These images last maybe a second each, easily missed with a blink of an eye. Both Nellie and Theresa pat me on the back with excitement.

Then the TV shows a close-up of Ms. Taylor, who is answering a journalist's question. I catch the first few words in English, which are quickly dubbed over in Cantonese. The Cantonese vocabulary is somewhat advanced for me, but she is saying something about more opportunities for Asian Americans.

"Why did Ms. Taylor get more time than Fei Ting?" Mom says. "If they wanted to ask questions, why not ask Fei Ting or me?"

"It's okay," Nellie says. "They featured Fei Ting. That's the important thing."

"Ms. Taylor rigged this," says Mom. "She's just using Fei Ting to get attention for herself." I quietly cringe at this unfair accusation.

"Let's see if Fei Ting was on the other channels," Nellie says.

"No," Theresa says. "I checked."

Mom looks hurt, a milder version of how she looked at Mr. Lai's butcher shop.

"Let's rewind the tape and watch Fei Ting again," Nellie says. Mom brightens. Theresa rewinds the tape a little, and we watch those few seconds again.

"Fei Ting, is your face really that chubby?" Mom says. She sounds surprised, like she's seeing my face for the first time.

"Theresa, rewind the tape." Theresa hesitates, but Mom waves her hand to hurry her along and she obeys. "There." Mom points at my face. "Don't her cheeks look fat?"

Stunned, Theresa, Nellie, and I stare at Mom for a moment. Then Nellie says, "Not fat. Just a little round. Very cute." She pinches my cheek as a show of affection. But she pinches too hard, bringing tears to my eyes. At least that's what I tell myself. It would be too humiliating to cry over this.

Now the picture changes to the anchorwoman. "Look at her," Mom says, pointing at the anchor. "She doesn't have fat cheeks. And Emerald Yeh and Wendy Tokuda, they don't have fat cheeks either." Mom holds my chin and turns my face towards hers, studying every contour. "Fei Ting will never get a TV anchor job looking like that. And look at that nose." She points at it, her index finger just an inch from my eyes. "Too flat. I always wished she had a sharper, prettier nose. And she has no double eyelids."

"Fei Ting looks okay," Nellie says. "You're just hypercritical because she's your daughter."

"No, you're under-critical because she's not your daughter," Mom says. "Because she is mine, I don't need to be polite. I can speak the truth. Dieting can fix the chubbiness. I bet plastic surgery can fix her single eyelids. How much would it cost?"

"Are you kidding?" Nellie shrieks. "That's dangerous! What if they make a mistake?"

"They're professionals," Mom says. "Professionals know what they're doing."

"But what if they sneeze or have a stroke?" Nellie argues. "Then Fei Ting will be deformed. Gracie, banish the thought!"

But Mom ignores her. "I wonder if freckles show up on camera," Mom says, squinting at my cheeks. "Fortunately, foundation can fix that."

After the dishes are washed, and the TVs returned to their original positions, Mom and I leave Nellie's house. As we're on our way out, Nellie pats my cheeks and says, "No plastic surgery for you." Then she says to Mom, "Right, Gracie?" She smiles wide, to make it seem funny, but underneath her jovial delivery is a mild worry, because she knows my mom. Mom ignores her and walks past me out the door.

Once we get home, Mom walks straight to the framed articles, scrutinizing my photos, her eyes darting back and forth between the two very similar pictures of me holding the trophy. "Gee, her cheeks do look big, bigger than the other competitors'," she mutters to herself. "Why didn't I notice that before?" Then she says to me, "The next time you accept your award, don't smile so big. It makes your cheeks look even bigger."

I blink back my tears and swallow the swelling in my throat. I scrutinize my face in those photos. I always knew that my face was round, but now it seems grotesquely swollen. The shine from my oily complexion makes my face look even bigger. In contrast, Diana has an oval face with sharp, chiseled features. Did Derek ever think that my cheeks were too big? How many times did I smile, making them even worse?

For half a day, I was Mom's hero. I had writing and speaking talent. That was all that mattered. Everyone else thought so—Ms. Taylor, Nellie and Theresa, even all those journalists and the CAA. If it's good enough for them, why not for Mom? How did my speech career suddenly become a beauty pageant? No matter how hard I work, at speech or my looks, I will never amount to those girls in *Seventeen* or *Cosmo*. Once again, in Mom's eyes, all my hard work is worth nothing.

Chapter Fourteen

The following Saturday morning, I feel my blankets torn off me, exposing me to the cold air. Mom pokes me in the arm. "Time to weigh," she says. Mom pulls the scale from under the bureau and stands behind it, waiting.

"Why?" I ask. She hasn't weighed me since I was fourteen, when I stopped growing.

"Because you need to lose weight if you want to be like Connie Chung, Wendy Tokuda, and Emerald Yeh," she says. "Now hurry up."

Slowly, I climb down from the bunk bed and approach the scale. Before I can step onto it, Mom begins unbuttoning my pajama top. Her fingers removing my clothes makes me feel dirty. I step away from her and close the opening of my pajama top.

"How can I know your true weight if your clothes are making you appear heavier?" Mom says.

How much can my pajamas weigh? Nonetheless, I obey and remove them. I am shivering in my undershirt and panties. Mom doesn't believe in using the heater in the wintertime. Why spend money on frivolous luxuries like electricity or gas when we could be spending it on my schooling? Then I stand on the scale. I shiver from the November cold while she bends over to read my weight.

"One hundred twenty-seven," she says. Her voice drips with disgust. "You should be one hundred fifteen. No wonder you look so fat." I flinch at the word.

"Get off," Mom orders. I do so. Mom kicks the scale back under the bureau. Then she writes my weight on a piece of paper on a clipboard. She pulls out a measuring tape from her pocket and wraps it around my bust, then my waist, then my hips, just as they do in beauty pageants. The tape feels like a creepy extension of Mom's fingers. Mom writes 34"-30"-35" on her chart.

"You should be thirty-six inches by twenty-four inches by thirty-six inches," she says.

Even if I did starve my waist down to twenty-four inches, how could I diet my bust from a thirty-four to a thirty-six, or my hips from a thirty-five to a thirty-six? Unfortunately, this logic escapes my mom.

Mom takes her clipboard to the kitchen and sticks my chart to the fridge with a magnet. Next to my chart, Mom adds a photocopy of something written in Chinese.

"What is that?" I ask.

"Your new diet," Mom replies. "This is the diet that Siu Fong Fong uses to stay thin." I have no idea who that is, but I'm assuming that she is one of those Hong Kong celebrities in Mom's magazines. I hate those magazines, with their skinny girls with fair skin and big eyes. Do their mothers weigh and measure them? Is that how they got to be so perfect, or were they born that way?

Mom twists a banana off the bunch sitting on the kitchen counter and tosses it onto the kitchen table. It lands with a thud. The edges of the banana are still deep green.

"That's your breakfast," she says.

That's it? I'm used to eating frozen waffles with margarine and syrup or a Tai's Bakery sweet bun with creamy filling. Nonetheless, I dutifully peel and eat the green banana. It tastes like paste rather than a sweet tropical fruit.

Halfway through the morning, my stomach growls voraciously. I try to focus on studying, but all I can think about is lunch, which would have been takeout *chow fun*. Instead, Mom serves me one slice of diet toast, one slice of diet cheese, and one tomato. The toast is dry. The cheese is tasteless and slimy. It looks as though it is melting, even though it is cold. The tomato tastes like cardboard.

That evening, Mom boils a chicken breast. She serves that to me—with no salt or pepper—along with the diet toast and a small salad made of iceberg lettuce, tomato, and nonfat salad dressing. She serves herself the same dinner. I'm glad. If I have to starve, then she should too. Maybe she will get tired of suffering and forget about this stupid diet. But Mom seems not to notice how bad the food is. Am I really spoiled, as Mom claims, or is Mom just incapable of tasting the difference between good and bad?

Then I remember what Mom said about eating bitter melon.

If I keep eating this, will I get used to it? Will I learn to like it? Somehow, I don't think so.

I expect Mom to serve me different low-calorie meals each day. Instead, she gives me the same low-calorie breakfast, lunch, and dinner every day. By Monday, my gastric juices are eating me from the inside out. My thoughts become frayed and frantic. Unable to bear my hunger any longer, I yank open the freezer door to sneak some Eggo waffles behind my mother's back. But the waffles are gone. Like a homeless person, I dig through the cold, wet trash under the kitchen sink, hoping to find the waffle box there. Unfortunately, Mom has already taken out the trash. My lonely green banana mocks me from my place mat. I attack it, ripping off the peel and stuffing the banana into my mouth. My tongue leeches what little sugar it can from the under-ripe fruit. I then grab the last banana on the countertop, which is supposed to be tomorrow's breakfast, and devour it.

During my morning classes, as my teachers lecture, all I can hear is the nagging in my stomach, which has escalated into a scream. As they write on the chalkboard, all I can see is *chow fun*, *cha siu*, and dim sum. My stomach growls so loudly that the other students turn to see where the noise is coming from.

Lucky for me, Mom did not factor in that Theresa and I always share our lunches. During lunch, Theresa opens her plastic container, revealing fried rice and barbecued shrimp. Its spicy, savory aroma fills my nostrils. I salivate so suddenly that I am unable to stop the small stream of drool that falls to my blouse. I hurriedly wipe my mouth with my napkin and remove my tomato, diet cheese, and diet bread from my brown bag. Theresa blinks in surprise and looks at me. I avoid her stare, discouraging any questions. Theresa hands me a small plastic fork. Eagerly, I attack her fried rice. I don't even bother to peel her shrimp as I shovel them into my mouth. Usually, I am careful not to eat more than half of her lunch, but this time, I can't stop myself from vacuuming up the whole thing. In just a few minutes, the container is empty, without even a stray grain of rice sticking to the edge. Theresa has probably had only a few forkfuls.

"Sorry," I say, red with shame.

"Oh, it's okay," Theresa replies. "I wasn't really that hungry today."

That evening, Mom notices that the last banana is missing. Her solution to the problem is to deny me breakfast the following morning. That way, the number of calories for the week can remain the same.

The following afternoon, I notice that Theresa's lunch, a thermos full of wonton noodle soup, is three times its usual size. I am able to eat to my heart's delight and still leave enough food for her. By Wednesday, Theresa is inviting me over after school. Nellie is waiting at home, where she happens to have leftover rice, vegetables, meat dishes, and pastries waiting for me.

Unfortunately, this means that the numbers on my chart stay

almost the same week after week at my Saturday weigh-ins. This vexes Mom to no end, especially because she is hungry and losing weight. On the fourth week, she announces that she will cut lunch from my daily meal plan to see if that will help. Now when I see my face in the mirror, my cheeks really do seem swollen. When I turn to the side and inspect my belly, it does seem to protrude a little. My thighs seem to jiggle when I jump up and down. I wonder why I never noticed these flaws before.

In addition to the diet, Mom has added other features to my beauty plan. Every evening, she cuts a lemon in half and makes me rub it all over my face. This is supposed to get rid of acne. I don't notice my acne getting better, but I do notice how much my skin stings afterwards, especially the pimples. I also notice how red and irritated my face is, which only makes my acne look worse.

Every now and then, Mom complains about my eyelids, which has caused me to have recurrent nightmares about botched surgeries. When I wake covered in sweat in the middle of the night, I comfort myself by touching my face and reminding myself that we are too poor to afford a plastic surgeon.

We have one more speech competition, the Saturday before Christmas break. Ms. Taylor has scheduled an after-school practice for today. I don't want to go. What's the point? Instead of focusing on my speech, I'll be obsessing about my eyelids, weight, and acne. I'll be wondering if my audience is really listening to me or if they're just counting my flaws. I'm reminded of this every day in speech, because I have class with Diana, the embodiment of everything I'm not. To make matters worse, Derek will be at the competition. Between him and my mother's beauty regimen, my enjoyment of speech has been squeezed out.

It's Friday morning. I'm at home, looking at myself in the bathroom mirror. I scrutinize my eyes. Do others think that I look disfigured because my eyelids have no crease? I cut skinny pieces of Scotch tape and apply one to each eyelid right above the lash line. It forces an unnatural crease to appear on each lid. Does this look better than no crease at all? Is this how my eyelids would look if I got them surgically fixed? It is certainly a safer alternative to surgery.

I walk into the kitchen for breakfast. Mom has already left for work. Sitting at my place setting on the kitchen table is my green banana. I gulp it down quickly, so as not to taste it. Then I go to the fridge to get my sack lunch. My chart, which is still stuck to the fridge, mocks me. I can't stand looking at those numbers. I jerk open the fridge door, only to see an empty shelf. That's when I remember that Mom is no longer making me lunch.

That afternoon, I do a run-through of my updated speech in Ms. Taylor's room. Now that Mom has decided that I will be a TV newscaster, I've had to change my lines about becoming a doctor. Normally, Ms. Taylor smiles after my delivery. This time, however, she frowns slightly.

"Frances, I keep feeling like something's missing," Ms. Taylor says. "You're saying all the right words in the right order, but your spirit is missing from those words."

Ms. Taylor has done so much for me. I shouldn't disappoint her. "Sorry," I say, trying to muster more enthusiasm. "I'll try harder."

Ms. Taylor's frown deepens. Then she beckons me over. I drag my feet to a desk next to hers and plop myself down. Ms. Taylor places her hand over mine. Her pale hands are soft and cool.

"What's wrong?" she asks.

I want to tell her, but how? Where can I start? I sigh and look down. Ms. Taylor startles. I look up to see what's wrong. Her face registers alarm.

"Frances?" she says. "Am I mistaken or are you wearing Scotch tape on your eyelids?"

Embarrassed, I look down again, but I know that that only makes the tape more obvious. I turn red and hot right up to my ears. Too mortified to speak, I nod.

"I've noticed some other Asian girls doing that lately. Why?"

"It's because . . . we don't have folds in our eyelids."

"What are you talking about?"

"See?" I pull the tape off my right eyelid. The adhesive stings and makes my eyes water. I blink and show her. "See how one eyelid has a crease and the other doesn't?"

Ms. Taylor looks closely. "Oh. I never noticed that before."

"Don't you think the right one looks weird?"

"No. In fact, I think it looks better than the left one, because it looks real."

"That's just a nice way of saying that it's ugly and that it looks even uglier with the tape."

"Frances! I've never heard you talk like this before."

Uh-oh. Did I overstep my bounds? "Sorry," I say.

"No, I like it. You're challenging me," Ms. Taylor says. "That means I've done my job. Let's examine this further. Go on."

"I'm five feet four and a hundred twenty-seven pounds, and I have a thirty-inch waist. I have freckles and acne," I say.

Ms. Taylor rolls her eyes. "First of all, you are not fat," she says. "Second, who in high school has never had acne? Third, no one can see your freckles unless they're close up. Besides, what's wrong with freckles? I have freckles."

I do a double take of Ms. Taylor's face. Up close, if I look carefully, I can see a light dust of cinnamon freckles across her cheeks and nose. Why didn't I notice them before? I'm embarrassed now. I hope I didn't insult her.

"You can get away with them," I say. "At least you're pretty. I'll never look like those girls in *Seventeen* or *Cosmo* or those female anchors on TV."

"Why do you need to look like those people?" she asks.

I open my mouth to speak, but I cannot supply a good answer. The more I try to explain, the more ridiculous I feel.

Ms. Taylor sighs. "Frances," she says, "I hate to say it, but in many cases, you're right. A lot of people do care about superficial things. But you don't have to buy into that just because they do. Okay?"

I grasp at Ms. Taylor's words as though clawing through a mist, feeling its cool moisture but unable to grip it with my hand.

Chapter Fifteen

I do not want Mom to weigh me right before my competition. It will only destroy my confidence. At the same time, I do not want to get into a fight with her. Mom's hysterics were bad enough right before my first competition. I don't need a repeat performance.

Instead, I neglect to mention that my competition is this Saturday. I wake before Mom does so that I am dressed and ready to go by the time she has pulled out the scale. Then I casually mention that the competition is today. She scowls at me. I make myself look flustered and disorganized, sorry that not only had I forgotten to tell her, I had even forgotten that I had forgotten. After all, what is she going to do about it, stop me from winning another trophy and hinder me from moving one step closer to a TV news anchor position?

"We'll do it tomorrow," she finally says.

I eagerly agree and slip out the door.

The December competition is at Washington High School, just a block from home. As I walk there, I give myself a pep talk. Maybe Diana is prettier than I am, but that doesn't make her a better person. She can't speak as well as I can. Her grades, though good, aren't as good as mine. Besides, who needs a boyfriend, anyway? Ms. Taylor is single, and she's intelligent, beautiful, and happy.

It takes me a while to find the meeting room, which is located in the school library, but once I do, I join Ms. Taylor, Salome, and Diana. Diana scans the room anxiously. Several minutes later, Derek arrives. My heart jumps from my chest to my throat. Diana gazes at Derek. Derek stares at me. I look away. Then Diana squeals, runs towards him, and throws her arms around him, almost knocking him over. They remind me of an octopus smothering a scuba diver. Ms. Taylor looks a bit uncomfortable. Salome rolls her eyes.

I used to see Diana as this poised dancer, a swan gliding across a still lake. Now all I see is a gawking, squawking goose. Feeling embarrassed for them, I look away again, only to see the other person I least want to see today: Sally Meehan, the dreaded red-haired girl.

Fortunately, I am able to pass two rounds without having to face Derek or Sally. After the second round, my stomach is growling. I follow the scent of hot dogs to the cafeteria and get in line to buy, only to realize at the head of the line that I don't have any money for lunch.

"Two, please," says someone behind me. It's Derek. He reaches over me and hands some cash to the girl selling the hot dogs. She gives him two hot dogs and he hands me one.

My pride tells me to reject the hot dog, but hunger takes over. "Thanks," I say.

Derek looks around the room and motions for me to follow him. We leave the cafeteria, pass a trophy case, and continue out of the building. Derek leads me to a set of bleachers facing a track field, where we sit down. Though it is sunny, the air feels cold. Even my hot dog is turning cold. We eat in silence as we watch sprinters and casual joggers run along the track.

"Can I ask you a question?" Derek says.

"Sure."

"Why did you give me a fake number?"

It takes a few seconds for his question to sink in. "What are you talking about?"

"When we exchanged numbers, on the last day of Princeton Review, you gave me a fake."

"No I didn't."

"I called you," Derek says. "The woman who answered said that there was no one there by the name of Frances."

"Could you have dialed wrong?" I say.

"That's what I thought at first, so I called again," Derek says. "The same lady answered the phone again and told me to stop calling."

I mentally reconstruct this strange scenario. Only one explanation comes to mind.

Mom.

I decide to test my hypothesis. "Did she have a Chinese accent?"

Derek thinks about this. "Yeah, now that you mention it," he says. "She sounds just like my friend's mom. Except she wasn't very friendly. Why do you ask?"

My eyes narrow. "Did she ask what you were calling about?"

"Yeah. I told her . . ." Derek sighs. "I told her that I wanted to ask you to the fall dance."

I pause, letting his words sink in slowly. He wanted to go to the dance with *me*. Me, not Diana.

"I meant to ask you in the car that night, but I ended up tripping over my own tongue," Derek says. "But wait, how did you know about the accent?"

Telling the truth will probably turn him off. But how else can I answer his question?

"That was my mom," I say.

"But . . . why would she say that I had the wrong number?" Derek asks.

"She doesn't want me dating boys."

"But if she won't let you date boys, then why would she let you attend a school dance?"

"Well . . . she didn't. I just went because . . . I thought you'd be there. And you were."

Derek looks down, ashamed. "I'm sorry," he says.

"Derek!" cries someone from around the corner. Derek jogs in the direction of the voice. Instinctively, I run in the opposite direction and hide underneath the bleachers. Diana runs into Derek's arms and begins sobbing. Derek turns her so that her back is to me.

"What is it? What's the matter?" he says to her. But Diana just cries inconsolably. He holds her awkwardly as she sobs into his chest. He looks pleadingly at me, as if to say, *What's wrong with her?* I shrug apologetically.

Then it occurs to me that I might know why Diana is upset. I rest my chin on my palm and roll my eyes like Sally Meehan. Then I imitate her facial tic. Derek's face lights up with understanding. He suppresses a laugh, because I've copied Sally to a tee. We smile at each other just a little too long. Then Diana tugs on his shirt. He turns his attention back to her, and I walk away.

As I make my way back to the library, I recall that horrible night at the fall dance.

Did any other boys ask you to dance? You know why? Your acne, your weight, and all that makeup on your face, which makes you look cheap.

If I were that ugly, then why would Derek want to ask me to the dance? In retrospect, Mom's plan was clever. What better way to convince me to give up on Derek than to squash my confidence so I'd never have the nerve to contact him?

What a sucker I was.

Well, not anymore.

Diana almost bows out of the third round, but Ms. Taylor talks her into staying. Though Salome does respectably in the semifinal round, only I make it to finals. Because today's tournament is in the city, Salome and Diana have the option of taking the bus home after being eliminated. Salome wishes me luck and heads home. Diana decides to stick around.

As I walk to the competition room, someone runs up from behind me and says, "Thanks." It's Derek.

"How's she doing?" I ask.

"Not great. At least she stopped crying."

As we round the corner, Derek places his hand on my arm. "Look," he says, "Sally's probably going to be in this round." My heart sinks. "I'm tired of watching her do this to people year after year. Let's put an end to it."

"But how?" I ask.

"First, we lift up the other speakers. Nod, smile, look attentive. Second, we give Sally a taste of her own medicine."

"You mean roll our eyes and do facial tics?"

"Not just any facial tic. *Her* facial tic. *Her* eye rolling. Remember when you were impersonating her in the hallway? You looked just like her! That gave me an idea. If we both imitate her at the same time, that would really mess her up. You in?"

The thought of transforming her evil eye into a boomerang is tempting.

"But it's too risky," I say. "What if we get caught?"

"Not if we sit behind the judge," Derek says.

"I don't know. I still think it's risky."

"How about this: we'll check out the judge. If the judge looks sharp, I'll shake my head and the deal's off. If the judge looks gullible, I'll nod and the deal's on. What do you say?"

I pause and consider his idea. Finally, I nod. Derek sticks out his hand. I shake it.

As we approach our room, Derek opens the door for me. Sure enough, there is Sally, sitting at the back. She looks away, pretending not to see us. A few seats in front of her is the judge, an old man with thin white hair and thick spectacles. He wears a gray cardigan sweater and a bow tie. He smiles a vague, kindly smile. His hand shakes as he holds his pen. He reminds me of a retired professor in an old folks' home. He lays down his pen and adjusts his hearing aid. Derek and I exchange knowing glances. There are two other competitors: a tall freckled girl with straight, mousy brown hair and a tall lanky black boy with gold-framed glasses.

Derek and I separate. Derek picks a seat a couple of rows to Sally's right. I pick a seat two rows to her left. To be honest, I'm more nervous about our plan than delivering my speech.

The round begins. Derek speaks first. Though I am not look-ing at Sally, I'm sure that she is pulling all her tricks out of her bag, but Derek is unfazed by it. Nonetheless, I nod and smile at him to show my support. As he returns to his seat, we exchange quick glances and smile.

Next it's the mousy-haired girl's turn. As she speaks, I look more attentive than ever. I smile and nod. I imagine sending pink clouds to her that serve as barriers to Sally's arrows. The mousy-haired girl does well in spite of Sally's eye rolling and facial tics. After her is the black boy with the gold-framed glasses. I continue to give nods of encouragement. His delivery is electrifying. He is as articulate and natural as Derek, but he has a different style. Derek's writing is stronger, but this guy has a more passionate delivery. I can picture him having a future in politics one day. He'll be tough to beat.

I am next. As I walk to the front of the room, I realize that I don't know what to expect from Sally. After our last showdown, will she give up sabotaging me, or will she reapply herself with a vengeance? I turn around, take a deep breath, and begin. As I speak, I ignore Sally entirely. Instead, I alternate eye contact with Derek, the judge, and the other contestants. Derek has a look in his eyes similar to the one he had the first day we competed together. It makes my fingers tingle. Towards the end of my speech, the judge's eyes glisten just a bit. Before I know it, I'm done.

Now it's Sally's turn. As she walks to the front of the room, Derek and I exchange glances. Derek raises his eyebrows. *Ready?* I nod. As Sally begins, the two of us simultaneously slouch, rest our chins on our palms, and sigh with boredom, just softly enough to escape detection by the judge's hearing aid. Sally hesitates a bit before finishing her first sentence, but she quickly recovers. A few paragraphs into her speech, I begin rolling my eyes. Then I do her facial tic. She continues reciting, but her face registers shock as her eyes oscillate between me and Derek. Her voice becomes less haughty and more tentative.

Suddenly, I flash back to my CAA competition. I am sitting onstage, staring at Stewart Chan's back as he delivers his speech. *Stutter, trip over your lines,* I think. Then he falters.

Then I'm back in the present again, staring at Sally, an injured animal that I am kicking. I stop doing my funny faces. My heart is pounding in my throat.

The boy with the glasses turns around slowly. The fluorescent lights dance on his frames, catching my attention. He eyes me, then Derek, then me again. My heart pounds more violently. I am sure that he is outraged, that he'll report us. Instead, a small smile creeps up on his face. He turns to face Sally again and leans back in his chair, as if enjoying a movie with popcorn.

By the end of Sally's speech, her voice is flat and barely audible. I look down, unable to watch. After she sits, the judge thanks us, and we all get up to leave—all except for Sally. On the way out, Derek sneaks a glance at Sally. He slips me a furtive thumbs-up, unaware that I deserted him halfway through our mission. But his triumph does not last long. Sally approaches the judge. The judge's brows arch in surprise. He asks Sally a question. Sally points her chin at Derek and me. The judge follows her gaze. Derek and I look away. A second later, I give in to my urge to look again. The judge is nodding and smiling while patting Sally on the shoulder. Sally becomes agitated. She points at us again, this time more emphatically, which seems to have no effect on the judge. Derek nudges me towards the door.

"That was close," I say to him as we proceed towards the gymnasium.

"Not really," Derek says. "These things are virtually impossible to prove. How else do you think she's gotten away with it all this time?"

ᖾᖽᖾᖽᖾ

During the awards ceremony, Derek wins first and I win second. The boy with the glasses, whose name is Derrell Johnson, wins third. As Derek shakes my hand, he presses something flat and square into my palm. At first, the feeling of the jagged edges startles me, but Derek fixes me with a knowing stare. I close my palm around it as he lets go, and slip it into my pocket. It feels like a folded piece of paper.

As soon as the awards ceremony is over, I ask Ms. Taylor to hold my trophy, and excuse myself to the bathroom. There I pull out Derek's note and read it.

Call me when your parents aren't home, okay?

My heart sings with excitement.

Then I realize that I threw away his number.

I flip the paper over, in case it is written on the back. But the back is blank.

I run out of the bathroom and back to the gymnasium. If I can just get him alone somehow, I can get his number again. As I'm about to enter, my team and Derek's team are exiting. Derek is walking out with Diana at his side. Diana links her arm with his. I step aside and let them pass. I walk behind Derek and

Diana and in front of Ms. Taylor and the rest of Derek's team. As we exit the building, Derek tries to disentangle himself from Diana.

"Wait," says Diana. "Ms. Taylor, can't Derek drive me home?"

"No," Ms. Taylor replies. "I'm responsible for making sure that you get home, and that's what I'm going to do."

As Derek pulls away, Diana blows him a kiss. Derek smiles politely but cringes a little.

"I can walk," I say. "I'm just a block away." I look at Derek as I say this. He understands my meaning and perks up. If I walk home, he can intercept me when no one's looking. Then I can get his number.

"No, Frances," Ms. Taylor says. "It's dark out. I can't take any chances."

Accepting defeat, Derek says good-bye to everyone and walks to his car. I force myself to follow my team to the van, knowing that as Derek waits for the call that never arrives, he will once again think I've rejected him.

❦

The moment I get home, I place my trophy on the shelf next to my other two trophies.

"What did you win?" Mom asks. She's lying on the couch, reading the Hong Kong magazines I hate so much.

"Second," I say, my voice nonchalant.

"How come you went down from first to second?" she asks.

She is comparing this win to my CAA win. She doesn't realize that this is a different kind of competition with a different pool of competitors. This win should be compared to my third-place win in my first competition. My initial urge is to tell this to Mom. Then I recall that she convinced me that I was ugly. Who is she to tell me that my second-place win isn't good enough?

About ten minutes later, Theresa calls. I want so badly to tell her about Derek. But I'll have to wait until the two of us are alone, out of Mom's earshot.

"How did it go?" she asks.

"I won second," I say.

"Oh. That's great." Her voice sounds flat; she's not her usual chipper self.

"What's the matter?" I ask.

"Oh, nothing."

"Come on. Tell me."

"It's stupid."

"How many stupid things have I told you?"

Theresa is quiet for several seconds. Finally, she says, "The Winterball was yesterday."

I completely forgot about that. Theresa hasn't mentioned Alfred since the week after the fall dance.

Suddenly, a cold realization dawns on me. I blame my mom for sabotaging me and Derek. Haven't I done the same kind of thing to Theresa? Theresa probably would have called Alfred had I not discouraged her. Then maybe they would have gone to the Winterball together.

I feel nauseous. My body breaks out in cold sweat.

"I'm sorry," I say.

"Oh, it's okay. It's not your fault," Theresa says. "I'm making a big deal out of nothing. I should just forget about it."

I say a silent prayer of contrition and ask for forgiveness. I vow to make this up to her somehow. I vow never to betray Theresa again.

The following morning, Mom makes good on her promise to weigh and measure me. I am shivering in my underwear as Mom hauls the scale from underneath the bureau, along with the measuring tape, which is coiled perfectly and perched on top. Though I am starving, I am not allowed to eat my green banana. In fact, I am not permitted even to drink a glass of water. Mom doesn't want me doing anything that might add an extra pound to the scale. I can have only a cup of tea, since tea makes me go to the bathroom, which may reduce the reading on the scale.

Of course, this is ridiculous. If I pee out a pound of urine from caffeine intake, I am not really a pound thinner. I am excreting water, not fat. And how can one banana affect my result? I watch Mom as she pores over my charts, analyzes my diet, and makes adjustments. Mom gestures towards the scale. I'm about to step onto it, but something holds me back.

You should be one hundred fifteen. No wonder you look so fat.

You should be thirty-six inches by twenty-four inches by thirty-six inches.

If that's such a big deal, then how come Derek likes me?

"Hurry up," Mom says.

A lot of people do care about superficial things, Ms. Taylor said to me. *But you don't have to buy into that just because they do.* I replay the awards ceremony from last night, except with a twist. Derek is about to slip me his note asking me to call him; then he stops himself and whips out a measuring tape. "Oh, wait, I forgot. I need to see if you measure up first," he says. Then he raises his hand, addressing the crowd in the bleachers. "Excuse me. Does anyone have a scale?" I stifle the urge to giggle.

"I don't want to do this anymore," I hear myself say.

"Yes you do," Mom says.

"No I don't."

"It's good for your future."

"I don't care. I don't want to do it anymore."

"Are you saying that you don't want to improve yourself? Even if you end up a *fei po*?" "*Fei po*" means "fat hag."

"Yes," I say, even though it sounds like *Yes, I want to be a fat hag.*

Mom flings the scale across the room. It crashes into the wall. Then she walks over to me, grabs me by the arm, and drags me towards the scale. I pull myself back. Mom grabs me by the neckline of my pajama top. It tears open down the front, sending buttons flying everywhere.

"Look what you did!" Mom screams, panting. "Do you know how hard I worked to buy you those pajamas?" I'm frightened by how far this has gone, but I force myself to meet her stare. "Fine, then," she says. "Be fat, disgusting, and pathetic." She turns and walks out the door.

I am shaking with terror and disbelief. This is the first time I've ever said no to my mother. I am also relieved. From now on, my mother can no longer poke and prod at my body. Someday, when I'm in college, I won't be living here anymore. My future home will not have a scale. I will never weigh myself again.

Chapter Sixteen

The following week, I notice a change in Diana's mood. She no longer smiles when she sees her classmates. Her shoulders slump when she sits and walks. The first time Theresa and I notice this, we exchange knowing glances. Though I am sad for Diana, I can hardly suppress my happiness for myself. That happiness is quickly followed by frustration, because without Derek's number, I can't take advantage of my opportunity. I try looking up his number in the phonebook, only to find a dozen Collinses. How many families would I have to bother before finding the right one? And what if I go through the whole list, only to discover that Derek is unlisted?

Mom and I pass Christmas Eve with Nellie and Theresa. Nellie gives me a leather-bound journal. Theresa gives me a teddy bear. Mom gives me a girdle. The following day, Nellie, Theresa, and Theresa's brother, Ben, fly to Hong Kong to spend the rest of winter break with Theresa's dad.

In January, speech class is over, and psychology takes its place as my senior-year elective. I still see Ms. Taylor on a daily basis, because she is also my English teacher. I remain active on the speech team and anticipate my February competition, when I will get to see Derek and finally ask for his number.

Unfortunately, I come down with stomach flu the day before the competition. As I spend the entire night on the toilet, I tell myself that my illness will pass by morning. The next day, I get dressed and eat a banana to give me energy, only to throw it up on my outfit. My fear of doing this during the competition is all that motivates me to give up. All day, as I lie in bed, I imagine Derek looking for me at the competition, wondering if I am avoiding him on purpose. During brief bouts of disturbed sleep, I dream that I am running to the competition, but my feet are heavy, as if anchored in wet concrete.

Mom is overjoyed that I have finally lost some weight. She is probably plotting how to keep me permanently ill so I can continue on this righteous path.

April rolls around and so does the next speech tournament. If I do well in this competition, I can go on to the state championship and then to nationals. A week before the tournament, Ms. Taylor beckons me to her desk after English class to schedule some after-school practice time.

"By the way, have you heard back from Scripps yet?" she asks.

"No, not yet," I reply. Not only have I not heard back from Scripps, I haven't received any word from any of the scholarship organizations. A sliver of worry scrapes against my chest. "Is that a bad sign?"

"No need to worry," Ms. Taylor says. "I have a good feeling

about this. I'm so excited for you. You're going to meet so many new and interesting people."

As I imagine myself at Scripps, I suddenly realize that I will know no one. This thought fills me with terror.

"I wish you could be my teacher in college too," I say.

"You'll have other great teachers in college," Ms. Taylor says. "I'll be a distant memory."

"No. I'll never forget you. Maybe I can visit from time to time."

"Well . . . can you keep a secret?"

I nod, eager to hear any of Ms. Taylor's secrets.

"I'm looking into getting a teaching job in North Carolina. My mother's sick, and I want to be closer to her. It's not finalized yet, but I'm getting some good offers."

My heart sinks. "I'll miss you," I say.

Ms. Taylor's eyes sparkle like sapphires. "You'll be fine. You'll have yourself and your achievements."

That afternoon, I search our mailbox as soon as I get home, hoping that today is the day that I will hear from Scripps. But all I see are bills and junk mail. I sigh and proceed upstairs.

Mom's company is forcing her to take some of her vacation days; otherwise she will lose them. That is why she and I join Auntie Nellie and Theresa for dim sum on 27th and Geary the following Saturday morning. We arrive by ten forty-five, because by eleven thirty, there will be a crowd of customers spilling out onto the sidewalk, waiting to get in. Already the restaurant is full. The body heat of the customers causes steam to form on the windows. Waitresses push their dim sum carts through the narrow spaces between tables while shouting out the names of their dishes above the loud hum of Cantonese conversation. We are sipping *gok poh* tea, a combination of chrysanthemum and *bonay*, while eating steamed dumplings.

"I have good news!" Nellie announces. "Theresa got into Berkeley!" She is so excited that she ought to be wearing a party hat and throwing confetti.

I look at Theresa with surprise. I'm her best friend. Why didn't she tell me? Theresa just looks at her lap.

"Have you heard back from Berkeley yet, Gracie?" Nellie asks.

Mom takes a careful sip of her tea. "No. Not yet." Her smile reminds me of cracked plaster.

Nellie shoots a nervous glance at Mom, then at me, and then at Mom again. "I'm sure that her acceptance package is coming soon," she adds quickly. "If they are willing to accept Theresa, then they would be foolish not to welcome Frances."

We eat the rest of our brunch in silence. Nellie is careful not to mention another word about Theresa's accomplishments. Mom strains to keep a composed appearance as her fault line of worry widens.

On our way home, Theresa and I walk ahead as Mom and Nellie lag behind. Nellie begins chatting about the latest Hong Kong celebrity gossip while Mom pretends to listen.

"Why didn't you tell me about Berkeley?" I ask Theresa.

"I figured you would ask me about it once you heard from them," Theresa says.

"But why wait?" I say. "Wouldn't you want to share your good news with me?"

Theresa squirms under her jacket. "Sorry. I didn't want to make you nervous."

"Nervous about what?" I try to sound curious, but instead, I sound irritated.

Before Theresa can answer, we reach Nellie's house. Nellie and Theresa part with Mom and me, and Mom and I continue to our apartment. As we get closer, the mail truck pulls away. Mom jogs to the mailbox. I jog after her. Mom fumbles through her purse for her keys and opens the gate. She rushes to our mailbox, wrenches it open, and pulls out some junk mail and a few envelopes. She sifts through the mail and finds what she is looking for. The legal-size envelope from Berkeley is skinny— not a good sign. My heart starts pounding. Mom climbs the stairs to our apartment and I follow.

Once inside, Mom sits down at the dining table and slices open the Berkeley envelope with her letter opener. With shaky fingers, she reads the letter. Her lower lip quivers. Her eyes register shock. Without seeing the letter, I already know what it says.

"How can this be?" Mom says. "Don't they know about your speech wins? Didn't they see you on the news?"

I don't bother to remind her that I wasn't featured on the mainstream news.

"Maybe . . . Maybe it's a mistake," Mom says. "Maybe they mixed you up with another applicant."

Mom looks helpless as she fumbles for a way to understand. I look away, as if avoiding the sight of a naked person.

Then it occurs to me that maybe this isn't so bad after all. If Berkeley is no longer an option, won't that increase the chances that Mom will let me go to Scripps? When will I hear back from Scripps? I notice another envelope next to the Berkeley envelope. Could that be the letter from Scripps? It is skinny, just like the Berkeley letter. Maybe Ms. Taylor is wrong. Maybe I didn't get in after all. I take a few steps to get a closer look.

Like a starved animal hoarding her food, Mom glares at me. "It's Ms. Taylor's fault," she says. Her voice is almost a growl. "If she had kicked you out of her class, you would have taken calculus. If she hadn't conned you into competing, you would have gone to Princeton Review and improved your SATs. See what happens when you trust other people besides me? You're an idiot."

My SAT score had improved by a hundred points. But because it wasn't good enough to get me into Berkeley, to Mom, it was non-existent.

Mom slices open the envelope I was eyeing. Inside are a letter and a check. Mom's eyes light up for a moment—until she reads the check.

"Damn them!" Mom says as she slams the check down onto the table. "Why would they be so stupid as to make it out to you? What kind of child has her own bank account?"

"What is it?" I ask, totally confused.

"It's your check. From the Chinese American Association."

"What's wrong?" I ask.

"I can't deposit it!"

"Why not?"

"Because your name is on it. Our bank account is in my name. They probably did it on purpose," Mom hisses. "The longer it takes for us to deposit it, the more interest they can accumulate in their bank account. That's probably why they waited this long to send it in the first place." I wouldn't have understood what she meant if Ms. Taylor hadn't explained what interest is.

Mom buries her face in her hands. Her shoulders slump forward in a defeated posture.

Finally, Mom sighs with resignation. "You will attend State." She is referring to San Francisco State University. "You didn't get rejected from that school. They have a good journalism program. Ms. Costello said. Maybe after a year, you can transfer to Berkeley."

My heart sinks. I already know from the finality in her voice that even if I am accepted by Scripps, she will not let me go.

In spite of my grim prospects, I check the mail every day after school for anything from Scripps. For five consecutive days, I receive nothing. I start to wonder if it got lost in the mail. Even a rejection would be better than this purgatory of not knowing.

The following Saturday, Mom drags me to the red fake-brick

bank on Clement Street to open a new bank account so she can deposit my check. Even though it's supposed to be my account, Minnie, our teller, talks mostly to Mom. She even hands the checks and check register to Mom. The two act as though I'm not even there. When we get home, Mom doesn't show me how to write a check or use the check register. She doesn't teach me how to use the ATM card. Instead, she just places my checking account materials in her filing cabinet. She never mentions my account again.

The following Monday, after school, I make myself a cup of tea to stave my afternoon sleepiness so I can study. I remove my tea bag from my mug of over-steeped tea and throw it into the trash. It is then that I notice a big, thick envelope in the kitchen trash basket. I brush aside the cold, wet food scraps on top of it and pull it out. The envelope is heavy and stuffed full. It is greasy from food and wet from tea leaves.

It is from Scripps. Inside are my acceptance letter, which states that I have been awarded a scholarship, my registration form, and a course catalog.

Like a terrier smelling a rabbit, I dig farther into the trash and pull out several damp, stained, and smelly letters addressed to me. They are all from various scholarship organizations. About two-thirds of them inform me that I have been awarded money to attend Scripps.

All that worry over the last month for nothing. How did this end up in the trash?

I think back to the check I got from the Chinese American Association. Mom was angry that the check was in my name and not hers. To her, it was ploy on the CAA's part to accrue more interest.

Interest is why it's in the lender's best interest to lend, Ms. Taylor said. Suddenly, this statement sounds like it applies to my mother. Has every penny spent on me been nothing more than a loan, something I must pay back with interest? Has every selfless act been merely an act of self-interest?

I play back all the times Mom has scoffed at how I don't understand the value of money. How could I understand if she never explained it to me?

Maybe she has withheld this knowledge from me on purpose. After all, I can't be independent without my own money, so wouldn't it be in her best interest to keep me ignorant about it? Along with keeping me dependent on her, it also gives her another excuse for criticizing me. That would explain why she was so angry about having to open an account for me. That would also explain why she neglected to teach me how to write a check or use an ATM card.

As the pieces of this mystery come together, a boiling anger erupts in my stomach. I can't let Mom get away with this. I'm going to go to Scripps, with or without her approval. But how?

The reason I got to do speech in the first place was that I hid it from Mom. By the time she found out, it was too late for her to wrench it away from me. Might the same tactic work for Scripps as well?

I decide not to fill out my registration form for State. If I am not enrolled, then Mom can't make me go. If her choices are Scripps or nothing, maybe Scripps will look more attractive to her. I fill out my registration form for Scripps. It is then that I hit another obstacle.

The form says that I must include a check. What to do?

I dive into Mom's file cabinet and ferret out the folder with my bank account materials. To my surprise, the checks have both my name and my mother's name on them. Maybe it's because I'm a minor. Unsure of how to write a check, I pull out a checking statement from Mom's account, which has mini photocopies of the checks she has written. I follow that format as I fill in my check. With shaky hands, I clip it to my registration form and insert them both into the enclosed envelope. With a pounding heart, I walk it to the mailbox down the street. I hold my breath, hoping that Mom won't find out until it is too late.

Chapter Seventeen

After discovering all my Scripps and scholarship materials in the trash, I have become much more diligent about checking our mail. It is a good thing too, because a week later, my first bank statement arrives. I open it and discover that, sure enough, the check I wrote has been listed and the money has been deducted from my account. I hide my statement in my backpack and blindly hope that Mom won't notice its absence.

I have been invited to compete in the state championship. This is the first time a St. Elizabeth's speaker has been invited to go. This year, it is being held at San Francisco State University, which is lucky for me, because I can take the bus there. Had it been held farther away, say in Los Angeles or San Diego, my mom probably wouldn't have given me permission to go.

Two nights before the competition, after Mom has gone to bed, I review my most recent draft.

My mother endures these hardships because she believes in my education. . . .

> *This is why she pushes me to strive for greater goals and never to rest on my laurels. This is why she emphasizes focusing on academics and forgoing the distractions of after-school jobs and dating. . . .*
>
> *My mother's perseverance and hard work are an example and inspiration to me. . . .*

A wave of nausea passes through me. After everything I've been through with my mother, none of this rings true to me anymore. To speak it, to argue it, to win with it would be a lie. The room is dark except for the beam of light radiating from my small desk lamp. I look at my trophies and the framed articles on the wall. They form long, ghostly shadows.

Over the last several months, I have made small alterations to this speech to reflect the new truth. First I changed the part about going to UC Berkeley. Then I changed the part about becoming a doctor. These changes seemed cosmetic at the time. But now, as I read this speech again, I realize that with my words and actions, I was chipping away at the old speech word by word until the whole thing came tumbling down. I take out a pen and a new sheet of paper and construct my new speech.

> *Ms. Taylor used to say that language gave us the power to reflect on the past and to shape the future. In other words, language had the power to change reality. Ms. Taylor also said that the key to empowerment was speaking one's truth.*
>
> *When I first heard those ideas, I was confused. Words were*

abstract, like fog. I could not grasp them with my hands, the way I could grasp money, food, or jewelry. Words could not feed or clothe me. How could they make me powerful and keep me safe? I became the rope in a tug-of-war between Ms. Taylor's thinking and my mother's. One offered me words, while the other gave me things.

Then I started to speak. I saw the effect I had on people who listened. Over time, I also saw the effect my mother had on me when she spoke. The former made me feel bigger, whereas the latter made me feel smaller. I realized then that Ms. Taylor was right, that words are more powerful than things precisely because they are abstract. Words are invisible wings, medicine for the soul. They can also be an invisible sword, spiritual mustard gas. They can also be used as a cloaking device. In fairy stories, witches use words to cast spells. I saw that this wasn't just make-believe. It was happening in the real world, every day.

Once I realized this, I didn't want to let my mother make me smaller anymore. If she made me any smaller than I already was, I would eventually disappear. So I fought back with words. Initially, I used them as a cloaking device, to hide and protect my true self, but my mother saw through them. It was at that point that I decided to make the truth my sword. The bad news is, the more truth I speak, the more she will try to smash my truth with her lies.

In spite of her efforts to crush me, I have to believe that my truth matters. I used to think that my mother always won

because my truth was not powerful enough. But now I suspect
that she beats it down because it is too powerful.

This is the true speech I want to deliver. But I can't. It's too late. I have already submitted my old speech to the judging committee.

The next day I tell Ms. Taylor after English class that I need to drop out of the competition.

"Frances, are you serious?" Ms. Taylor's eyes shine like flashlights. "You're the first speaker at St. Elizabeth's to be invited to go to the state championship! You have a chance to go to nationals. The competition is tomorrow. This is not the time to quit!"

"You said that we should speak our truth," I say. "Well, this speech no longer speaks my truth, so I can't use it anymore."

"Frances, think it over," Ms. Taylor says. "I know you can do it. This is a winning speech."

"But it's no longer *my* speech. Remember your pep talk? You said that success is measured by others' judgments but real success is measured by internal standards."

"But . . . Look, I'm glad that you're speaking your truth, but"— she sinks her head into her hands—"do you have to do it *now*?" She shakes her head and heaves a long sigh. Finally, she looks up at me. "Okay. Which part of your speech is no longer true?"

"All of it," I say.

Ms. Taylor's bright eyes search an invisible spot on her desk. She is pulling up my speech from her memory and reviewing it silently. After several seconds of silence, she says, "What if you revise parts of it to reflect your new truth?"

I start to object, but she puts up her hand to stop me.

"You don't need to throw out the whole thing," she says. "Start with the same question, but end with a different conclusion. Think about it. Okay?"

That night, I wait for my mom to go to bed. In the darkness, I place my old speech next to a clean sheet of paper under my desk lamp, and I begin again.

I thought that public high schools had large campuses, but they don't compare to college campuses. This one has several buildings separated by large stretches of lawn and concrete. I have to consult a campus map to find the correct building. Eventually, I find Ms. Taylor in an auditorium-style lecture hall. At the front of the lecture hall is a large raised stage that reminds me of the CAA competition.

At about nine o'clock, the speaker assignments are posted onto the part of the stage facing us, and all the competitors migrate towards the postings. As I walk up to the stage, I spot Derek approaching from the opposite side of the room. Without thinking, I turn away from him and face the chart. As soon as I find my room assignment and speaker order, I hurry out of the lecture hall, hoping that he didn't see me. He is probably mad at me for not calling. I already have enough stress, worrying about my speech, without having to think about how to explain why I didn't call. With luck, he won't be in my first round.

Fortunately, my first round is located just down the hall, so I don't have to worry about getting lost. The judge is a woman in her early twenties with long, straight dark hair, an olive complexion, and green eyes. She wears jeans, tennis shoes, and a sweatshirt that says SFSU in big block letters. I pick my usual seat off to the side. So far, there are three other speakers in the room, but I recognize only one. The others must come from different parts of California.

Then Derek enters. My heart beats faster as he approaches. Instead of picking a seat near mine, as he usually does, he moves to one on the opposite side of the room. This only confirms my suspicion that he is angry with me.

The first speaker delivers a powerful speech about his parents' involvement in the civil rights movement and the legacy of that movement today. When Derek is called to speak next, my heart starts pounding again. Usually, he makes eye contact with me from time to time while delivering his speech. But this time, he doesn't look at me at all.

They don't call this the state championship because the

competition is weak. The following two speakers are also excellent. For the first time, I cannot even be 100 percent sure that Derek will win. And here I am, test-driving a revised speech.

As with death, my number comes up eventually and it is my turn to go. I assume a kamikaze attitude as I march to the front of the room. I push Derek out of my mind and recite the first half of my speech as I usually do.

> "This is why she emphasizes focusing on academics and forgoing the distractions of after-school jobs and dating. This is why she insists on doing all the housework, though she is exhausted every day after work, leaving me more time to study and do my best."

I am approaching the edge of the cliff. Looking over the edge, I take a deep breath and jump.

> "But this sacrifice does not come for free. In return, I am expected to get straight As, so I can get into UC Berkeley."

Derek shoots me a startled look.

> "I am expected to go on to medical school or journalism school," I continue. "Afterwards, I am expected to embark on a successful career, so that my future income will support her and she won't have to work and suffer anymore. When I feel tired or daunted by my quantity of schoolwork, I am

expected to remember that my hardship can't be half as hard as my mother's and that someday, when my hard work pays off, so will hers."

Derek fixes me with his piercing stare.

"Where do these values come from? Much of our sensibilities about family and education come from Confucianism. Confucius taught that the remedy for social chaos was for each individual to live a virtuous life and to follow the moral "dao," or way. His instructions on what constituted moral behavior were based on relationships between emperor and subject, father and son, husband and wife, elder brother and younger brother, and elder friend and younger friend. The former had to provide just leadership and good example. In return, the latter had to respect and obey the former and never usurp his authority. In so doing, members of society could maintain harmony with each other and with the heavens.

"Most American teens would find these expectations to be oppressive. Are they? Here is what my mother would say. In the pursuit of individualism and focus on the self, they have lost focus on their families and feel no obligation to reciprocate their parents' financial and emotional investment. They care more about their peers' opinions than their parents'. Parents defer to their children instead of the other way around, so they don't discipline or push them. Nothing is denied to them. As a result, they become complacent. Their energies become diffused,

even stagnated. This is true not only of American teens but of
American society.

"That is my mother's answer to that question. What is mine?"

The air becomes thin. I am gasping for what little oxygen is
left in the room. This time, I cannot blame Sally Meehan for
my stage fright. My nemesis is within. I look to Derek. He nods
slowly.

"On paper, the Confucian way looks good," I continue.
*"But it has one fatal flaw. It assumes that the authority figures
are always just. What if that assumption is wrong? What if
their judgments are wrong? What if their expectations are unre-
alistic or unfair? What if they are selfish or dishonest? Under
those circumstances, should the people they lead still follow them?*

*"In a perfect world, one can be both an individual and a
member of a family or community. One can choose both what is
good for the self and what is good for the family. But in real life,
that isn't always the case. Sometimes choosing one means choosing against the other. Then the question of whether to choose
one's family at the expense of oneself or oneself at the expense
of one's family has no easy answer. It is like choosing whether
to cut off one's right hand or one's left hand. It is like having to
decide whether to save your drowning mother, knowing that you
may both drown, or swimming to shore alone, knowing that
you can only save yourself. If that is your dilemma, which way
is right? Which way would you choose?"*

I look down, signaling the end of my speech. When I look back up at my audience, everyone is giving me a blank stare, including the judge. Several seconds pass in silence. Then, slowly, Derek begins to applaud. One by one, others in the room also clap but with lukewarm hands.

When the round is over, I keep my head down as I exit the room, as if doing so can make me shrink and disappear.

⸎⸎⸎

I find out later that I placed dead last in the first round. In the second and third rounds, I place fourth, which is second to last. I don't even make the cut to the semifinal round.

It's three o'clock, and for the first time, I am going home from a competition before dark. Ms. Taylor and I exit the lecture hall and make our way to the bus stop. Outside, the sky is overcast, but there is no wind. I am unable to look at Ms. Taylor. I just stare at the concrete under my feet as we walk.

"You okay?" she asks me. Her voice is like cool water on a burn.

"Sorry," I say.

"About what?"

"About losing. About letting you down."

"What did I say about success and winning?" she reminds me.

Suddenly, I hear someone behind me calling my name. I turn around and see Derek several feet away, running up to us. He is the one spot of sunshine in a landscape of gray. When he finally catches up, he is bent over and breathing heavily.

"Derek, are you all right?" Ms. Taylor asks.

Derek waves his hand, brushing off her concern. "My fault," he says. "Should've studied harder in PE."

Unsure of why he has run after us, Ms. Taylor and I wait for Derek to explain. Meanwhile, Derek's eyes shift nervously back and forth between Ms. Taylor and me. Finally, he says to me, "Have a minute?"

I look at Ms. Taylor, who looks at Derek and gives me a knowing smile before continuing towards the bus stop. As she walks away, I expect Derek to ask why my speech is different or to console me on my loss. Instead, he asks, "Are you mad at me about something?"

"No. Why would I be mad at you?" I ask.

"I don't know. You seem to be avoiding me."

"Oh." I blush, remembering my overreaction earlier this morning. "I was worried that you might be mad at me."

"What made you think I was mad?" he asks.

"You sat at the opposite side of the room like you were avoiding me."

"I was trying to give you space because I thought you were mad at me. Besides, why would I be mad at you anyways?"

"Because I didn't call." I replay the memory of Derek's number, torn to shreds, drizzling into the trash. "I lost your number. Sorry," I say.

"I'll accept your apology on one condition," he says gravely.

"What's that?"

"From now on we don't assume that the other person's mad."

"Deal." I stick out my hand. He shakes it.

"When you didn't call," Derek says, "I figured that either you changed your mind or you tried calling me and got caught by your mom. I thought about calling you, but I figured that I'd just be told that there was no one named Frances there and that I should stop calling the Wong residence."

I chuckle. Only Derek can make my family situation funny.

"When you didn't show at the next competition, I really started to worry," Derek continues. "Maybe your mom was holding you hostage. Or maybe you had the good sense to change your mind about me. That would be a tragedy. I mean, who would help me pick on Sally?"

He means it as a joke, but I can't help feeling guilty.

"Derek, I have a confession to make," I blurt out.

"Don't tell me. You ripped up my phone number and threw it away."

I freeze, my heart in my throat.

"I'm just kidding," he says. "But seriously, what's your confession?"

"Um . . ." I mentally erase how close I came to revealing what really happened to his number. "Halfway through Sally's speech, I . . . aborted our plan. I felt . . . sorry for her."

Derek's face falls. He becomes silent and distant.

"I'm sorry," I say.

"No, don't be sorry," he says. "I see your point. We don't want to become the people we're trying to defeat, right?"

I nod. Little does he know that I've already become that person.

"I'm sorry," Derek says. "It's my fault. It was my idea."

"You don't need to be sorry," I say. "You tried to do a good thing."

Derek's eyes soften. "Thanks," he says quietly.

We've run out of things to say, but I don't want to part, and he doesn't seem to either, so we just stand awkwardly in silence.

"I wanted to ask you . . . ," Derek says. "I know I shouldn't, considering the wrath of your mother, but . . . would you like to go to the prom with me?"

My heart starts pounding. I give him the answer that will get me into deeper trouble, the answer I can't stop myself from giving.

Chapter Eighteen

I am so happy about Derek's invitation to the prom that I have to exert tremendous effort to suppress my joy at home. It isn't until I go to bed that I realize what a hole I've dug myself into. I will have to take the sneaky route to the prom, which means overcoming a few obstacles. For example, how will I get a dress? And what will be my alibi for Mom?

As I ponder the first question, it occurs to me that though I have neither a job nor an allowance, that does not mean I don't have money. I have a bank account. I should have more than enough money to buy a dress at Macy's.

I move on to my second problem, the alibi for Mom. I could tell Mom that I am sleeping over at Theresa's. That would mean Theresa would have to be in on the plan. But how can I possibly ask Theresa for another favor regarding Derek, especially after how things worked out between her and Alfred?

I delay problem solving, hoping that a solution will magically materialize.

A few weeks pass. The magic solution does not materialize. Derek's prom is tomorrow. I must think fast.

Maybe I should rethink the assumption that asking Theresa for help is the same as taking advantage of her. Getting Theresa to go to the prom could be a great way to make up for standing between her and Alfred. After keeping them apart, I would now have the chance to bring them back together.

In the locker room, before first period, I ask Theresa, "Are you free after school?" I already know the answer to this question. Her social life isn't any more active than mine.

"Sure!" she says. "What do you have in mind?"

"I thought we could go . . . downtown!" I infuse my voice with enthusiasm.

"Downtown? What for?"

"I thought we should be adventurous and venture out of our neighborhood," I say. "What do you say?"

After school, Theresa and I take the 38 Geary bus to Downtown. Downtown tends to be sunnier than the Richmond District. That is the certainly the case today. Nonetheless, it actually feels colder than home, because the tall buildings block the sun and form long tunnels for the icy wind, which cuts through my pants and blows my hair in all different directions. As we walk by Macy's, we conveniently pass a window with two mannequins wearing prom dresses. One is wearing a formfitting knee-length velvet navy blue dress. The other is wearing a silky ankle-length black dress that reminds me of Audrey Hepburn.

"Wow, how beautiful!" I say, eyeing the dresses.

Theresa's eyes sparkle in agreement.

"I think you'd look great in the navy one," I add.

"Wow. You think so?"

"Absolutely," I say. "We should go inside and check it out."

Suddenly, Theresa becomes hesitant. "Oh, I don't know."

"Come on."

"Well . . . maybe for just a little while."

We enter the store and ride the escalators to the juniors level. The whole juniors section is the prom version of Disneyland. The dresses are clustered into groups based on style and color. Each group of dresses has its own size-two mannequin modeling the style. The dresses come in mostly dark colors, like black, navy, royal blue, burgundy, and emerald green. I can't resist the urge to touch the various materials. Many of the dresses are silky and shiny. Some are crinkly and rough. The velvet dresses remind me of pets—you can stroke them one way but not the other. The sequins remind me of fish scales. They sparkle like Christmas tree decorations.

Other girls are shopping for their prom dresses with their moms. These girls look giddy with excitement. The moms look at their daughters, some with girlish enthusiasm, some with bemusement, and some with annoyance. Nonetheless, they are all there, helping their daughters. Most of them hold their daughters' dresses as they follow them around. A few of the girls are heavier than I am, but their mothers aren't berating them about it. They just select larger sizes in a matter-of-fact manner. Can these girls confide in their mothers about school or even boys? Will these mothers let them go to whichever colleges they choose? I feel a stab of envy that hints at depression, the way heavy clouds signal rain.

I quickly brush away this feeling. I seek out the navy dress that most resembles the one worn by the mannequin. I grab one in Theresa's size and one in my size and hold the smaller one up to Theresa. "Hey, this looks like the one we were admiring," I say. "Why don't we try it on together?"

Theresa backs away from the dress. "Oh, that's okay. You can try yours on. I'll just wait outside."

"You don't have to buy it," I say. "Just try it on for fun." I hold the dress up to her face the way one might hold a bone to a dog's nose.

"I don't understand," Theresa says. "What's the point of looking at prom dresses when we aren't even going to the prom?"

"Well . . . I was thinking that"—I take a deep breath—"maybe I was wrong. About the Alfred thing."

Theresa winces. "I-I've already forgotten about him," she says. Her tone, however, suggests the opposite.

"What if he lost your phone number and was hoping that you'd call?" I say.

"But . . . that was five months ago," Theresa says. "I don't understand. Why are you bringing him up now?"

Should I tell her about Derek now or later? I hesitate, unable to decide.

"Because this is your last chance ever to do a formal," I say. "You won't get that chance back. You wouldn't want to wonder what if, right?"

Theresa crosses her arms in front of her chest. "I thought you were my friend," she says.

"I am!" I say.

"Then don't make me feel worse."

"What do you mean? I'm only trying to help."

"Yeah. By telling me not to call him when it would have mattered and now telling me to call when so much time has passed that he won't even remember my name. Thanks for your help."

I plop the dress back on the rack. "Fine. We can do something else," I say. Though I try to make my voice cheerful, it ends up sounding hard and flat.

"No, I don't feel like it anymore. Let's go home," Theresa says.

"But we just got here! We just wasted our time coming all this way!"

"It was your idea!"

Theresa walks away. My eyes dart between Theresa's receding back and the navy dress draped over my arm. If I don't buy this dress now, I will have nothing to wear tomorrow. But if I do buy it, I won't be able to catch up with Theresa before she boards a bus home. Besides, how will I explain the new dress while trying to placate her?

Panicked, I hang my size-eight dress in the size-two section of the rack and race past the openmouthed stares of the prom girls and their mothers. Theresa nimbly runs down the escalator like a mouse while I gallop after her.

"Theresa," I say.

But Theresa ignores me. I follow her out of Macy's and all the way to the bus stop. Theresa stands with her back to me, her arms crossed and her foot tapping.

"I'm sorry," I say to the back of her head. "Don't be mad, okay?" I hate the whining, begging sound in my voice, but at the moment, I don't care.

Theresa's head bows. Her shoulders slump. Finally, she turns to me. "No. I'm sorry. It's my fault."

"No it's not."

"Yes it is. It's not your fault that Alfred didn't ask me to the Winterball," she says. "I shouldn't be taking that out on you."

I avert my eyes from her contrite gaze.

"You were just trying to help by suggesting that I go to the prom with him," Theresa says. She sighs. "It's bad enough that he rejected me the first time. If he rejects me again . . . I'll just die of humiliation. I just want to forget about the whole thing and put it behind me, okay?"

I am so grateful to have her friendship back that I give up pushing her further. I banish the possibility of telling her my true predicament. Instead, I take the bus home with her, silently wondering what to wear and what my alibi will be for Mom.

As soon as I arrive home, I open the closet door. I sift through my side of the closet, only to find a uniform blouse and the button-down shirt and skirt that I wear to speech competitions. I also see the dress I wore to my eighth-grade graduation. It is off-white and pink and very lacy and frilly. Desperate, I take it off the hanger and try it on. I can barely pull the dress past my hips, much less pull up the zipper. I suck in my belly as hard as I can as I force the zipper up. Then I look in the mirror.

I look like I'm ten years old. All I'm missing are the Shirley Temple sausage curls.

I squirm my way out of the outfit and hang it in the closet. Desperate and irrational, I start sorting through Mom's half of the closet. At first, I find Mom's work clothes, a series of drab but inoffensive blouses and slacks. Then I find casual clothes that she must have brought over from Hong Kong in the sixties, polyester button-down shirts and bell-bottom pants with paisley patterns and elastic waistbands—definitely not prom material. I almost give up hope.

It is then that I notice a chest sitting under Mom's clothes. It is made of lacquered wood and has an intricate carving of women in a landscape. The women are dressed in traditional attire, the kind imperial women wore during the dynasties. I open the chest, releasing the strong scent of mothballs. The first thing I see is a sleeveless navy blue dress with large round collars made of white lace. I decide to try it on.

It doesn't look quite like the dresses at Macy's. The material is thick and coarse, and the collars are distracting. Nonetheless, it does mimic the sleek form-fitting shapes of the Macy's dresses, and the dark color is slimming and formal looking. I put on my black flats and scrutinize myself in the mirror. Not great, but not bad. I turn to examine my back side. Unfortunately, the dress is short, barely covering my behind. The slit in the back makes the problem even worse. I guess that makes sense. This was Mom's dress, and she is six inches shorter.

It occurs to me that my mother used to fit into this dress when she was young. If she was my width but shorter, then technically, she was actually fatter! What right has she to be so critical of my weight?

I fold the dress carefully and place it in my backpack. Then I close the chest and arrange Mom's clothes to look exactly as they were before. In the evening, I ask Mom if I can spend the night at Theresa's tomorrow. As usual, she hassles me about it before giving her consent. Then I add my casual clothes and my toothbrush to my backpack to keep my actions consistent with my story.

My plan, though clever, isn't perfect. If Mom isn't expecting me home tomorrow, where will I spend the night? I hope that if I remain calm and resourceful, all other obstacles will be easy to overcome.

Chapter Nineteen

The next morning, I shower and style my hair. Though I still have the makeup Theresa and I used at the fall dance, I decide not to put it on. After all, I used it at the fall dance and got nowhere. In contrast, I didn't wear makeup at any of my speech competitions, but I still got Derek to like me. So what's the point? Instead, I wear a tinted lip gloss to give my face a little color. Before leaving home, I double-check my wallet to make sure I have enough change for the pay phone.

During the school day, I move slowly, so as not to sweat, which would necessitate another shower. After school, I hang out in the library until all the students have left campus. Then I change into the navy dress in the bathroom. Because I didn't have the chance to air out the dress, it still smells like mothballs. I fan the dress with my hands to diffuse the smell. Afterwards, I call Derek on the school pay phone and ask him to pick me up at school. Then I wait outside. Though it isn't warm, at least it's not too cold. The sunshine helps make up for the occasional wind.

About a half hour later, Derek's car pulls up in front of me. He looks handsome in his black tux and crisp white shirt. I climb in and he pulls away.

"Where are we going?" I ask.

"You'll see."

We continue west until we reach Ocean Beach. At the Great Highway, Derek turns right and drives us up the hill, which eventually veers to the right. At the top of the cliff, he turns left into a parking area. He pulls into a spot facing the ocean and parks. There is a forest and a hiking trail to our right. In front of us, giant rocks jut out of the ocean. Every violent wave that slaps these rocks sends a fan of white spray in all directions.

"Wow," I say. "Nice view."

"Yeah."

Derek leans towards me. As his face gets closer to mine, I stiffen, my heart racing, but he ends up reaching behind my seat for something on the floor. It's a corsage made of tiny bloodred roses and baby's breath.

It occurs to me that amid the drama of getting a dress, I forgot to get him his boutonniere.

"May I?" Derek asks.

I nod. Derek pins the corsage onto my dress.

"I forgot to get you one," I say. "Sorry."

"That's okay," he replies. "I'd look silly wearing a corsage."

I chuckle. We stare awkwardly out the window, unsure of how to pass the time.

"Are you hungry?" Derek asks me.

"Sure." Actually, I'm so nervous that I can't imagine eating anything.

Derek climbs out of the car, walks to the passenger side, and opens the door for me. I take his arm and we begin walking down the steep hill.

We reach a boxy two- or three-story building at the bottom of the hill. It seems to be jutting out over the ocean. "The Seacliffe. We talked about it when I drove you home, remember?"

Though I'm excited about going to this restaurant, I'm also nervous. Are there special rules or rituals we should follow that only I don't know about? Automatically, I stand up taller, as if preparing to deliver a speech. If I present myself with poise, maybe Derek won't notice that I've never been to a classy restaurant.

When we enter the restaurant, we are greeted by a woman standing behind a podium. A man wearing a long white half apron leads us upstairs and into the dining area, which has large windows revealing the big white waves. Usually when I enter a restaurant, I am bombarded with bright lights, the sounds of people shouting and food sizzling, and the smells of grease and all things savory. In contrast, this room is quiet, cool, dark, and completely void of smells. The server guides us to a small round table next to a window. Simultaneously, the server pulls out the chair closest to the window and Derek pulls out the chair facing the window. I sit down on Derek's chair. Awkwardly, Derek sits on the chair that the server pulled out for me.

The server then hands us our menus. Another server fills our glasses with ice water and lays down a basket of bread. The menu is heavy, firm, and bound in leather, not flimsy and laminated like the menus I am used to. I marvel at the plates and silverware in front of me. The plates are bright white, matching the tablecloth. Three forks lie on the left side of the plates, while a knife and two spoons lie on the right. Why so many pieces of silverware? At home, we either use just a pair of chopsticks or a fork and a knife.

Derek opens his menu, and I copy him. Some of the items I am familiar with, such as steak and chicken. But what is filet mignon, confit, or hollandaise?

"What looks good to you?" Derek asks me.

"Uh . . . what looks good to you?" I say, hoping to glean a cue from him.

"I always like steak, so I think I'll get the filet mignon and lobster tail."

"But if you like steak, why are you getting filet mignon?" I ask.

Derek looks at me strangely. "Filet mignon is a kind of steak," he says.

"Oh." There's more than one kind? "Then . . . I guess I'll get the same."

Derek scrutinizes me with a piercing expression. Suddenly, I feel naked, humiliated. I look down, ashamed. We are silent for what feels like several minutes.

Finally, Derek says, "My friend David's family took me to a Chinese restaurant once. We were all perusing the menu, which, fortunately, was bilingual. Otherwise, I would have been lost. Anyway, Dave's dad started rattling off to the waiter a list of menu items in Chinese. I asked Dave what he was saying and Dave translated. I went through the menu, furiously trying to find these items, but I couldn't find them. I asked Dave where he found those items, and Dave pointed at the wall. Turns out there were all these pieces of paper taped to the wall with dishes written entirely in Chinese."

I smile. I know exactly what he's talking about. "Don't feel bad," I say. "My mom and her friend order from them all the time, but I can't read them either."

"Unfortunately, it gets worse," Derek says. "Everyone started eating except for me. I just sat there staring at my food. Finally, Dave's mom asked me what was wrong. I had to explain to her that I didn't know how to use chopsticks. They had to order a fork especially for me."

Poor Derek!

"Once I got my fork, I ate everything in sight," Derek says. "Everything was so good that even though I was full, I couldn't stop eating. I was so enthusiastic that when the next dish arrived, I began helping myself. It looked like some kind of brown broth with lemon slices. So I spooned it into my bowl and began drinking. Then I noticed David's family and the waiter staring at me with eyes wide as saucers. Turns out that the soup was actually tea and lemon—for washing our hands."

I burst out laughing. "I'm so sorry," I say.

"It's okay. It wasn't as bad as the time when I went to a sushi restaurant and mistook the wasabi for green tea ice cream."

I laugh even harder. Maybe he's not looking for a Princess Grace or a Princess Di. Maybe I don't need to pretend to be like him, because in some ways, he is like me.

A waitress comes to take our order. Derek orders his filet mignon, and I do the same. Derek adds two salads to our order. As we wait for our food, he encourages me to enjoy the view. I stare past him at the crashing waves going in, out, and in again, the foam forming lace patterns along the water. When I snap out of my trance, I notice Derek gazing at me with a tender and serious expression. As soon as he catches me watching, he shifts back to his comic grin.

Our food arrives, and Derek gently points out which utensils to use for each course. Halfway through the main course, Derek says, "There's something I've been dying to ask you. Why did you change your speech?"

I cringe at the memory of my last competition. "In my old speech, I said that I wanted to attend UC Berkeley and go to med school so I could—"

"Become a doctor and take care of your mother," Derek says. "When your hard work pays off, so will hers."

I am stunned. I think back to the pain I felt when I delivered this speech to my mother at the Chinese American Association only to find out that she hadn't heard a single sentence. In contrast, Derek remembers and understands every word.

"Well, the more I thought about it, the more I realized that I didn't really want to go to UCB or med school. That's what my mother wanted," I say.

Derek nods. His piercing gaze is unblinking.

"When I won the Chinese American Association competition, my mom was starstruck by the judges, who were all TV journalists,"

I say. "Now she wants me to be the next Connie Chung."

Derek grimaces. "I can't see you wearing all that makeup," he says.

"She tried to make me beautiful and glamorous so I could look good on TV," I say. "But it wasn't what I wanted."

"So, what do *you* want?"

"I want to go to Scripps College."

"And how about your career?"

"I don't know. But not medicine and not TV journalism." I groan. "But instead of making the speech better, I just made it worse."

"Don't say that."

"It's true," I insist. "At the end, everyone just gave me this horrible blank stare. The only reason anyone applauded was because you did it first. I didn't even make the first cut." My face burns with humiliation at this admission of defeat.

"It wasn't a bad speech," Derek says. "It just felt . . . unfinished. People didn't applaud because they were still waiting for the ending."

I give Derek a quizzical look.

"People like certainty," Derek explains. "People like answers. In your speech, you started asking a lot of difficult questions and then you just ended the speech without answering any of them."

"That's because I don't have the answers!" I say defensively. "What was I supposed to do, lie?"

Derek stares at me for a long while. His expression morphs through many shades of thought. It is like watching a flower blossom on fast-speed video.

"Maybe you're the real winner here," he says.

"How so?"

"Do you remember what my speech is about?" he asks.

"Compassionate conservatism. Corporate greed."

"Guess what my dad does?"

I shrug. "CEO?"

"He's a corporate lawyer. He runs his dad's law firm. Guess what they want me to do?"

"Be a lawyer in their firm."

"Bingo. My grandpa went to Harvard. My dad went to Harvard. Guess where they want me to go?"

"Harvard."

"Right again."

"So . . . what are you going to do about it?"

"Oh, I'll be attending Harvard this fall," Derek replies. "Then I'll probably go to law school and eventually join their firm. In the meantime, I vent by winning contests speaking out against what they do—all the way to nationals."

"Does your family know what your speech is about?"

"No. It's my own dark secret."

"So you're living a double life," I say. "Speech is where you can be a better version of yourself. Like Clark Kent versus Superman."

Derek nods.

"I understand," I say. "But what if your family is like a small, cramped house, and what if speech is a window giving you a view to the outside? What if, one day, that window opened and you could just fly out?"

Derek reaches for my hand. His is hot and dry. In contrast, mine is embarrassingly cold and clammy. I think he will pull his hand away, but instead, he rubs my fingers to warm them.

After dinner, we walk hand in hand back up the hill to Derek's car. By now, the sun is beginning to set. Derek turns towards the ocean and points to a labyrinth of rocky paths that are partly submerged in water.

"That's the Sutro Baths," he tells me. "It was this huge swimming facility that burned down years ago." I try to imagine how the building must have looked when each rock path was the foundation of a wall. "And there are some cool caves over there," he says, pointing to the right of the baths. "I'll take you there sometime."

The wind whips my hair in all directions. Derek brushes my hair out of my face and rests his palm against my cheek. His eyes pierce into mine. He leans in and touches his lips to mine. They are soft and hot, just like his hands. At that moment, I no longer feel the cold of the wind. The roar and crash of the waves go silent. So do my thoughts. So do my worries and everything that has ever made me unhappy.

Derek drives me to the St. Francis hotel. From the parking lot, we walk towards the banquet hall, where the loud bass vibrates against my chest. The entry is decorated with gold and white balloons.

A long line of people snakes from the entrance to the banquet hall, where the prom is held. My eyes travel to the head of the line, where a couple is posing for pictures. The photographer is cracking jokes to make them smile before snapping his flash. I imagine myself posing before the camera with Derek's arm wrapping around me.

"Let's dance first," Derek says. "We can take pictures later, when the line is shorter."

As we pass the photo line, a few of the girls gawk at my dress. Suddenly, I become hyperaware of my large round white lace collars and the shortness of my hem. In fact, out of all the girls here, I have on the shortest dress. I become paranoid that my underwear is showing. I consider excusing myself to the restroom to check, but decide against it. If it is indeed showing, there is nothing I can do about it, so it is best not to know.

On the way to the banquet hall, Derek is greeted by his friends. He introduces me to each of them, even Dave, the friend who took him to the Chinese restaurant. Inside the banquet hall, there are round tables and chairs lining the periphery of the room. At the center of the room is a large dance floor. The room is dimly lit, just bright enough so that you can see everyone in their formal attire.

It is then that I notice that the disco lighting makes my white lace collars glow neon violet. Embarrassed, I cover them with my hands.

Derek leads me past the tables to the dance floor. I feel awkward, hearing the thumping beat of the bass and not knowing how to dance to it. I look around to see how others are dancing. They just bob up and down, not touching each other. Derek peels my hands from my collars and begins moving as though dancing to a big band song. He doesn't worry about not looking like the others. I decide to let go and let him swing me. He spins me around counterclockwise and then clockwise. As my body becomes warmer, the mothball scent in my dress becomes even stronger. I hope that the distance between us is wide enough that he can't smell it. We dance several songs like this, never stopping to catch our breath.

Eventually, a slow song comes on. Derek slowly brings me towards him until our bellies are touching. At first, I am self-conscious about the mothball smell and the sweat dripping down my back. Then I notice that the back of his coat is also warm and damp. Though my dress is drenched, he does not move his hand or shrink away from me. A thin line of sweat runs down his cheek in front of his ear. And to my utter relief, the perfume in his deodorant is actually overpowering my mothball smell. We are perfect in our collective imperfection.

Just as I think this, we bump into a couple behind Derek. Derek turns around and so does the boy we bumped into. He is a heavyset Asian with metal-framed glasses. He is wearing a dark suit and a boutonniere of white roses that are red at the tips. He looks strangely familiar.

"Hey, Derek!" shouts the boy over the music.

"Alfred!" Derek replies.

Alfred. Immediately, my body tenses up.

Derek and Alfred shake hands.

"Hey, I want you to meet Frances," Derek says to Alfred.

As Alfred offers his hand, he squints and frowns, as though reading through a foggy lens. "Have we met before?" he asks me.

"No, I don't think so," I say, shaking his hand firmly, to communicate certainty.

"So, who's your date?" Derek asks Alfred.

"Oh, uh . . ." Alfred turns around and steps aside. "This is Theresa," Alfred announces. "Theresa, this is Derek and, uh, Frances."

Theresa is wearing the exact knee-length slim-fitting navy blue velvet dress that I picked out for her at Macy's. She is wearing matching pumps. A corsage of white rosebuds with red tips decorates her dress. Her thick black hair, which is clipped back with a matching rosebud barrette, cascades past her shoulders in long, loose tendrils. I've always thought of Theresa as childlike, but suddenly she looks glamorous and sophisticated—unlike me in my sixties minidress and white collars.

But what is most striking about her is how she is staring back at me, her eyes wide and her mouth in an O of shock.

Chapter Twenty

I paste on a smile. "Hi," I say.

Theresa's mouth slowly closes. Her round eyes narrow.

"Well, good to see you," Alfred says. He turns his back to us and continues slow dancing with Theresa. Derek puts his arms around me, and we start swaying again. But I'm unable to melt back into my previous happy state.

"What's the matter?" Derek asks.

"Can we take a break?" I say.

Derek guides me off the dance floor to one of the round tables. We both sit down. I turn my seat so my back is facing the dance floor.

"What's wrong?" Derek asks again.

"Nothing," I say. Then I ask if we can leave.

"Now? Don't you want to stay for the last dance?"

"I don't feel too well."

Derek looks disappointed, but he goes along with my request. On the way home, my heart is fraught with worry. How will I repair my friendship with Theresa? Will she squeal on me to my mom? A couple of times, Derek asks me if I'm feeling okay. I tell him that I just have a bad headache but it's getting better.

When Derek turns onto Balboa, I ask him to stop a couple

of blocks away from my apartment. Derek turns off the engine and gazes at me. He is expecting me to get out of the car and go home. Mom is expecting me not to come home. What to do now?

"Derek, I have a confession to make," I say.

"Don't tell me you have another boyfriend."

I smile. "No. My mom doesn't know that I'm at the prom with you. She thinks that I'm spending the night with a friend." I conveniently leave out that the friend is Theresa.

"So she would wonder why you were coming home when you're supposed to be at your friend's house," Derek says.

I nod. Derek rubs his chin and frowns.

"How about this?" he says. "Let's just hang out for the night and I'll drop you off in the morning."

"Are you sure?" I ask. "You won't get in trouble with your parents?"

"I can just tell them that I was hanging out with friends," he replies. "That's what I did last year and they didn't mind."

Last year? Who did he take to the prom last year? I suppress my jealousy and force myself to think of something else.

"What will we do all night?"

"Let's play it by ear. I'll surprise you."

Derek drives me towards Downtown. He then makes a turn into the tunnel leading to Chinatown. Derek keeps driving until I no longer recognize my surroundings. I see a tall, skinny, loud blinking sign showing a scantily clad blond woman. She has two red blinking lights where her nipples would be. I look away and blush. There are a lot of Western restaurants and cafés brimming with people. They remind me of Paris, though I've never been to Paris.

"Where are we?" I ask.

"North Beach," he replies. "You've never been?" He sounds surprised. I shake my head, embarrassed by my ignorance. Though I've heard of North Beach, I've never thought of San Francisco as consisting of more than Richmond, Sunset, Downtown, and Chinatown.

As we pass certain restaurants and landmarks, Derek tells me stories about them. Some stories are personal, like the one about where his dad proposed to his mom. Other stories are historic or legendary.

Derek manages to find parking, and he takes me to a café for a cappuccino and a dessert called tiramisu. I've never had coffee before. I feel deliciously naughty, like I'm having a beer or a cigarette.

Afterwards, we get back in the car, and Derek drives me to the top of a very steep hill. As I look down, I notice that the street is composed of a series of hairpin turns. As Derek drives down slowly, it dawns on me that we are going down Lombard Street, the famous "crookedest street in the world." Until now, I've seen it only on postcards. I can hardly believe that this street is lined with houses. I try to imagine what it is like for the residents to bring their groceries home every week. Once we reach the bottom of the hill, we continue north until we get to the water. Derek points out Ghirardelli Square,

Fisherman's Wharf, Pier 39, and the Bay Bridge. Everything glitters with yellow lights that sparkle like jewelry. He finds a place to park and we walk along Pier 39, even though it's closed and deserted, even though it's cold. Derek lets me wear his jacket. He puts his arm around me to help me keep warm. We stay at the pier, where the sea lions hang out, and watch the sun rise.

Derek drives me back to the Richmond District. We have breakfast at Mel's Diner. I order pancakes. Derek orders bacon and eggs. We both order coffee. My eyelids are heavy, but my heart is still giving off fireworks. I can't tell if it's from the coffee or from being with Derek.

After breakfast, Derek drives me home. We park along 32nd Avenue between Balboa and Cabrillo.

"Thanks," I say.

Derek grabs my hand. "Is your mom home?" he asks.

I shake my head. "She's working," I reply. "Why?"

"I want to see your place," he says.

On one hand, I'm excited that he is curious about where I live. On the other hand, I'm worried about what he'll think. He drives a BMW. He probably doesn't live in a dilapidated one-bedroom apartment.

As we approach my building, I check the second-story window to make sure that Mom is indeed at work. We climb the dark painted-green concrete stairway. I open the door to the apartment, and we step inside. The horizontal blinds hang crooked. Some of the pieces are bent from years of use and abuse by previous tenants. I wonder what Derek thinks about our linoleum floors and our saggy green love seat.

"It's not that impressive," I say.

"It's not that bad," Derek says, choking on the words. We stand there in silence for several awkward moments.

Finally, he asks, "Do you mind if I use your bathroom?"

I show him the way. As he relieves himself, I imagine what he must be thinking about our cracked pink and maroon tiles, our worn and stained yellow bath towels, and the rust running down our tub underneath the faucet. Derek emerges a minute later. His hands smell like the sandalwood soap we buy from Chinatown.

"Where's your room?" he asks.

I guide him to our narrow trapezoid-shaped room. Both mattresses in the bunk bed are covered with orange and pink blankets.

"Do you sleep on the top or the bottom?" he asks.

"The top."

"Does your sister sleep on the bottom?"

"I don't have a sister."

"Then who sleeps on the bottom?"

"My mom. This is a one-bedroom apartment."

Derek says nothing. His expression seems sad.

At that moment, the door begins to jiggle. There is no place for Derek to run or hide. The door opens. Mom is carrying a box of pastries, which emit a sweet, buttery aroma. Her eyes zero in on me and Derek. Then she focuses on me, her bottom lip quivering. This confuses me, until I realize that she is staring at my dress. But it doesn't last long. Soon her expression becomes cool again. She takes slow deliberate steps towards us, like a stalking predator.

"So, who is this?" she asks, her voice silky and dangerous.

Derek puts on his most charming speech-persona smile. "Hi, Mrs. Ching," he says, extending his hand. "I'm Derek."

Mom's eyes travel down to Derek's hand and back up to his face. Her look is withering. Derek's smile wilts. His hand falls limply to his side.

"You don't deserve a friend like Theresa," Mom says to me, completely in English so that Derek can understand. "You're so absentminded. You left your pajamas on your bed. I called Nellie's house. Theresa answered. When I told her about your pajamas, she was quiet for a long time. Poor Theresa. She didn't know what to say. When I told her to tell you to come back and get them, she said that she could lend you a pair." Mom sniggers. "Imagine, Theresa lending you a pair, when she is so thin and you are so fat."

I wince, wishing that I could just disappear.

"I called in sick today," Mom continues. "I wanted to see for myself." She shakes her head and clicks her tongue against the roof of her mouth. "Poor Theresa. She is such a bad liar, not like you."

I burn with humiliation. Will Derek make the connection between the Theresa Mom is referring to and the Theresa we met at the prom? I don't dare look at his face. I am too scared to see his reaction.

"Not only do you lie," Mom says, "you lie to sleep over at a boy's house. How about all the other times you 'slept over at Theresa's'? Were you sneaking off to sleep with boys all those other times too?" She emphasizes the s in "boys," to make it unequivocally plural, while turning to stare at Derek. Derek shrinks as Mom hovers over him, even though Derek is probably six feet tall, whereas Mom is only four foot ten. "Is that why you invited him over," Mom continues, talking to me while staring at Derek, "so that you can sleep together here too?"

"I should go," Derek says, slowly walking sideways towards the bedroom door while giving Mom wide berth.

"Yes, perhaps you should," Mom says. "It was nice meeting you." She smiles at him, eyes wide and unblinking like spotlights, lips parting to show all her teeth.

Derek darts out of the apartment and down the stairs. I hear his footsteps, which end in a loud trip at the bottom.

Then Mom turns to me.

"Nothing happened," I say.

"Funny. He did not defend you. In fact, he abandoned you," Mom says, switching back to half Chinese, half English. "Why is that? He must not care much about you or your reputation."

"That's not true," I say.

"Is it not? Has he introduced you to his parents yet, or is he sneaking you around like he's ashamed of you?"

How can I answer that question without making him look bad?

"Hm. I see," Mom says. "I can understand his point of view.

After all, he is high class, not like you. I can tell by his clothes and his manners. Where is he going to college, Harvard, Princeton?"

"Harvard."

"Ah, yes. Why would he want to bring home someone like you, some poor Chinese girl who only got into State? Why not have his fun with you right before leaving for Harvard to meet someone proper?" Then Mom sighs, adding dramatic effect. "I wonder what he thought as he looked at this apartment. Did he feel pity, disgust?"

I think about the look on Derek's face as he saw the bunk bed. Could pity and disgust be the emotions it elicited from him?

Then I stop myself. This is what she wants me to think. She is trying to brainwash me, just as she always has. I won't fall for it.

But just as I think this, Mom's tone changes.

"That is why I told you not to date boys," she says. Her eyes turn red. Her voice is no longer mocking. Instead, it is choked with disappointment and anguish. "That's why I told you to go to Berkeley and become a doctor or TV journalist," she says. "Then no one could look down on you, not even Derek. You could do better than Derek. You could get a Chinese Derek. You could have your pick of many Dereks. They would line up at your door, begging to take you home to meet their parents. But you throw it away. And once you sell yourself cheap, no one will ever believe that you are valuable. Who pays full price for a used car?

"That dress is cursed, you know," Mom adds. "I know. I attracted your father with that dress."

Suddenly, the dress feels cold and creepy against my skin. The smell of mothballs makes me nauseous.

Mom turns away and exits the bedroom. Her posture is slumped and her footsteps are heavy, painting the picture of defeat.

I hurry to the bathroom and remove the dress as quickly as possible. No matter how much I rub my skin with my wet washcloth, I can't remove the mothball smell.

Chapter Twenty-one

I wish I could call Theresa and cry on her shoulder about what happened after the prom, but I don't dare. The Monday after the prom, I see her in the locker room before first period.

"Hi," I say. My voice is tentative.

Theresa doesn't look at me. She continues placing her books in her locker.

"Look, about the prom . . . ," I begin, but the end of my sentence drifts away from me.

Theresa is now reorganizing her things, even though they were perfectly organized to begin with. After about a minute, she finally looks at me. Her eyes are hard and cold.

"If Derek hadn't asked you to the prom, would you still have encouraged me to call Alfred?" she asks.

Ashamed, I look down.

"And if you had met someone at the fall dance, would you have discouraged me from calling him in the first place?" she adds.

Again, I say nothing.

"That's what I thought." Theresa goes back to reorganizing her books. Then she closes her locker door just a little harder than usual. Though I am still looking at her feet, I can feel her eyes boring into my forehead. "You're selfish," she says.

I nod. "I'm sorry," I say.

I hope that this admission will dissolve her anger. Instead, she turns on her heel and walks away. I feel as though she is pulling my skin with her, tearing it off my body, exposing all the ugliness underneath. I blink back my tears as I sort out my own books. I lost Derek, and now I've lost Theresa too. Theresa is probably the nicest person I've ever met. She was my best friend, perhaps the only real friend I've ever had.

A few seconds later, I hear a small voice behind me.

"You were right."

It's Theresa.

"The night after we went to Macy's, I called Alfred," she says. "He didn't call me after the fall dance because he lost my number, just like you said. He forgot to retrieve my number from his pants pocket. Then his mom forgot to check his pockets before washing his pants. I would never have called him if you hadn't encouraged me."

"I'm really glad that you got to go to the prom with him," I say. "I only wish I had encouraged you to call him sooner."

"I'm sorry too," Theresa says. "I can understand why you didn't tell me that you were going to the prom with Derek. After all, when Alfred invited me, I did the same thing. I didn't want you to feel bad because I had someone and you didn't."

"I guess we should have just told each other the truth," I say. "Then we could have double-dated."

"Yeah," Theresa agrees. "It would have been fun."

"So, how did it go?" I ask.

Theresa goes on and on about her date with Alfred, about what they ate and what they said. She tells me about the two-hour phone call they had the next day and the date they went on the day after. I swallow my own anguish as she tells me her good news. I focus on listening. I focus on being happy for her.

I don't call Derek for the next week. I tell myself that I need time to let things cool. Deep inside, though, I'm scared. What if he does think I'm cheap? Is that why he avoided taking photos, not because he wanted to wait for a shorter line but because he didn't want any evidence of our being together? After a week, I consider calling him, but every time I think about it, all my doubts creep up. A week becomes two weeks, then three weeks, then a month.

Derek doesn't call me either. I tell myself that it's because he doesn't want to get me into further trouble. Deep down, however, I hear a nagging whisper telling me that he hasn't called because my mother has sullied his image of me. The more I think this, the more afraid I am to call him.

In June, I am chosen to give the valedictorian speech. This means that I got the highest grade point average in the class, even higher than Theresa's.

Over dinner, I decide to tell Mom. We are having clay pot rice with Chinese pork sausage and Chinese broccoli.

"I'm going to be the valedictorian at my graduation," I say, using my most casual voice.

Mom doesn't look at me. She just continues chewing, as though I have said nothing. Perhaps she doesn't know what valedictorian means.

"It means that I got the highest grade point average," I add.

Still no reaction from Mom. Could it be that she is distracted by her own thoughts and did not hear me?

"I'm going to be—"

"I heard you the first time," Mom retorts. "Do you think I'm deaf?" Then she continues eating.

I swallow the lump in my throat. I remind myself of her muted reaction after my CAA speech win. Maybe she is happy for me but is hiding it. Maybe this weekend she will tell Minnie at the bank, Mr. and Mrs. Tai at the bakery, or Lynn at the grocery store.

"What's so great about getting the highest grades if they can't get you into Berkeley?" Mom says. "Theresa didn't get the highest grades, but she took calculus and she got the higher SAT score. That is why she got into Berkeley. So if I were you, I would stop bragging like a hotshot and acknowledge the truth—that the last four years have been a complete waste."

I brace against the sting in my eyes and blink back my tears. The following Saturday, we go to the bank, the bakery, and the grocery store. Mom says nothing to Minnie, the Tais, or

Lynn about my valedictorian status. I start to wonder if I ever achieved anything at all.

A week before graduation, I am supposed to practice my valedictorian speech with Ms. Taylor, but I have to postpone our meeting, because I've been blocked and unable to write my speech.

"Frances, graduation is just one week away," Ms. Taylor says.

Though I already know this, hearing her say it makes me panic even more.

"Do you want to meet and brainstorm this?" she asks.

"No. Just give me a couple of days. I'll get it done," I say. I sound way more confident than I feel.

But Ms. Taylor doesn't buy it. "Is everything okay?" she asks.

"Yeah. Just under a lot of pressure. Don't worry. I'll get it done." Before she can argue, I add, "I need to hurry home now so I can work on it."

On the way out, I see Derek, leaning against his car, which is illegally parked in front of the school. The moment he sees me, he straightens up and peers at me, his eyes searching and unsure.

He didn't abandon me, as Mom had predicted. He came back for me. Everything I feared is untrue.

My heart is singing as Derek drives me home. He reaches over and places his warm hand on my cold, clammy one.

"Sorry my hands are cold," I say.

"It's okay," he replies. "I'm always too hot, so it's refreshing to be with a girl who acts as natural air-conditioning."

I blush.

"Don't start blushing," he says. "Then it'll get hot again and I'll have to roll down the windows. Speaking of windows, I've been thinking about what you said. About the cramped house and the window. I think you're right, and I'm making some changes."

"Oh yeah? Like what kind?"

"Maybe I don't have to surrender to the Dark Side after college. I'll still go to Harvard, and I may still end up studying law, but that doesn't mean that I have to go work for my dad. I could work somewhere else. I could even work for the Other Side." Derek glances at me from the corner of his eye and grins.

"Or you could work for him and insist on doing only pro bono work," I say.

"Yeah," he says. "He'd love that."

We are silent for a few blocks. Then Derek says, "You're still going to Scripps, right?"

"Yeah."

"How does your mom feel about it?"

"She doesn't know."

"Really? How are you going to pull it off?"

"I'm just going to keep it a secret until the last minute, when it's too late for her to stop me," I say.

Derek nods. "I assume she's not paying for it, then."

"No, but that's okay," I say. "I got some scholarships. I'm hoping to get a campus job too."

"So you could use a summer job, right?" Derek says. "That way, you could start saving up money sooner."

A summer job. I can't believe I didn't think of it sooner! "But how do I get one?" I ask.

"My dad's looking for someone to shelve books, run errands, and photocopy. He usually hires teenage aspiring lawyers. You could be the first TV newscaster."

I roll my eyes. "Nice of you to think of me," I say.

"Actually, I'm only thinking of myself. I'm shelving books over the summer. I'm just trying to improve my work conditions."

He pulls over a couple of blocks away from my apartment.

"I won't ask if I can come inside," he says with a wink.

I'm relieved that we can talk about that horrible morning with my mother.

"I am so sorry about what happened that day," I blurt out. "I'm so embarrassed."

"Don't be. It's not your fault."

"I was so afraid that she had turned you off."

"She did. But you don't."

I let his kind words anoint me. But I need to make myself worthy.

"I have another confession to make," I say. "When my mom talked about Theresa . . . that was the same Theresa that you met at the prom. You know, Alfred's date?"

Derek takes a moment to remember. Then he shrugs. "I figured as much."

"You mean . . . you knew?"

"In retrospect," he says, "the way she looked at you plus your eagerness to leave right afterwards . . . I figured you weren't strangers."

He knew all along. I blush with shame.

I hear Mom's voice in my head. *Poor Theresa. She is such a bad liar, not like you.*

"I'm afraid that what my mom said about me is true," I say.

Derek smiles. "That you're a slut? I think not."

"No," I say, blushing even hotter. "That I'm a bad friend."

Derek looks surprised. "Why do you say that?"

"Theresa's done so much for me and I . . . haven't exactly returned the favor."

"Do you think friends should be keeping score?"

"She's not like that," I say. "She met Alfred at the fall dance. They really hit it off, but when he didn't call her . . . I discouraged her from calling him."

"How come?"

"Because . . . I didn't want to be the only one without a boyfriend."

Derek's face becomes serious, but he says nothing. I am revealing the ugliness in me. I'm on the verge of losing him again.

"She's always been better than me," I explain.

This is the truth that I've never been able to speak to anyone, not even myself. I hope that he will say, *No she's not*, or something like that.

Instead, he says, "Why is that a bad thing?"

I open my mouth to respond, but no words come out.

"It's good to have someone around who's better than you. It gives you someone to chase. It's like what you said in your old speech," Derek points out. "At the top, where else is there to go except down? If I knew each time I competed that I would win, I'd probably quit. I mean, what would be the point? There would be nothing to strive for."

"Really?" I say. "I would love to enter competitions knowing I would win all the time."

Derek laughs and touches my cheek. I find this gesture very endearing.

"What are your plans tonight?" he asks.

I groan. "I need to write my graduation speech. I was supposed to practice today, but I had to postpone, because I've been totally blocked."

"Maybe Theresa should do it instead, considering that she's so much better than you," Derek says, keeping a straight face.

"Yeah," I agree, even though Derek is joking. "Even when she's not better than me, she's better than me. Last November, we competed in this Chinese American speech tournament. I won, and she didn't even place, yet . . ."

Then, little by little, an idea for my speech begins to form.

"I gotta go," I say. I give him a peck on the lips and rush home.

The following Monday afternoon, I meet with Ms. Taylor in her office after school. She sits at the back of the room with her cup of strong black coffee. I stand at the front of the room, gather my breath, and begin.

> "Many of our coed peers probably wonder why we chose to go to a school like St. Elizabeth's. Did our parents force us to come here so that we could be cloistered from boys? For some of us, that may be the case. But that's not the reason St. Elizabeth's exists. An all-girls school is not so much a safe haven from boys and dating as it is a safe haven for learning and achievement. Without boys to distract or eclipse us, we could speak up in class, assume leadership positions, and achieve high academic goals. This achievement will contribute to our self-confidence, self-esteem, and self-efficacy. It will help us to achieve economic freedom and personal empowerment.
>
> "School is supposed to be a place of achievement. We work hard to get the highest grades. We join sports, academic decathlon, and speech teams, and we compete to win. Later, we compete to get into the best colleges. Then, after college, we compete to get the best jobs and earn the highest incomes. We are always striving to be number one.
>
> "There's only one problem with this model. Not everyone can win. In every competition, there has to be a loser. So if fifty students compete in a speech contest, and only one person

wins, are the other forty-nine contestants losers? Were their efforts completely pointless? How about the basketball team that got into the finals but lost the championship? How about the team that did its best but never won a single game during the whole season? How about the student who ran for school president but lost the election, or the student who didn't get the highest grade point average? How about the students who didn't get into Harvard, Stanford, or Berkeley? If we can't be the best, are we just wasting our time?

"Maybe there is a deeper lesson to learn here, a lesson that can't be graded or measured. I was chosen to give this speech because I have achieved a lot, and I'm going to share something I've learned on this path of achievement and success.

"It isn't enough.

"I'll give you some examples. A C student who gets a B is thrilled. An A student who gets the same B is devastated. A shy first-time speaker is thrilled just to get through a speech contest. A winning speaker has to worry about defending her title. Same with the champion tennis player or basketball team. And let's face it: don't we have higher expectations of our winners? Don't we feel disappointed when they do well but not great? It's not fair, but that's how we think. So how do you know when you're a winner? Easy. It's when good is not enough.

"I had to reevaluate what it meant to be a winner. I remember what a great mentor of mine said. She said to me, 'Competition is about comparing people, judging who is the best. According to those rules, whoever wins is successful, and everyone else loses.

"'But I want you to think about success differently. Winning is part effort and part luck. What judges think, how well other competitors do, that's luck. Talent, that's also luck. Some people are born with more and some with less. Luck is totally out of your control. What is under your control is your effort.'

"She also said, 'Reward time isn't after the competition, when they hand out trophies. Reward time is now. It's the thrill of competing, the opportunity to show them what you've got. Relish this time. Don't worry about how other people are doing. Focus on what you're doing. If you're doing your best, if you're having fun, then you're a success.'

"When I look back, my greatest accomplishment in high school has nothing to do with competition and winning. I learned to use my own judgment and not to follow others blindly. I learned to judge myself based on my own standards. I learned to find my own voice. I learned to speak my own truth. I have nothing to show for these achievements, no grades, no medals, trophies, or diploma. Yet these are the achievements that can't be taken away by loss, failure, or misunderstanding.

"In my future, I know that I will have both wins and losses, good times and bad. But if I remember to think for myself and speak my own truth, I can't go wrong. I can still be proud of myself. When I look back on what I got out of my high school education, this is what I am most grateful for."

I look to Ms. Taylor for feedback. She nods. Her stained-glass eyes glisten.

"Well," she says quietly, "I guess I accomplished my mission."

ᖓᖓᖓᖓᖓ

The following Saturday, I deliver this speech in a cathedral to a congregation of classmates, teachers, and family members of the graduates. The congregation is large and far away. I must speak into a microphone to be heard. I cannot see where my mother is, much less what her reaction to my speech is. Sometimes I wonder if she is even listening to my words, if she understands them. I will probably never know. And perhaps that is okay.

Though Theresa is the one who got into the coveted school of all Chinese families in San Francisco, for the first time, I don't begrudge her for it. I don't even mind when Mom rubs my face in Theresa's success. I just agree that Theresa is great, even when Mom says that she is better than I am. The first time I do this, Mom does a double take, and I pretend not to notice. Over the next several weeks, Mom's comparisons of Theresa and me become less and less frequent. Eventually, they stop altogether.

Chapter Twenty-two

A few days after graduation, I get a card in the mail from Ms. Taylor. On the cover is a large white crane with its wings spread out. Inside, it says, *Congratulations, Frances, on all your achievements, both inside and out.* Underneath her signature are her current phone number and her future address in North Carolina.

The following week, I go to my first job interview and get my first job, at Derek's dad's law firm, which is is located in a high-rise building in the financial district of Downtown. The job is pretty boring. All I do is shelve books, file, pick up lunch, deliver interoffice memos, and look up and photocopy articles. Nonetheless, I look forward to going to work every morning, because Derek is there. Every day, we exchange glances and smiles between bookshelves when no one is looking. During lunch, we walk to the nearby sandwich stand and eat sandwiches and frozen yogurts.

Every Saturday, while Mom is at work, Derek and I pick a different place in the city to visit. On the first Saturday, we visit the Sutro Baths and the caves nearby. The following Saturday, we hike Lincoln Park and visit the Legion of Honor. The following Saturday, I ride the cable car for the first time. Then we visit Golden Gate Park, then the Exploratorium, then Alcatraz, and the list goes on. By the end of July, we are venturing across the Golden Gate Bridge to Sausalito and Tiburon. The more places I go with Derek, the more the Richmond District seems to shrink in comparison, until my spirit in Mom's apartment feels like my body in the girdle Mom bought me for Christmas.

The whole time, Mom thinks that I am staying at home, doing nothing. I leave the apartment after Mom leaves for work and get home before she does. For the first two pay cycles, I hide the checks in my backpack, along with my bank statements, unsure of what to do with them. By the fourth paycheck, I know I have to do something. The most obvious option would be to go to the bank and ask a teller. I picture myself entering the bank timidly, asking Minnie for guidance. Very likely, the next time Mom visits, Minnie will mention that I came by. Then Mom will be on to my scent.

So instead, I consider asking Theresa. Then I remember that I never did tell Theresa that I had applied to Scripps. Initially, I figured that if I didn't get in, it wouldn't matter. Then, when I did get in, I was so caught up in the roller coaster of state championship, prom, and graduation that I didn't have time to figure out when and how to tell her. Strangely, Theresa hasn't brought up the subject of college either. And now that I am working on weekdays and seeing Derek on Saturdays, and Theresa is taking summer school and seeing Alfred, we rarely talk on the phone, much less see each other. Consequently, the opportunity to discuss my Scripps acceptance—and my subsequent escape plan—never arises.

Despite our busy schedules, Theresa and I finally make a date to hang out at her place in late July. In her kitchen, I help myself to custard tarts while Theresa makes Ovaltine, which tastes like malted hot cocoa. As Theresa stirs the Ovaltine powder, hot water, and condensed milk, I stare at Nellie's corkboard, which still displays the articles about my CAA speech win in November. The paper is already starting to yellow. I stare at the round-faced girl holding the first-place trophy. My eyes lose focus, causing the articles to blur, until the CAA winner in the photo fades and disappears.

Theresa sets down two mugs. My cold fingers absorb the heat emanating from one of the ceramic mugs.

"So, are you excited about Berkeley?" I ask.

Theresa hesitates. She seems to be studying my face. Then a big smile erupts. "Yeah, actually I am! Alfred is going too. Isn't that lucky?"

"That's great!" I say. I hide my own sadness about not being able to go to the same college as Derek. *I applied to Scripps, but they rejected me,* Derek said when I commented on this to him. *Which is too bad, because if I did get in, I'd be the envy of every freshman guy!*

Theresa goes on to tell me about the Berkeley campus, orientation, and possible majors.

"You know, I'm so happy that you're happy for me," Theresa adds.

"I'm happy that I'm happy too," I say. "I'm also happy that you're happy that I'm happy. But most of all, I'm happy that you're happy."

We both double over laughing.

"When I heard from Mom that you didn't get into Berkeley, I was afraid to bring up Berkeley at all," Theresa says. "I didn't want you to feel bad."

"You shouldn't feel that way," I say. "I mean, look at what happened when you thought that way about the prom."

Theresa laughs again. "Yeah, you're right," she says. "I'm bummed out that we can't go to the same school. On the bright side, Berkeley isn't far from State, so we can still see each other on the weekends."

Suddenly, my laughter stops. I forgot that Theresa, like Mom and Nellie, would assume that I would be going to State.

"State has a good journalism program," Theresa adds. "But if you don't like it, after a year or two, you can transfer to Berkeley. I hear that your chances of getting in are stronger as a transfer student."

For a moment, my jaw almost drops in shock. That's almost exactly what Mom said!

I realize then why I haven't shared my Scripps plan with Theresa. Underneath her skin, Theresa is like me, but in the marrow of her bones, she is more like Mom and Nellie. By helping me with speech, Theresa has already swum against her conscience. She probably rationalized that speech would help me get into Berkeley. But to expect her to help me with Scripps would be like expecting her to paddle up a waterfall.

I think about how things went when I asked Theresa to hide my first speech trophy. Maybe I could get Theresa to help me get to Scripps if I applied enough pressure, but I would once again be causing her to suffer more so that I could suffer less.

"Yeah, I guess I could transfer in a year or two," I say. I take a quick gulp of my Ovaltine. It scalds my tongue, but instead of spitting it out and making a mess, I swallow it, sending a streak of fiery burn down my throat.

Because I am desperate, I end up explaining my situation to Derek the following Monday.

"I thought about asking Theresa," I explain, "but she doesn't need the stress of having dim sum with my mom while knowing that she's an accomplice in my mother's demise."

"That's okay," Derek replies. "I'm definitely the better candidate for the job. I'm not planning to have dim sum with your mom anytime soon."

Derek shows me how to endorse my checks and deposit them using my ATM card. When the ATM spits out my receipt, I feel a dizzying excitement at seeing how much money I've accumulated. I'm rich!

In mid-August, Derek must leave for Harvard. We agree that he should wait until I settle down at Scripps and give him my address and phone number before he gives me his. If he were to send me his contact information any sooner, it would likely end up in Mom's hands. As with my Scripps package, it is not likely that she would pass it on to me.

For the last several months, I have been like a sleeper agent. Orientation at Scripps will be starting in less than a week. Now is the time to strike.

I find a travel agency close to where I work, and book a one-way flight to Ontario, which is east of Los Angeles, for one p.m. the next day. I hide my plane ticket in my wallet. That evening, after Mom has gone to bed, I write a letter telling her that I am leaving for Scripps. I will place the letter on the dining table tomorrow morning, right before I leave. But for now, I hide it in my backpack, next to my wallet.

Before going to bed, I review my secret itinerary. My flight is at one p.m., so I need to be at the airport by eleven a.m. I should leave the apartment by nine thirty, which means I should start packing at eight at the latest. Mom leaves for work at four thirty. So that gives me plenty of time in the morning.

I wish I could say good-bye to Theresa before leaving. Mom and I are supposed to spend this Sunday with her and Nellie, but I will be gone by then. I'm not sure when I will see Theresa again.

Once in bed, I am unable to sleep. I make myself unnaturally still, fearful that any tossing and turning will give me away. I close my eyes and pretend to sleep as Mom wakes and gets ready for work. As soon as she leaves, my exhaustion settles in, weighing down my head and my eyelids. When my alarm goes off, I nearly jump out of bed, as if hearing a fire alarm. I quickly climb down from the bunk bed and get dressed.

Fortunately, I don't own a lot of things, so I am able to fit my clothes and toiletries into Mom's old suitcase. Giddy with excitement, I drag the suitcase to the front door. Then I search my backpack for my letter to Mom. To my surprise, it is not there. Could I have forgotten to put it away? With a pounding heart, I search my desk, but it isn't there either. Where could it be? Instinctively, I search my wallet for my plane ticket.

My plane ticket is gone. So is the cash in my wallet.

Images from the past school year flash before my eyes. My mother forbidding me to get a job, claiming that it would interfere with my studies. My mother's eyes as they look me up and down before she asks me if any boys asked me to dance. Derek asking me why I gave him the wrong phone number. My Scripps package and my scholarships rotting in the garbage can under a pile of kitchen trash. My mother cornering Derek and me in the apartment after the prom. The crane on Ms. Taylor's card.

My mother named me Fei Ting. Fly stop. The girl who stopped flying. My mother is clipping my wings. Again.

I can't give up now. I can buy another plane ticket. I grab my backpack and run to the nearest ATM, which is several blocks away on Geary Boulevard. Sweat drips down my forehead and back as I insert my card. To my surprise, the ATM tells me that my card is invalid and spits it back at me. I try again, but the same thing happens.

Suppressing my panic, I board the bus to the red bank on

Clement Street. A half hour later, I enter the bank. Minnie is sitting at her usual spot. Fortunately, there is no line. I approach her. She smiles at me until she sees the look on my face.

"Minnie," I say, skipping formalities, "my ATM card isn't working." I keep my voice low so that no one else can hear.

Minnie's jaw drops for a moment. Then, slowly, her look of surprise is replaced by a sad expression. "Frances," she says gently, "your mommy closed the account yesterday."

"But . . . it's my account," I say. "How can she do that?"

"It's a joint account," says Minnie, "so it's hers too."

"But . . . don't we have to agree to close it? Don't I have to sign off on it too?" I keep hoping to find a rule that was broken that will invalidate what my mother has done.

"No. Either person can close the account," Minnie says.

"So . . . where did my money go?"

Minnie sighs. "Your mommy consolidated the accounts."

"W-What does that mean?"

"She put the money in her account."

I back away from Minnie slowly, until I trip over a crowd-control post. As my bottom hits the marble floor, that post and a couple of adjacent posts come crashing down. Everyone in the bank turns and stares at me. The security guard helps me to my feet and asks me if I'm okay. Ignoring him, I run out of the bank and lean my back against the wall. I slide down the wall until my bottom rests on my heels, and bury my face in my hands.

As I look down at my feet, I notice that I am standing in

a puddle of dried urine. It reminds me of the homeless man Mom and I passed many months ago at this very spot, before school started. *His mother should have helped him more,* Mom said, *and he should help her more. That's the problem with this country. No family loyalty.* As bystanders walk past, they look down on me with expressions of surprise and disgust, the same way I looked at that homeless man.

Humiliated, I pick myself up and take the bus home. Along the way, I reflect on my hopeless state. In the past, whenever my mother sabotaged me, I always comforted myself with the promise that I would escape one day. How will I survive if that is taken away? I wish I could call Derek, but he is too far to help me. Besides, I have no means of reaching him right now. Who else can I turn to?

Ms. Taylor.

I get off at the bus station near my apartment, which has a pay phone. Once again, the bus stop's plastic covering has been shattered by vandals. The broken pieces, which blanket the concrete like snow, crunch under my feet. The phone has been scratched up. The receiver has that nauseating homeless smell. I dig through my backpack and fish out Ms. Taylor's card.

With trembling fingers, I dial her number.

I get a recording saying that this number is no longer in service. Ms. Taylor has already moved to North Carolina. Though I have her new address, I don't have her new number.

I burst into tears. I am angry with her for abandoning me, even though it isn't her fault. My plane leaves in just a few hours. My window of opportunity is closing. Orientation and fall semester will begin without me. Should I just admit defeat and give up?

Wait. I have one last resort: Theresa.

I run from the pay phone to Theresa's house. Each time one of my feet hits the pavement, a jarring sensation goes through my body. When I finally reach Theresa's house, I ring the doorbell. Theresa opens the door. Her smile vanishes the moment she sees the look on my face. I blurt out the whole Scripps story, from the time I applied until now. Then I pause, hoping that she will have another clever idea that can save me.

Theresa gazes at me with a sad expression. "Frances, I'm so sorry to hear about what happened," she says.

Once again, Theresa understands. She always understands. Tears of gratitude come to the surface.

"But you did get into State too," she says. "Maybe you should just forget about Scripps and go to State."

My hope begins to fracture. I fight to hold all the pieces together. "But . . . I never sent in my registration for State."

Theresa gasps.

"It's still possible," I say. "To get to Scripps, I mean. Maybe you could give me a ride to the airport."

"But what will you do once you get there?" Theresa says. "How will you fly to Scripps with no plane ticket and no money?"

"Maybe you could lend me some money," I say. "I'll pay you back."

Theresa sighs and shakes her head. "Frances, this is more

serious than just sneaking around to do speech. How will your mom feel when she comes home and finds you gone?"

My splintered hope erodes to sand. The harder I hold on, the more it slips through my fingers.

"You're the only family she has," Theresa says. "What will she do without you?"

I want to say, *Well, what if you were me? Wouldn't you do the same?* But I know that were our situations reversed, Theresa probably would stay home and endure. The gap between us is only a few feet, but the real distance is the width of a canyon, too great to bridge with arguments.

"I know you want to be like Ms. Taylor," Theresa says. "But that's just an ideal. That kind of goal isn't practical for us. Even Ms. Taylor went home to take care of her mother when she got sick. Can't you follow her example in that way?"

This is too much. I run away from Theresa's house. The houses in front of me blur from my tears. At the end of the block, I double over, gasping for air. As long as Theresa, the perfect daughter, was on my side, I could convince myself I was in the right. Now I must face my self-doubt on my own.

If I forge ahead, everyone at home will see me as the bad daughter. I will have to face a year—actually, four years—of uncertainty, with no one to back me up. And what if I don't like Scripps? Unlike Ms. Taylor, I wouldn't be able to call home to cry about it.

But what will my life be like if I quit now? I will go to State, then transfer to Berkeley, then go on to med school or journalism school. My mother will stand over me, triumphant, her lips curled into a smile, saying *I told you so.* Any tiny victory I have will be like all the others, short-lived. Mom will find another way to get back at me and make me small again.

I look up, as if asking God for guidance. Black telephone and electric bus wires mar the gray sky. The jagged poles supporting them look like they're leaning, ready to fall on me. The two-story homes that line the streets look like an army of bullies hovering over me.

Either I leave today, or I never leave. My window may be closing, but I need to squeeze myself through, before it closes completely. I have spent the last year sneaking around, battling Mom's lies with my own. Now is the time to speak my truth.

I return to the apartment and sit on the couch. I make myself like a leopard hiding behind a bush, waiting for the wildebeest to cross the river.

Several hours later, my mother arrives. She is carrying her purse and the takeout for tonight's dinner. I watch her as she closes the door and tosses her purse and the takeout on the dining table. She acts as if nothing unusual has happened. She expects me to play along. This makes me increasingly angry, until my anger overrides my fear.

"I want my money back," I say. My voice is shaky.

Mom's eyes are round with innocence. "I don't know what you mean."

She's trying to convince me that I'm imagining things. But this time, I won't be fooled.

"You went through my backpack and stole my cash and plane ticket," I say, my voice growing louder. "You closed my account. You took my money. I want it back."

Mom laughs. "Everything you have, you have because of me," she replies. "So your things are actually my things. How can I steal something that already belongs to me?"

"I earned all that money," I say.

"How can you earn all that? You don't even have a job."

"Yes I do. I've been working all summer."

Mom's eyes narrow to slits. "You lie."

"No, *you* lie!" I say.

Mom gasps in shock. My heart pounds and my knees shake violently. Now that I have vomited these accusations, I cannot swallow them back down.

"You've always discouraged me from getting a job," I say. "You said that you wanted me to focus on school, but you were just trying to keep me helpless and dependent on you. You lied about the porcelain bowl after the earthquake. You knew that you broke it, but you just accused me because you lost your temper and needed someone to blame."

She glares at me. "How dare you!" she shouts. Then she slaps me hard across my left cheek. It stings, and my skin feels hot and tingly. But I refuse to cower as I did when she beat me with my trophy.

"And you lied about Derek," I continue. My speech is slightly slurred from the numbness in my cheek. "He called to ask me to the fall dance, but you told him that he had the wrong number and then you told me that he didn't like me."

Mom slaps me across my right cheek, snapping my head in the opposite direction. My neck makes a cracking sound. The stinging in my eyes causes a tear to roll involuntarily down my cheek. "Shut up!" she says.

"You even lied about my acceptance to Scripps," I say. "You threw away my acceptance package without telling me."

Mom slaps me again across my left cheek. The room spins as everything around me fades. I struggle against my dizziness to remain standing.

"You useless idiot! I'm doing this for you!" Mom screams. "You wanted to go to some no-name college. Everyone would have laughed at your Mickey Mouse degree. And if you ran off with that Derek, you would have lost focus on your schooling. You could have spoiled your reputation. You could have gotten pregnant. How do you think I got stuck with you?"

Tears pour down from both my cheeks, splashing onto my shirt.

"You were about to ruin our life," Mom says. "I had to stop you."

I fight the urge to break down. "I still want my money and my plane ticket back," I say between swallowed sobs.

"What's the point?" she says. "Your plane already left. It's too late."

And with that, she turns around and begins setting the table. Once again, she is acting as though nothing happened. She is expecting me to drop this and go along. And why shouldn't she? Everyone always has.

Even Nellie and Theresa.

After Mom beat me with my trophy, Nellie was sympathetic to me, but in the end, she defended Mom. *It's because she loves you so much that she gets this upset,* Nellie said. *So be good and don't upset her anymore.*

Even Theresa defended Mom. *You're the only family she has. What will she do without you?* Even though she saw my mother beat me. Even though she knows that my mother hid my acceptance package and stole my money.

I know that inside, you're a good girl, Nellie said to me. Why is everyone telling me to be a good girl? Why doesn't anyone tell Mom to be a good mother?

Like hot liquid boiling over a pot, my hatred rumbles in my stomach, erupts, and fills my entire body. Ms. Taylor's advice to speak one's truth has deserted me. I speak swords and stare daggers, yet my mother does not bleed. She can do whatever she wants and get away with it. Meanwhile, everyone thinks she's so great.

Then it occurs to me that maybe Ms. Taylor's advice has not deserted me. Maybe I have deserted her advice. I never told anyone the truth about my mother, not even Ms. Taylor. I never openly disagreed with Nellie or Theresa about her. I am partly responsible for nobody's seeing through Mom's mask. What would happen if I yanked it off, exposing her true self to the world?

Slowly, a plan comes to mind.

Chapter Twenty-three

I spend the next few days playing the role of the defeated one. I swallow the hurt of my last confrontation with Mom, funneling my rage into revenge.

The following Sunday, Mom and Nellie decide to go jewelry shopping. We meet at Tai's Bakery to get breakfast. Theresa averts her gaze when she sees me, but I ignore this. I have a plan to execute, and I can't allow any distractions. Nellie orders the curry buns behind the glass. Theresa chooses her favorite, barbecued pork. Mom orders her *gai mei bao*. Now it's up to me to choose.

"So, speech champion, what will it be? Another *gai mei bao*?" asks Mr. Tai.

"I'm sorry, but I can't have any," I say. "My mother says I'm too fat."

Mr. Tai's, Nellie's, and Theresa's friendly expressions distort into shocked looks.

Mr. Tai packs a bun for me anyway and smiles politely. "You don't mean that, Little Sister."

"Of course I do," I say loudly. "My mother calls me a liar, so I have vowed to speak only the truth. I only hope that she will do the same."

Just then, Mrs. Tai enters from the back. She is unaware of what happened just moments ago. "Fei Ting," she says cheerfully, "you must be excited about college!"

"No, not really," I say. I project my voice to speech level so that everyone can hear. "Originally, I was looking forward to going to Scripps, but my mother threw away my acceptance package to make me think that I got rejected."

Their jaws all drop simultaneously.

"I'm sure it was an accident," Nellie suggests. "Your mommy must have thought it was something else."

"No, I don't think so," I reply, "because when I brought it up, she slapped me hard across the face."

Now other customers are staring at me.

"I got scholarships to relieve her burden," I announce to everyone in the bakery. "I even worked a summer job to pay for airfare and my books. But she stole my money and my plane ticket and refuses to give them back to me."

The other customers look away or walk away from me like I'm crazy. I endure this discomfort the way I endure Mom's insults. The only pleasure I get is seeing Mom look down, helpless and ashamed. What is she going to do, hit me in public?

I pick a table near the front window and sit down, pretending not to notice people's reactions to me. Nellie grabs my *gai mei bao*, and she, Theresa, and Mom join me. Nellie and Theresa eat quickly, making themselves look busy. Mom just stares at her bun. I ignore mine and gaze nonchalantly out the window.

After Nellie is done licking her fingers and picking up crumbs, she says to me, "Fei Ting, eat your bun."

"I would love to but I can't," I say. "My mother will call me lazy and ugly." I push the bun towards Nellie. "Here, you eat." With hesitation, Nellie wraps up the bun to go.

"Well, let's hurry," Nellie says. "The jewelry shop will open soon."

Immediately, I get up and walk to the door first. Instead of holding the door for my mother, I let it swing back in her face, walking away as if she doesn't exist. Nellie catches up to me. "Fei Ting, please stop! This is cruel," she hisses.

"Tell her that the next time she beats me with a sharp object," I say.

As we wait for the bus, I never stand less than a few feet away from my mother. On the bus, Mom spots a vacant double seat and sits down. Rather than sit next to her, I pick an empty single seat a few rows up. In contrast, Nellie and Theresa sit side by side in one of the double seats. I do not allow myself to see their expressions.

We get off at Union Square in Downtown and connect to the 30 Stockton bus to cross the long, dark, echoey tunnel into Chinatown. Union Square has theaters and department store window displays. Each window looks like an inviting make-believe world. Chinatown, on the other hand, is lined with pavement littered with dirt, trash, fresh spit, and old wads of chewing gum. Honking horns and loud talking people litter the air the way the trash litters the streets. The crowds of people form conflicting currents of foot traffic that push me this way and that.

When we get to the jewelry shop on Stockton Street, the storeowner, Mr. Wong, greets Mom. Mom pastes on a big smile and introduces me as her daughter, the winner of the Chinese American Association speech contest. Doesn't he remember seeing me on Channel 26? Mom asks him. Mr. Wong covers his confusion with feigned recognition. Of course he remembers me. What a smart girl I am. Just lucky, Mom says. Instead of nodding and smiling, denying my excellence, I turn away and walk to the opposite side of the room. I focus my eyes on the loud red carpet, the garish gold accents throughout the shop, and the sparkle of gold and gems in the display case. Mom explains that I graduated at the top of my class, that I deserve a pretty necklace as a reward. Mr. Wong heartily agrees. I roll my eyes.

As Mom and Mr. Wong peruse the jewelry, I peruse the jade bracelets from several feet away. They come in different shades and marbled combinations of green, violet, white, and brown. They also come in different sizes, from adult to infant. I remember my childhood bracelet and the way Mom left it on me until it threatened to crush my growing wrist. Suddenly, that too takes on symbolic significance. How many other ways has she harnessed me, hindering my growth?

"Fei Ting, look at this one," Mom says. She is holding up a twenty-four-karat gold necklace with a jade pendant. "What do you think?"

Her voice is too kind, almost pleading. In return, I shrug, looking bored.

Mom smiles a polite, fragile smile for Mr. Wong. "Come over here and try it," she says to me, the way lenient parents coax tantruming toddlers.

I walk towards her, but I make each step look like an inconvenience.

Mom holds the pendant up to my face. "It's Gwun Yum. Remember Gwun Yum?" This Gwun Yum is the highest quality jade, bright green, like a traffic light. I am mesmerized by its greenness for a moment before I recover my composure.

"I'm allergic to gold," I tell her.

"But Theresa's wearing one, see?"

Across the way, Nellie is trying on a twenty-four-karat necklace. She holds one up for Theresa to try on, but Theresa shakes her head. She looks like she's trying not to cry.

"I'm not Theresa," I say.

Despite my protestations, Mom clasps it at the back of my neck and turns me to face the little mirror on the glass display case.

"Isn't that pretty?" Mom says.

I see my own reflection in the mirror, with Gwun Yum perched an inch below the space between my collarbones. I remember the last time I wore her image around my neck, when Theresa lent me hers for good luck during my first competition. She would never behave this way. I can't bring myself to think about what she might be thinking now. Above

Gwun Yum, I see my face. Its expression looks pouty, selfish, cruel . . . ugly.

"You're so lucky to have such a generous mother," Mr. Wong says. He probably feels contempt for me for not being more respectful. But I don't let him shame me. He's not morally superior. He just wants to make a sale and I am merely his obstacle.

"Do you like it?" Mom asks me.

"It's okay," I say.

"Mommy will buy it for you, okay?"

"With what, the money you stole from me?" I say. "I would much rather you spend it on my education than on a piece of jewelry."

Mr. Wong's smile disappears. Quickly, he recovers and nods at Mom, the one holding the purse strings. Mom tries to smile back, though her effort is strained. Then Mom pulls out hundred-dollar bills to pay for the necklace. Is it the money she stole from my account? This thought burns my chest like a branding iron.

"All that cash, gone just like that," I say. "Do you know how many hours I had to work to earn all that? You must not know the value of money." I relish turning Mom's own words against her.

Mr. Wong takes out a pink silk pouch with elaborate embroidery to package the necklace, but Mom stops him. "Fei Ting, don't you want to wear this home?" She's almost begging me now.

"No thanks," I say as I walk out the door. I let it close before Mom can follow. She hurries to catch up with me, but I do not wait for her. Instead, I keep a steady pace, staying a few feet in front of her, as if she has nothing to do with me.

There are groups of old people walking side by side, some friends and some couples, wearing dark silk vests, with their backs hunched over and their hands clasped behind their backs. Immigrant mothers have infants tied to their fronts or backs in cloth bundles. Adult and teenage children are walking with their mothers and grandmothers, guiding them gently by the arm as if their mothers were frail and might fall. Theresa walks with Nellie in this way. They are just a couple of feet behind Mom. Only I am walking alone.

As we board the Stockton bus, Nellie grabs my wrist and hisses, "Fei Ting, stop!" She tugs on my hand, urging me to go sit with my mother. I wrench my hand from her and pick a solitary seat far away. Finally, *she* is following *me*. I am breaking her. *How does it feel?* I think as I watch her hunch over, clutching her stomach.

Before entering the tunnel to Downtown, the bus pauses. Through the window, I see an elderly woman sitting on the street. Her thin white hair is cut in a bob, like Mom's. She is wearing a black Chinese jacket, just like the one worn by Popo in her photo, only this woman's jacket is faded and tattered. Her skin is littered with age spots, and the creases on her face remind me of the skin of an elephant. She looks straight at me. Her old brown eyes have faded to blue. She has no teeth, except for a few gold ones. She reaches out her hand to me, as if begging for help.

She is all alone, with no one to help her. Does she have children? Did they leave her too?

The bus starts up again. We enter the tunnel, leaving the woman behind. I sternly remind myself that if Mom had the upper hand, she would not be merciful towards me. I crush any seed of compassion that might germinate.

Once we pass the tunnel into Union Square, I step off the bus without waiting for Mom, as if the bus could carry her away and it wouldn't be my concern. Mom follows me passively, like a stray puppy.

We transfer to the Balboa bus. Finally, Nellie and Theresa exit at the 30th Avenue stop. Theresa runs home with her hand over her mouth while Nellie chases after her, huffing and puffing. Seeing Theresa this distraught sends a sour pain through my chest, but I force myself to endure it. I exit at the 32nd Avenue stop and let the door close on Mom's face. The moment we walk through the front door at home, Mom's shell of dignity collapses. Sobs escape from her as she hunches over, with one arm clasping her belly and the other grabbing the doorknob for support.

"You're killing me," she says between sobs. She slowly sinks to the floor until she is kneeling. "You are my life," she says. "I have given you everything. What more do you want?"

"I want my money back," I say. "I want to leave."

Mom sobs some more.

"Now," I say.

"I can't. All the money is in the bank."

"Write me a check."

"But you have no account."

"I'll get a new one." Without her name on it.

"How will you get a plane ticket with no cash and no bank account?"

"I'll figure it out."

Weakly, Mom pulls her checkbook out of her purse and writes me a check. I make sure it is the right amount, and it is, down to the penny.

"Everything I did, I did for you," she says.

"No," I say. "You did it for yourself."

Mom looks at me, her eyes wide with confusion. "Aren't the two the same?" she says.

I stuff my backpack with my clothes and toiletries. Whatever doesn't fit I decide to leave behind. It seems hypocritical to accuse Mom of stealing my money and then take her suitcase without her permission. Of course, she could argue that I shouldn't be taking my backpack or my clothes, for that matter, because she paid for those too. A half hour later, I am ready to go. My plan is to take the bus and the BART to the airport and to purchase a plane ticket there. I don't know exactly how I will buy the ticket, but I hope that if I ask the right person, I can figure it out.

I put on my jacket and backpack and head for the door. Mom

is lying on the couch, clutching her stomach. She looks wilted and trampled upon, very much like she did when I came back from my first speech competition. I feel my mother's helplessness like an octopus arm wrapping around me. I feel her hold tightening, cutting off my circulation. Without looking at her, without saying good-bye, I walk out, tearing myself away from her, away from this apartment, until the part of me that she is holding on to snaps off. Though it hurts, though I bleed, I continue down the stairs to the security gate.

To my surprise, I find Theresa standing outside the gate, peering in. The fog outside is so thick that the water droplets dot her jacket and hair like glitter. Her car is illegally parked behind her.

Without words, we climb into her car.

As Theresa drives me through Golden Gate Park, I watch the fog accumulate on the windshield until Theresa has to turn on the wipers.

"Thanks," I say.

"Don't thank me," Theresa replies. "If I had driven you to the airport when you asked me to, you'd be at Scripps now, and none of this—" Her voice catches. She swallows to regain her composure. "Come to think of it, if I hadn't helped you with speech in the first place, you wouldn't have gotten close to Ms. Taylor and she wouldn't have persuaded you to apply to Scripps."

It is amazing how that first day in Ms. Taylor's class changed the course of my life.

"Theresa, do you regret helping me?" I immediately regret asking this.

Theresa sighs. "I shouldn't have helped you with speech. I shouldn't have helped you with Derek. And I shouldn't be driving you to the airport."

We are silent for the rest of the drive. As we approach the 280 freeway, I hear echoes of my speech.

> "It is like choosing whether to cut off one's right hand or one's left hand. It is like having to decide whether to save your drowning mother, knowing that you may both drown, or swimming to shore alone, knowing that you can only save yourself. If that is your dilemma, which way is right? Which way would you choose?

We finally approach the airport signs that say ARRIVALS and DEPARTURES. Theresa steers into the departures area and pulls up to the curb. She reaches into her purse, takes out a thick wad of cash, and tucks it into my jacket pocket.

"It should be enough for a plane ticket and cab," she says.

"Thanks," I say, "for all the things you shouldn't have done."

I take one last look at her long face and crescent eyes, which remind me of the moon. I take a mental photograph of the green pendant that sits right below her collarbone, resting on her pink angora sweater.

"Good luck, Frances," Theresa says. Then she turns away from me, directing her gaze to the road ahead of her.

I exit the station wagon and step onto the curb. All around me, people are rushing back and forth while dragging their suitcases. Horns honk. Engines rev and idle. People shout. A sharp whistle slices the air. A thick cloud of cigarette smoke fills my nostrils and lungs. My heart starts racing. Can I do this?

Then I take a deep breath and gather my energy. I assume my speech posture, spine erect and shoulders back, and I march into the airport.

⁓⁓⁓

A few hours later, I step off the plane in the Ontario airport. Outside, the first thing I notice is the blue sky. The bright light and intense heat are dizzying. The hot sun bakes my cold skin. I close my eyes and turn my face to the sun for a moment to soak up its rays before hailing a cab.

Epilogue

FEBRUARY 1991

Though the temperature has cooled down, it is still sunny and warm, about seventy-five degrees. I am finishing up my campus tour. After the crowd thanks me and disperses, I check my watch and notice how tan my arm has become. To remind myself of how I used to look, I peel back my wristband, revealing a strip of white skin made even whiter by the caramel brown next to it.

On the way to the cafeteria, I pass a long row of orange trees and admire the mountains, which were invisible until winter, when the smog cleared. I decide on the spur of the moment to stop by the mailroom first. In my cubbyhole is an envelope addressed to me. I am eager to open it, thinking that it is from Derek. Once I pick it up, however, I recognize right away my mother's lean, sharply slanted handwriting. My heart starts pounding.

Nervously, I walk back to my room, squeezing the envelope with my fingers, trying to make out its contents. I imagine a letter several pages long. I hear Mom's voice, sharp as her penmanship, reciting this imaginary letter. She complains about how much she is suffering. She tells me that this is all my fault. Mentally, I prepare a defiant response.

Then again, maybe it's not an angry letter. My mother's

imaginary voice takes on a pleading tone. Again, she tells me how much she is suffering, but this time she says that she needs me. She begs me not to turn my back on her again. Her voice breaks into sobs. The ink on the letter bleeds and runs where her tears fall. I picture her doubled over, clenching her stomach, which is bloated with spasms. My defiance deflates.

By the time I've reached my dorm, I've imagined half a dozen bad letters and am drenched in sweat. I hold the envelope up to the window the way a farmer holds an egg up to the light, but it's a security envelope and does not reveal what's inside. Which of my imaginary letters does this letter most resemble? Am I better off opening it or throwing it away?

Finally, I open it.

It is a shiny red envelope with gold Chinese brushstroke characters. Inside the red envelope are ten crisp hundred-dollar bills folded in half.

Why? What for?

Then it hits me. It's Chinese New Year. I completely forgot.

Every New Year's Eve, we would wash our hair and eat a big fancy meal at Auntie Nellie's. On New Year's Day, we would eat vegetarian food and abstain from washing our hair. On the day after New Year's, we would eat another elaborate nonvegetarian meal similar to that of New Year's Eve. It wasn't until the third day that we were permitted to wash our hair again.

Another New Year's practice was the giving and receiving of *laycee*, or lucky money in red envelopes. Older and married people would give *laycee* to younger and unmarried people. The cash was always crisp and new, never old and wrinkly. Each couple would give two envelopes, one for each spouse. I always got two envelopes from Nellie, but Mom would only give me one. She refused to pretend that my father had anything to give to me. But she always made a point of giving me twice the amount that Nellie gave me. Looking back, I think that was her way of showing that she was compensating for my father's absence, to prove that I wasn't being cheated.

Ms. Taylor always emphasized the power of words and the importance of having a voice in society. For Mom, money was her voice, her words. As I hold these crisp bills in my hand, their fresh ink filling my nostrils, I wonder: what is my mother saying to me? Is this another ploy, or is Mom being conciliatory? Should I accept her money or should I throw it back in her face? Should I do nothing or should I acknowledge her gift, and if I should acknowledge it, how? Via a letter? A phone call? What should I say to her? What would she say back to me?

I don't have the answers to these questions. But I do know one thing: no matter what, I will finish my education here. In the worst-case scenario, Mom could take me down a few notches, even reduce me to tears, but she cannot take me back to where I was a year ago.

I close my eyes and take a deep breath, repeating this promise to myself. Then I dial my mother's number, which is seared into my memory, like her voice.

She picks up after the first ring. She doesn't say hello or ask who it is. She doesn't need to. She knows it's me.

Acknowledgments

I am very grateful to Stephen Barbara, my agent, who is the greatest advocate, teacher, and friend a writer could ever have.

I am also thankful for Elizabeth Law, my editor, whose intuitive and insightful comments pushed my manuscript to the highest level. Her brilliance, enthusiasm, tact, and sense of humor made the revision process illuminating and fun.

Terry Wolverton has shepherded this book from its inception. She has taught me everything I know about writing and being a writer. Her influence over the years has also made me a better teacher and person.

My classmates in Terry's class, One Page at a Time, patiently slogged through numerous drafts of this book. I am so thankful for their friendship and critiques.

Thanks to the PEN Emerging Voices Program, through which I developed the early drafts of this book, and to Leslie Schwartz, my PEN EV mentor, for her generosity, support, and meticulous attention to detail.

Christine Lee and Barbara Willson were my go-to people whenever I had questions about Chinese culture and speech competition respectively.

This book could not have been finished without a mom's best

friend: child care. And for that great gift, I have to thank Katie Leigh Webb, Karen Chow, Hugh Kunkel, Walter Snow, and Christine Lee.

And finally, I must thank my husband, Eddie Nishi. Eddie was the one who told me that I should be a writer. He encouraged me to leave my full-time job and, later, supported my decision to work part-time so I would have more time to write. He sacrificed many evenings and weekends to watch our son so I could complete my revisions. Without him, I would have never become a writer and this book would not exist.

About the Author

CARA CHOW was born in Hong Kong and grew up in the Richmond district of San Francisco, where *Bitter Melon* is set. She was a PEN Emerging Voices Fellow and currently lives in the Los Angeles area with her husband and son.